Our Mersey Shore

A Novel

Keith Ryan

With Best Wishes,

Keith Ry

CAMADERRY
PRESS

A catalogue record for this book is available from the British Library.

Our Mersey Shore/Keith Ryan - 1st ed
ISBN: PB: 978-1-9162796-2-9

Thank you for supporting independent publishing.

Cover Design by Ann Glynn Design.

For Vera and Ollie

The Mersey Shore

They came in droves upon the sea,
Their longships resting on the tide.
Anlef and Constantine, Viking and Scot,
With mighty roar they filled the Mersey Shore,
The greatest army ever seen.

On land, the Saxon force,
White Dragons flying in the wind,
King Aethelston at the head,
And by his side his brother,
Edmond the First, future King of England,
Smote six Kings and seven Earls,
Hacked and hewed the mighty battle through,
And claimed the Mersey Shore.

Sky and Water
Joined as one.
Tide, cloud, sun,
Oozed crimson.

Put to sword by Saxon hands
Invaders panicked, fled.
White Dragons flew from every pole
Above the gore, the banked dead,
Along the Mersey Shore.

The day was won
For England to begin.

Battle of Brunanburh, 937AD

Sky

CHAPTER ONE

Bootle
Liverpool
December 1940

Maggie

It was the dog that saved me. He ran into the doorway of a shop where I had taken shelter on Stanley Road. In the gathering darkness of the blackout, I could make out the sharp face of a brown-and-white sheepdog filled with intelligence and fear. I cursed my new slingback shoes now covered in dust and rubble. I tried to smooth the dress I had just bought, the one that lay crumpled over my arm. Having worked all hours making barrage balloons in Littlewoods, and saving coupons all year, I wasn't about to let it go.

My world had gone silent, a strange no-sound in my ears, while explosions shook the ground beneath my feet. That first one landed close, without warning. Probably a parachute mine blown in from the Mersey on the sea breeze. No air raid siren. No high-pitched screech. Close. My head was swimming in sound, as if someone had slapped me in both ears. A low, rumbling fear rolled over me in waves. I must have skinned my knees when I hit the ground, but I couldn't feel them. That didn't matter. What mattered was saving the dress. I couldn't wait to see Billy's face when he saw me in it on Christmas Day.

When the landmine hit I scrambled up through the choking air, my nose and mouth filled with dust and grit, and ducked back into the shop doorway. People ran down the street, heads low; gesturing to those around them to hurry up, mouthing words I couldn't hear.

There were no dogs on our road anymore. A few scrawny cats used to sit on the high walls of the back alley, staring suspiciously with their yellow-black eyes and high-arched, sooty bodies... witches' cats that were up to no good, spying on everything that moved. The bombs took care of them.

But before the bombs, were there dogs? The man from the bottom of the road, Mister Goode, had a white and black Jack Russell that used to sit on his knee. He rubbed tobacco with his dark brown thumb and yellow forefinger, talking to the dog like it was a child. They used to sit like that on the park bench before it was removed and replaced with searchlights and a gun emplacement. When Mister Goode struck a match, his pipe flamed and then settled, sending spirals of sweet-smelling smoke into the air. I loved the aroma of it. I was transported to the exotic place in the Americas where it had come from, cut, dried, and carried on one of my brother's ships across the oceans to the great port of Liverpool.

On this winter evening, with bombs falling thick and fast, pipes and dogs were far from my mind. And then there was this one dog by my side.

The dog saved me. He stared at me with shining green eyes, then took off across the road. The painted kerbs were barely visible in the near pitch-black evening. I hobbled after him as fast as my new slingbacks would let me. I ran after him for fifteen minutes, though it was raining bombs that Saturday evening. I never stopped until I reached the road in front of our house.

Raining isn't the right word. More like a stampede of bombs, a mad charge through people's homes, lives and businesses. Shrapnel fell like hailstones and I knew that the anti-aircraft guns were firing from the park where I used to play before all this madness. I ran on up through the town, propelled by blind panic, expecting at every moment that the shadow of death would fall on me from the sky.

My brother Tom had come ashore earlier in the day, having been shipwrecked in the Atlantic. He was going on fire-watch down at the docks. I ran in to him at the front of our house, catching my breath. He grabbed me by both shoulders and shook me hard. My old boots, wrapped in brown paper, had been blown out of my arms when the first bomb fell. I had been stupid enough to wear the new shoes out of the shop. They cut deep into the soft flesh around my toes, but my dress seemed to be in one piece.

"Maggie, are you mad? Where did you run from?" he shouted.

It sounded like a distant echo from a lost time.

"Stanley Street," I sputtered.

His eyes widened and he squeezed me tight.

"There's a shelter there," he said. "Why the hell didn't you go to the shelter, under the arches of the railway bridge?"

The dog had disappeared.

Tom guided me through the house and into our Anderson Shelter half-buried in the back garden, and planted me into the strong, country arms of my mother.

"Well, I see you saved the dress," she said. "Thank God for small mercies."

Our mother had a great sense of irony about her. Tales were often repeated of her upbringing on a small farm in Ireland "*where we grew thistles for a living,*" as she often said. Of her uprooting to the *second* greatest city of the Empire. Of marrying a man of few words from the home country.

"*He did manage to say 'I do,'*" she would laugh.

She often spoke of bringing forth a Catholic family of ten children into "*this Protestant world.*" She was off then on a rant.

"Cooking and cleaning and surviving the Great War, and the Great Depression. And now this."

It was true that she had earned the right to carry her dishcloth draped over one shoulder and her irony perched on the other. Two formidable weapons always primed to strike.

I sat shaking on the edge of the bunk as she washed my feet, the cold water numbing the pain. Afterwards I curled into a ball on the bunk, my head wrapped in my arms. I was careful not to touch the curved metal roof of the shelter, which was always cold and wet. Mum's machine-gun voice, giving a running commentary on everything from queuing in the rain for food to Hitler's bomb that had flattened her second-favourite shop in the city, drowned out the worst of the raid.

In the morning Tom appeared in our steaming hot back kitchen while we ate breakfast following early Mass. He was black from head to foot; even his red hair was singed brown at the edges. He peeled off his scorched uniform like a snake shedding its skin and stood in his white vest that contrasted with his blackened hands and sooty face. They told a story of the night's heavy bombing. Once again, Jerry had dropped thousands of incendiaries, then followed up with high explosives and parachute mines.

"I swung by Stanley Road on my way up this morning," said Tom. "The shelter took a direct hit and the railway bridge collapsed. They're still digging like crazy, but it looks bad. They don't know how many were in there… The guess is over fifty.'

He looked at me long and hard.

"When this is all over you need to seriously consider entering the Olympics," he said. "Jessie Owens isn't the only one to give the two fingers to Hitler."

I never saw that dog again. When I told Tom, he said I must have imagined it.

Sometimes when I wake in the dark with sirens wailing and bombs screaming louder as they get ever closer, I see those green eyes in the split second between fitful sleep and wide awake.

In the peace-filled years before the war, Sunday Mass was a serious event in our house. Fasting from midnight and with no breakfast, the family, dressed in our Sunday best, would walk together down the deserted, terraced streets and across the park to the church. There, squeezed in between my mother and my sister on the smooth wooden bench, I would feel their strength and warmth and thank God for my family.

I used to love listening to my sister Mary going on and on about being in love. She was in love with Johnny Connolly. I was in love with Billy Newsome, although he didn't know it at that time. He had recently moved to Bootle following the death of his father. The way he held the paten under my chin at communion and looked at me with those clear blue eyes... He didn't smile, but I knew that he wanted to. He was a regular altar server and had spoken to me once when I met him in the park.

"Are you all right, Miss?" he'd asked as he looked down at me from the far side of the railings.

I'd been reading Agatha Christie's *Death on the Nile* and not watching where I was going. I loved the detective Hercule Poirot, the way he solved the murder mystery with so many exotic suspects. Poirot was in the middle of revealing who done it when I fell over loose clay from the anti-aircraft diggings. And there I was, sat, mortified and red-faced, in the muck. Billy Newsome asked me again but I was too flustered to answer. If a bomb had landed right there and then and blown me to smithereens I would have been eternally grateful.

Mary and me were both in love with Dixie Deane and the whole Everton team. We spent the first half of each week arguing about the match on the previous Saturday, and the second part focused on the coming weekend fixture... who should be playing where and why. We could go on for hours.

As a girl with seven older brothers and a father who were all mad into football, a sister who was a fanatic, and a mother whose regular comment was *"It's only a bag of wind,"* I was brought up to live and breathe the air of Goodison Park.

Blue, blue, my team is blue,
Everton Three and Liverpool Two...

That was one of the more polite songs we sang.

The talk in those years before the war was grounded in the relentless progress of Hitler, his ambitions and his strength. Being the youngest in the family, with brothers who continually travelled the world, I hung on to their tales of adventures in far-flung places. Back in those days I was good at staying quiet, tucked up in the corner seat behind the door. I heard an awful lot more than people would usually say in the hearing of a fifteen-year-old, as I was back then. Tom, Pat and Liam often argued with Dad about Hitler. It usually got hot.

"Look what he did in Guernica," Tom said on one occasion. "We need to act now to protect the civilian population. Nothing we've done so far will be enough. We need a war-time plan and we need it now."

"Look son, it may not come to war."

"But Da, you know better than anyone what war is like. And what's coming out of the sky isn't like anything we've seen before. And he is going to bomb the docks."

"Please God, it may not come to pass."

"But Da..."

"Just leave it, son. I think Hitler will be satisfied now that he's got what he wanted."

"I hope you're right Da, but the talk on the ships is all about the coming war – and what it will mean for us."

Dad shook his head.

Later, sitting on the steps outside our front door, in the warm summer sun, Tom put his arm around me. He had lived in America since I was seven or eight and had only recently come back.

"Don't worry, Mags," he said. "Everything will work out okay."

"What happened in Guernica, Tom?" I replied. "And don't treat me like a baby, by the way. I'm nearly sixteen."

Tom laughed.

"You were fifteen last month, remember. And Hitler is a long way from here."

"Tell me. I want to know. I'll ask Mary and she'll tell me if she knows."

"Hitler bombed a town in Spain," he said. "That's all. Now, don't worry, it'll be fine. It's a million miles from here."

I remember the look on Tom's face that day. He was wishing for a future he knew was already behind us. I had known all along what had happened in Guernica; that the Luftwaffe had bombed the city, destroyed it and killed the civilian population. I knew that it could happen here, but I didn't believe it until that moment on the steps of the house and the look on my brother's face. A trench opened deep inside my world and something evil took root in that dark part of me, a place no longer safe and hidden from the world. I felt sick to the pit of my stomach.

On another occasion I was in my usual place behind the door, pretending to study for my exams, when a fierce row broke out between Tom and Liam. What was really frightening was that this time Mum did nothing to stop it.

"Look, Hitler is not going to be satisfied with the Sudetenland," reasoned Tom. "First the Rhineland, then what he did in Spain, then Austria, and now Czechoslovakia. For once I agree with Churchill when he said we're '*like a flock of sheep on the way to the butcher*.'"

"Tom, listen to what Chamberlain said: *'Peace in our time,'*" countered Liam. "We have an agreement in writing from Hitler. Not just his word. It's over. Things will be fine from now on."

"Oh, for God's sake, don't be so naïve, Liam!" Tom retorted. "Why do you think they're still digging trenches in the park and issuing these things to every house?"

He pointed to a box of gas masks that sat on the kitchen table, unopened.

Then he dropped his voice and said slowly, "Because they know what's coming and they know that we're not ready for it."

I was dying to open the boxes, but I didn't move a muscle. I held my breath.

"You're being pessimistic, as usual," countered Liam. "Hitler wouldn't dare risk war with us and the Empire and France. He's not a complete lunatic."

Tom took a deep breath and sighed audibly before replying in a low and steady voice.

"Liam, I'm only going to say this once: Hitler *is* a lunatic. He's counting on us not having the stomach for a fight. And he's not going to stop at the gates of Prague."

"Tom, this is not our fight! It's got nothing to do with us! Chamberlain has succeeded where you said he couldn't. Britain and Germany will never go to war."

I looked at my mother glaring from one angry face to the other, a rising panic in her eyes. For once, the lethal weapon that was her dishcloth was not deployed, but lay limp and lifeless over her shoulder. I believe that she knew then, just as I did, that none of Liam's silvery wishes would stand in the way of Adolf Hitler. She sat between them, speechless, as the awful spectre dawned that her sons could be sacrificed to the Gods of Sky and Water.

A few days after that row, the shelter arrived.

"Look what the Lord Privy Seal in charge of air raid precautions – that Mister Anderson – has sent to keep us all safe from harm,"

Mum stormed. "A giant tin can, God help us! We'll be squashed in like sardines. I'll sleep in my own bed if you don't mind."

Liam, a ship's engineer, supervised the building of the shelter. He had recently returned from Singapore and was getting ready to sail for New York. He knew a lot about engines, but not a lot about air raid shelters. The boys dug for days. They sank a drain pit and laid a concrete base with steps down to it, then placed the shelter on the base and piled earth over the top. They assembled metal-framed bunks inside the galvanised shell. Liam even put in a spot for a heater, a small oil lamp and a bucket for a toilet. Luxury. Seeing that swell of soil and listening to the news, which got worse every day, my stomach twisted in a knot that didn't go away night or day.

Nothing that was thought of back then, no imagined future place, could prepare us for the terror of what was to come. For months now, since the end of summer 1940, the peace of our evenings was shattered night after night by the wailing of sirens and the menacing growl of approaching planes. They flew in high over the barrage balloons that I helped to make in Littlewoods, where I have worked since I turned seventeen. My teacher training has been put on hold until after the war. It felt good to be part of the fight against Hitler.

I hated the scramble in the dark down into the Anderson Shelter. It was cold and damp there. The air smelt of fear. We sat and waited in the stifled darkness, afraid to lie down. It was here, in this hole dug into our back garden, in a giant metal can piled over with earth, that we passed our nights of disturbed sleep.

The Blitz had visited our city and our town nearly every night since August. The newspapers were filled with stories of destruction and personal heroism from other parts of the country. London, Coventry… The censorship that hid our pain from the world added to my mother's anger and the anger on our streets.

A growing sense of despair hung in the murky air that fell across crumbled walls and broken footpaths and deep-cratered roads. It could be seen in the severed sewers and mains, in burnt-out homes and businesses. The stench of smouldering lives hung over the dust of fallen houses. Dust, chased from random corners by the sea breeze, swirled in spirals through the filthy air of shattered streets.

Over time a deep dread gripped my mind. Nowhere was safe. My father and brothers, those who weren't at sea, were out night after night on fire-watch. Those on land were directly in the path of the bombs. Those at sea were at the mercy of dive-bombers or U-boats. Our lives were shattered by madmen who desired nothing but death for me, my family and the entire population of our town, Bootle, and the city of Liverpool.

And then I was saved by a very smart dog. It was the most terrifying moment of my seventeen years on earth, but at least I had saved the dress.

The next morning we set out to early Mass. It was the fourth Sunday of Advent, the Sunday before Christmas. Maybe because of all the bombings, or because it was the start of Christmas week 1940, Father Breen was preaching the gospel of love and forgiveness.

He spoke from the pulpit. *"For God sent his Son into the world not to condemn the world, but so that through him the world might be saved. No one who believes in him will be condemned; but whoever refuses to believe is condemned already…"*

I desperately wanted to believe in a God who would save us.

Later on that evening, I sat at the kitchen table with my sister Mary. She was four years older than me and at twenty-one, married and pregnant, knew everything about life and love. Sitting there in the blacked-out room with her two hands wrapped around her mug of black tea, her smile beamed from ear to ear. She was staying with us while her Johnny was out on fire-watch.

"I love your dress," she said, looking at where I'd hung my prized possession on the back of the kitchen door. "Just look at that sweetheart neckline! Maybe I can borrow it in six months' time when I get over this bump? Only kidding. It's gorgeous. It'll turn some heads."

"Just one will do me," I said.

"And are we talking about Billy Newsome, by any chance? I hear that he's crewing on Tom's next ship. The one we can't name, of course, in case we're overheard. 'Loose lips sink ships,' as Tom says."

"Stop kidding, Mary. You know how it is. It's an official secret."

I gave a quick glance in the direction of the ceiling. Dad had spent seven nights straight on fire-watch along with his job of running the docks all day. He was exhausted. Tom had taken Dad's place tonight down at the docks to give him a night off.

"Mum and Dad are in bed, remember. For our ears only, okay?"

Suddenly, our world exploded just as the air raid siren went off. We jumped under the kitchen table and grabbed on to each other in the pitch black. A great wind whipped through the house, smashing cups, saucers and glass as it crashed through our home, followed almost immediately by the sound of the ceiling collapsing around us. It was like a rumble of thunder followed by massive hail hitting the floor and table, knocking over chairs.

As soon as everything stopped moving, I crawled out from under the table and pulled Mary out backwards as the other side was blocked. We scrambled our way through the dirt and rubble out into the hall.

"Mum! Dad! Where are you? Are you all right?"

Looking up as the dust began to clear, stars appeared through the blackness. Part of the roof was gone and the stairs were blocked with fallen timber. There was no smell of gas. Through the hole in the roof, the stars were watching.

"We're all right, but the stairway is blocked," Dad called. "Go out and get some help."

Outside on the pitch-black street there was panic. Sirens wailed and bombs continued to fall down on the docks. In towards the city, searchlights chased the shadow of death across the skies. The ack ack of anti-aircraft guns and the shriek and roar of high explosives filled the air. The furnaces of hell burned in a great ring of fire. Houses were blazing further down the street. The crowd was herded back with talk of UXB's.

"Unexploded bomb. Everyone out!"

Except that there was no way out, as our road ended on the railway and it seemed as though the whole world was on fire up there.

"Who are ye? Who *are* ye?"

It was the familiar Belfast twang of our neighbour two doors down.

"It's Mary Connolly and Maggie Brady. Are you all right, Mrs Waldron?"

Mrs Waldron had her hands on our heads, feeling the soft contours of our faces.

"Have you seen my Kate? Kate, where are ye?"

She moved on to the next group.

"Who are ye?"

It was pitch black, but as the light from the fires grew stronger and my eyes adjusted, I could make out that we were moving slowly through a shadowy crowd silhouetted against the burning buildings. It was only later, when I realised that we were all covered from head to foot in soot, that this biblical scene was complete.

Soot, like a great shadow of death, was forced by the blast down the chimneys of all the houses in the street and covered everything and everyone. We had crossed the Great Divide and were descending into Hades.

And then I remembered.

"My dress!"

The realisation struck me hard like shrapnel. I screamed, but no sound escaped my parched lips.

At that moment I could have killed Hitler with my bare hands.

"Maggie! Mary!"

It was my Billy. He'd been on fire-watch at the warehouse that was now blazing at the top end of the street.

"Are you all right?" he asked.

It sounded like a snarl from a wounded animal.

"Do you know where we can get a ladder?" I asked him. "Mum and Dad are trapped upstairs. We need to get them out now."

"Wait here."

The local fire-fighting team had arrived and were busy trying to connect their water pumps. Hungry, angry, red flames leapt through windows and doorways. Roofs were blazing, their dry, aged timbers feeding the conflagration.

Yet with all this fire, it was freezing cold under the stars.

Billy came back with a ladder, swung his coat around Mary and managed to get inside our house and up the stairs. Dad had rolled out of bed and was dressed. The impact of the blast had blown the glass out of the bedroom window, even though it had been taped, and a large shard had embedded itself in the wall a foot over their heads. With Billy's help, he managed to clear the rubble off the stairs and somehow got Mum down safely. He led her out the back and into the shelter.

She never said a word. That would come later.

"God bless you, lad," said Dad.

"You're welcome, Mister Brady."

CHAPTER TWO

Summer 1939

Looking back now to that innocent time before the war, the most abiding memory I have of our home is walking into the warmth of the back kitchen in the early morning. Mum would have been up for hours, rising early in the half-light of summer or the pitch-black of winter and silently breathing the range back to life. She cooked Dad's porridge all year round and sent him off to work on the docks with a full stomach and a packed lunch. As soon as I opened the door, the heat would hit me in the face. It would draw me in and wrap me up in its comforting blanket.

There was bustle and clamour in that little space. The clatter of dishes, pots and pans was like a rhythmic beat that drew words into the air. The talk was always lively. My brothers would argue the football gossip about how bad Liverpool was and how good Everton was, and the upcoming Derby. Then they'd move on to the war in Spain and the terrible things Hitler was doing, bombing Barcelona, Guernica or Madrid. There was talk about tides and weather, the latest shipping news, and their upcoming trips to exotic places; Alexandria, Casablanca, Boston, Bombay or over the pond to Dublin or Belfast, bringing coal, sugar, timber, or cotton in those peace-filled years before the war.

An enormous pot of steaming porridge sat on the stove, feeding an army of mouths. Mum, like a four-star general, dished out orders by the ladle while I sat in the corner, quiet as a mouse, pretending to read some schoolbook, hanging on every word.

She was a great shot with her dishcloth. If talk became too heated or turned to politics or religion, she could repeatedly fire off that dishcloth like a machine gun.

"No room in this house for Mister Chamberlain," she'd say, the lilt of her Irish accent rising above the din. "Am I the only person in the world going to do any work today?"

That was the end of it.

There was a general clear-out. I joined four of my brothers Liam, John, Pat and Luke, who were on shore leave, as they passed me at the door. They were off to the park for a kick-around before heading out to sea later in the morning. They were in buoyant spirits.

"I bags be Dixie Dean." I let them know I wasn't going to be goalie again.

They say that some things are fated to happen. When it came to Billy and me, I believed that was true. The midsummer fete was held each June in the school hall adjoining the church, and as in every year since I can remember, I had been volunteered by my mother to help. So on Saturday 24th June 1939, I found myself working with a group of other volunteers, mostly my own age, who had also been volunteered by their mothers. We put up bunting, carried tables and sorted boxes of old toys and books and clothes. We set up stands of home-made bread, cakes, sweets and novelty stalls. I mention this date because it's our date.

I was putting up bunting, standing on a chair, struggling to reach a hook high on the wall of the hall. Suddenly Billy reached over, saying, "I'll do that for you, Miss," and then it was done. He smiled as he caught my hand and helped me down. It was a moment of pure magic.

"I'm Billy," he said. "Don't want you falling again, do we?"

My heart felt like it had jumped into my mouth as I stepped down off the chair. Billy held on to my hand for a split second longer than he needed to.

"I'm Maggie. Thanks for the hand."

He beamed an even broader smile. Looking back, that was the moment when it first began, our love for each other. That is, if you still believe in love after all that has happened. It was as if a tide had come in and lifted our boats and we were powerless to stop it, even if we'd wanted to.

For most people, the summer of '39 is remembered for the hapless drift into war, when nations forged relationships built on hate or fear. But for us it was a time of awakening, of young love waltzing on the bandstand in the park to the sound of the summer breeze. It was as though summer itself had taken a deep breath of sea air, spread itself prostrate on the estuary sands, looked up at deep blue skies and sighed. It was hard not to believe that things would stay that way forever.

We met outside the cinema the following week. He'd asked me if I'd like to go and see *Goodbye, Mister Chips* and I didn't have the heart to tell him I'd already seen it with my friends. This was a date and with Mary as chaperone, we sat holding hands and watched the drama unfold. In the film, Mister Chips falls in love with Katherine, a young woman he meets on a mountain in Austria. Despite their age gap, they pass the test of true love when they both see that the colour of the River Danube is really blue. It was a bit corny second time round, but there wasn't a dry eye in the house. I think we were all in mourning for the *world* of Mister Chips, a world where it meant something to be English. A world in which you could carry on teaching Latin while a Zeppelin dropped bombs outside. A world slipping silently by the stern of our boats, as we headed out into the channel and on towards a choppy sea.

Afterwards, as we walked by the docks, it was clear to both of us that the river was cold and grey, tinged with angry white horses, the forerunner of a squall that was coming in off the sea. We found an area outside the high walls where piles of timber blocked us from view. Billy pressed himself against me and we kissed. It was like an explosion of blue. Then Mary's urgent voice called that it was time to go.

I often think of that time now, the two of us, red-faced and laughing, linked either side of Mary as we walked back to Bootle. It's an image I carry in my head, a still photograph carried in memory, frayed and fading at the edges, but the definition sharp and clear. Mary, then getting ready for her upcoming wedding, looked beautiful in her fawn gabardine coat with a fur collar and her elegant hat, for all the world looking like Greta Garbo. We laughed all the way home.

"Goodbye, Mister Chips."

"Goodbye, Miss Chips."

"You two are completely bonkers!"

"You're the best sister, Mary. Just the best."

The sharp evening air that blew in off Liverpool Bay carried with it a hint of salt and the smell of the sea, while overhead seagulls wheeled and squawked to the Gods of Sky and Water, screeching for their supper. But to us, that coming night exhaled the promise of love like smoke rising from the portions of chips we held in our hands as an offering to the gods.

We didn't notice the hard words printed in black ink on the pages of the newspapers. It was the delicious taste of freshly cooked chips with the whiff of vinegar and the hungry bite of salt that made up our world. A banquet fit for a king and queen.

CHAPTER THREE

September 1939

That summer seemed to last forever. Time stood still and gazed out to sea, into the shimmering haze where sea and sky mixed and intertwined. The tidal flow of the estuary rocked us as we lay on the wet sand. Lukewarm water lapped our thighs, rolled on to our stomachs and nudged our hands intertwined in the mix of sea and sand. We were King and Queen of a vast kingdom of sea and air that swirled and spun in the blue that stretched to the blur, so that sky and water joined in an ecstasy of happiness, our fingers buried deep in the sand, anchoring our bodies to each other.

But summer ended like the blink of an eye on lookout, with unknown dangers lurking about, hiding beneath the surface of the sea and in the burning face of the sun.

Then the world went dark.

Like the shadow of a solar eclipse spreading across the face of Europe, a malevolent force of unspeakable evil came knocking on our door.

Billy and I cycled out to where the estuary meets the open sea on the Saturday morning of that fateful weekend, to a section of beach that we called *Our Shore*. We laughed and joked that it would possibly be the last swim of the year. It was the second day of September, a weekend that changed our world forever. What would normally have been a quiet cycle was interrupted by a stream of lorries heading towards the shore full and returning empty. Billy was forced to swing in to the side of the road in front of me, then back out to cycle alongside, and back in again every time one of them came to pass us. Soldiers shouted, whistled and laughed out of the open back and sides, waving as they passed.

We eventually reached the sand dunes and raced each other to the top in our excitement to catch a glimpse of Our Shore. Once there, we stood hand-in-hand panting and breathless, dumbstruck, gazing in silence out to sea. A line of breakers was visible in the middle distance across the wide expanse of beach, broken in several places by long slivers of shallow water left behind by the retreating tide.

Spirals of barbed wire were being unfurled the entire length of the sands, where they stood naked, shivering, abandoned in the full glare of the midday sun. New concrete bunkers and gun emplacements were being dug into the dunes and *Keep Out* and *Danger* signs had sprung up everywhere. We sat in silence, our legs dangling over the edge of a half-built bunker, taking in the wide sweep of the scene before us. Soldiers moved like crabs across the sands. A glint of silver from the wet rivulets mixed urgently with cruel flashes from the barbed wire, sending a warning in Morse code from the Gods of Sky and Water. I closed my eyes against the glare.

The Vikings had stood on this very spot over a thousand years ago. Anlef, Viking King of Dublin joined forces with Constantine, King of Scotland, and landed a huge army in the Mersey with the intention of conquering England. The Saxon army had other ideas and defeated the invaders in a ferocious battle that resulted in Edmund the First being crowned first King of England.

The Vikings believed in the vengeance of their sky god Odin, and of their warriors' God-given right to wreak havoc in his name, but they got their comeuppance here on the Mersey Shore. Mary had got me reading about them and their female warriors, the Valkyrie. They followed Odin everywhere, even into battle, and carried the bodies of the dead to Valhalla, the Norse version of heaven. Strong women, clearing up the mess made by violent men. In another life I could imagine myself as one of the Valkyrie. I would have the power to choose who would live and who would die.

Billy's elbow dug into my side.

"I'm starvin'!"

Not even the desolation of the scene before us could dampen our spirits. I carefully laid the picnic rug on the bare concrete and began to set out our celebration lunch. Billy scrambled to his feet, waving like a person possessed. A large passenger ship was making its way down the Queen's Channel, the narrow channel that runs down the Mersey parallel to the coast, and on out towards the open sea. Crowds on the ship could be clearly seen and heard as they cheered and waved. Billy jumped up and down and cheered and waved back.

"That's the *SS Athenia*," he said. "It came down from Glasgow. It's heading to Belfast now and will sail for Montreal later today. There's a lot of people on board heading for Canada to escape the coming war. Must be over a thousand men, women and children on that ship. Come on Maggie, wave back."

Billy had just finished his studies as a radio operator and knew everything about every ship that sailed in and out of the port. We were celebrating his graduation. It was like his job and his hobby and his passion all rolled into one.

It struck me then that Our Shore was being transformed into our very own concentration camp. The ship and its fortunate passengers were making a great escape beyond the rolling barbed wire and sailing into a new life far from the threat of bullets and bombs. They would be watched over on their journey by the god of water Aegir, but with the threat from his wife Rán who captured stray sailors in her net. They could be in for a rough passage from their nine daughters whose various names I couldn't remember, who depicted every kind of wave. The sea was a fickle and dangerous place. The

Vikings knew that from bitter experience. A shiver ran the length of my spine.

Passengers gathered along her starboard side and lined the decks of her stern. The ship ploughed down the Queen's Channel and on into Liverpool Bay and the Irish Sea beyond, steam pouring black from the one large funnel mid-ship. The *Athenia* gave a long farewell blast of its ship's horn. She swung away from the shore, headed straight out into the clear blue sea and sailed on into the mix of sky and water in Liverpool Bay. A trailing cloud of smoke rose in a column behind, marking the sky like a dirty smudge on the living seascape.

"*SS Athenia* to Canada via Belfast, one pm Saturday, the Second of September. All aboard!"

Billy, pretending to shout into his cupped hands, was in his element.

I gazed in wonder at the stern until it disappeared into the hazy blue, leaving only the black funnel visible. When I looked again, that too had disappeared into the shimmering ocean, leaving only a wisp of grey smoke dispersed and hanging in the vast ether. I wanted more than anything to be stowed safely on board that ship with Billy and my whole family, sailing over the horizon and on to the New World. I wanted to leave behind forever the knot at the bottom of my stomach, and the terrible dreams that have haunted my broken sleep for such a long time now.

We sat motionless long after the dark swirl was eaten up. I was watching the shadows of the clouds, black on the surface of the sea, chasing after the ship where it had disappeared out towards the horizon. I shivered again for no reason, as it was a warm day. Billy put his jacket around me, gently wrapped me in his arms and kissed me. I felt myself falling backwards in space, rolling on to my side and kissing him back. Then my elbow gave way and we both slipped sideways into the sandwiches. At that very moment, a truck screeched to a stop beside us and a group of soldiers armed with picks and spades trundled past. We ate our dishevelled sandwiches and drank our lukewarm lemonade. Try as we did to recapture it, the moment was gone forever.

The sun shone for the first Sunday in September. My parents had gone to early Mass as they wanted to be home in time to hear the broadcast. I'd arranged to meet up with Billy after eleven o'clock Mass, but there was no sign of him at the church. It wasn't like him. Mass was a rushed affair. Father Breen walked off the altar and into the sacristy straight after communion, which was unusual. Then he came back out with a serious face and said a quick blessing.

"Go home to your families," he said. "We are a nation at war. May God help us and keep us safe from all harm."

Outside, on the steps of the church, I strained my eyes into a sky filled with puffy white clouds floating carefree across the deep blue yonder. There was no sign of enemy planes. Halfway home, however, the piercing sound of air raid sirens shattered the peace of our world. I ran through the shocking noise, convinced that bombs would fall at any moment.

My memory of that day is etched on my soul. I remember crying to myself with terror as I ran home that sunny morning. I gulped the air filled with the shrill sound of sirens. I ran, looking up and back over my shoulder, expecting German planes to appear and bomb us all into annihilation right there and then. I reached the safety of our back kitchen, leapt into my seat behind the door and put my hands over my ears.

I strained to hear the peaceful peal of church bells, but they had fallen silent that morning. If heard at any time in the future, they would be the signal that an invasion was underway, telling us that Stormtroopers were at our door, warning us that our very civilisation was about to be destroyed forever. All I could hear were the low rumblings of enemy aircraft somewhere deep inside my head.

I should have known that nothing is forever.

"They've turned off the sirens. It was just a drill. Nothing to worry about. Mags. Are you okay?"

I looked up at the calm face of my big brother Tom; the taut, white face of my father and the red, angry face of my mother, and then my other brothers jostling for positions in the confined space.

"Remember, things change, but we remain the same."

That was a big speech for my father. He was wearing his cap in the house, which I had never seen him do before, like he was ready to leave at any moment. Then he took it off, scratched the top of his bald head and put it back on again.

The bombs did not fall on us on that day, the first day of the war. Nor the next. We did not know then that they wouldn't come till long after my seventeenth birthday, deep into the following summer. Our peace was already shattered and our sacred space invaded with the shadow of death that September Sunday morning. I could see it in my mother's eyes.

How do you send your seven sons out into the perils of the North Atlantic, or the Mediterranean, or the Indian Ocean? How do you say goodbye with a casual nod in the knowledge that there is a very good chance that you will never see each other again? How do you send your husband off to work at the heart of the biggest German target outside London? Those docks were only a mile away from our home as the crow flies. The Gods of Sky and Water were angry. Nothing short of human sacrifice would satisfy them now. The bombs would surely come.

There was no doubt that the U-boats were deep under Atlantic waters. Tom and all the others would have to face them down. Tom laughed it off.

"Oh, the Atlantic is a very big ocean. Nothing to worry about, Ma."

He grabbed her and swung her around in the little space and the faces of her children turned into men were laughing at the sport of it all as they whizzed by in a blur. Dad had taken his cap off again and was scratching his bald head, wearing an expression that confirmed to me that the world had gone completely mad.

"That's the end of the football season," he said. "Bad cess to ye Hitler."

Everyone laughed, but to me sitting in my snug, it felt like a death. Our death. Nothing would ever be the same again.

CHAPTER FOUR

December 1940

The all-clear brought much needed relief from that hellhole. Mum never spoke a word the whole night in the shelter. I lay on my side, with images of fire and bombings flashing on the inside of my eyelids, wishing that she would be her usual self and lash out about the war, using her sharp tongue as a weapon to fight back at Hitler.

Not a word.

We stared in silent disbelief at the scene that greeted us when we scrambled through the back kitchen and out into the hall. Part of the roof was gone. There were broken timbers and glass everywhere… everything ruined and covered in soot. It is a terrible thing, losing your home. And yet we were among the lucky ones, Dad said. Miraculously, we had all escaped injury. Our home was the worse for wear, but still standing.

Johnny arrived and guided Mary through what was left of the house. Tom, Pat and Peter arrived back up from the docks, where they had been on fire-watch, and had a good look at the damage. They climbed on to what was left of the roof and declared it fixable. Talk was of a new section of roof and something to replace the glass that had been blown out of every window. They cleared the rubble from the stairs and I climbed up to see for myself the broken glass and soot, cold air and empty window panes. We had been violated by Hitler and his filthy Luftwaffe. Then I saw a pane of glass lodged in the wall a few feet above my parents' bed. I started to shake with anger and something resembling shock set in, only it wasn't, more like disbelief that this could happen in our home.

I was concerned about Billy and his own place, a few streets away over the far side of the railway. He worried a lot about his mother up there on her own and his brother somewhere in the South Atlantic. His father's death had hit her hard. I needed to see him and hold him, but that would have to wait. There was a great debate about what we should do. The talk was of going to the church hall until the house was repaired and sleeping in the crypt, as it was as good as any air raid shelter. Then my mother found her voice again.

"I'm not going anywhere out of my home to have looters and god knows who traipsing through the house, going through my drawers," she said. "If the bombers come back tonight, there's not a lot more that they can do to us. Tom, can you get that stove cleared and we'll see if it's working?"

Thus it was decided to stay. With a gigantic team effort, we cleared most of the rubble out of the kitchen. My dress lay on the floor under plaster and brick, torn and covered in timber and soot. It looked like a sad rag, a reminder of a life that would never be. I grabbed it and stumbled out the door and on through the hall, fighting back tears with every stride. And with every stride, something broke inside me. By the time I got to sit on the front steps, tears were flowing freely down both cheeks.

The next thing I remember was Mr Watts, our local air raid warden, who ran the corner shop at the end of our street, and Father Breen, standing with Tom, Pat and Peter out on the road, discussing the nights of destruction that we had lived through. More than two hundred people were dead in Bootle alone. Eight people had died at the other end of our street. Two air raid shelters took direct hits, as did the railway arches. The docks took another heavy beating. Hundreds more were injured and thousands left homeless.

The men approached the house.

"Maggie, are you all right?" asked Father Breen.

"I've been better, Father," I said. "Thanks for asking."

They went past me into the house and Tom sat down beside me. He put his arm around me and I let myself be wrapped up into the safety of his strong arms.

"It's normal to feel like this in battle," he said. "This is what war does to people. If it doesn't kill you, it can damage your spirit and break you inside."

"What kind of God would allow this to happen?" I snapped.

"Hush now, Mags. This isn't the time to start loose talk like that. We need to pull together."

"I want to ask him."

"Who?"

"Father Breen. I want him to explain to me how God loves me today."

"Let's go for a walk, Maggie."

He led me down our street to where the bomb had landed on the houses that had been on fire last night. Three of them were gone, reduced to nothing but a mound of bricks, with smoke rising from the rubble in the cold morning breeze. It sent a chill through my bones. Other houses were black and smouldering, their roofs and insides burnt asunder. I could see a picture still hanging on the wall of Number Six. The faces were fused to the cracked glass.

Before the war there had been life in this space. Children tumbling down steps, Sunday dinners cooking, thoughts of Christmas week... Now, loved ones were away at war. Josie Morris, who had been in my class at school, was dead, along with her whole family. Josie and I used to walk her little sister to school. She'd never stop talking. She used to skip down the pavement, laughing and singing nursery rhymes, holding my hand. God, the smallness of it. I remembered how sweet and gentle she was. Little Beth, now away in Wales and her family dead. All dead.

"Tom, it's not normal to feel like this. Why did you say that just now? Are you not angry or afraid or anything?"

"You're right, Mags, it's not normal, but there is no normal right now. This is Hitler trying to break us – and whatever happens, we can't let him win. We can't let him break our spirit."

I looked at Tom and knew that he was crying silent tears that he would never let the world see.

"Truth is, sis, I'm getting so used to seeing this that I'm not thinking about it so much. Just keep on doing what you can to not let these bastards get to you."

I had never heard Tom curse. Mum would have brought the dishcloth into action had she been within earshot.

"Wash out your tongue!" was her stock answer to any profanity, and the dishcloth would snap at the perpetrator in the same breath. The brothers called the dishcloth 'Sting' and had all felt its sting at one time or another.

We walked on through the park where the searchlights and ack ack gun emplacements were throwing new diggings around like graves in the cemetery, getting bigger and deeper with each passing raid. Down at the docks, it looked like the end had come. The Overhead Railway had been hit again and a large warehouse was on fire. Fires burned or smouldered all along the length of the river. Across the Mersey in Birkenhead and Wallasey, it was a mirror image.

"Cotton," Tom nodded towards the warehouse. "It'll probably burn till Christmas Day."

The exhausted firemen had given up trying to save the building and were concentrating on containing the hungry fire that snapped and snarled along the roof and screamed out through every window.

It was mid-winter, the shortest day of the year. The weather seemed content that there was no lift in the light. The sun hid his face behind black smoke interspersed with dark clouds that formed a gloomy frame within which the city landscape and seascape could be mistaken for a black-and-white photograph of the great catastrophe.

The roads were littered with random bomb craters. Near the docks, we came across an ambulance halfway down in one of the craters. A team of men strained and pulled on ropes and pulleys, lifting the heavy vehicle inch by inch.

"The crew of that ambulance were taking an injured mother and two children to hospital last night," said Tom. "Their first car was hit during the raid and they had to transfer to the ambulance which then drove into the bomb crater in the dark. The patients had to be carried out of there, then transferred to a hand cart, and continued to the hospital on foot."

"That's a terrible story," I said.

"It's true," he said. "I was here last night when it happened. I helped to get them out, as it was impossible to put the fire out in the warehouse. I wanted to bring you here, Mags, because this is what we do. No matter what they throw at us, we'll never give in and we *will* win this war. Good will win true in the end. We're fighting for our very existence here. Don't you see that we can never let this beat us?"

I looked at the earnest face of my big brother, strained and taut from nights of fighting fires from thousands of incendiary bombs, of being blasted by hundreds of high-explosives and parachute mines. He was doing this while on shore leave, having had his ship torpedoed in mid-Atlantic.

I felt my eyes welling up again, this time in anger.

"I'm going to look for work in the munitions factory in Kirkby tomorrow," I said. "They're asking for volunteers and I'm going, so don't try to stop me."

Tom laughed in spite of everything.

"You can't work there, Mags. It's too dangerous. Besides, you're under eighteen. You know the rules."

It was my turn to laugh now, though it felt and probably sounded like a snarl.

"Look at you lecturing me about danger," I replied. "You, who's just off a ship that was sunk in the mid-Atlantic! You, who comes down here every night on fire-watch as if you're going to the football up at Goodison. You put out hundreds of incendiary bombs and place yourself in the direct fire of the HE bombs, not to mention the parachute mines and shrapnel from our own guns".

I paused for breath.

"Tom, I may be the youngest in the family, but I'm not a baby. I have to do something that will help to hit back at him. Making barrage balloons is important – I know that – but to be honest, I always thought they were more for show than anything else. I'm determined to go out to Kirkby tomorrow. There's a general call-out and I'll tell a white lie about my age. After all, I'm in my eighteenth year. Besides, I heard that you get better coupons if you work there."

He laughed at my poor attempt at a joke, and then yawned.

"Come on. Let's get you to Mary's place," I said. "At least you can have a proper sleep there. She's on duty in the library today. That's if there's anything left of it this morning."

The journey through the broken city was like walking in a dream through a Pathé News report. It reminded me of scenes from the crumbling streets of the East End of London that Billy and I had watched on the big screen last week, when we went to see *Gone with the Wind*. On the way up to Mary's place, Tom stopped to help pull a broken handcart out from under a collapsed wall. The air was pitch black. Breathing it seemed to suck the lifeblood out of my body. I could taste dust, soot and grit in my teeth and on the roof of my dry mouth. He was in the midst of it all, a handkerchief tied around his mouth, stripped to his vest, his muscles rippling under the strain.

I knew that something terrible had happened in America to bring Tom home. I often tried to find out what it was, but always drew a blank. I couldn't get a word out of Tom about that. I felt an enormous swell of pride rising in me that he was my brother. He was a hero if ever there was one.

One thing that struck me as we picked our way through the rubble-strewn streets was the randomness of it all. Here, a whole street was spared. There, one side was spared and the other smashed and broken. In one direction, everything was destroyed, while houses on the other side of the impact site were left untouched. Here a bomb, there an unexploded bomb. This street blocked, that street gone. Apart from Father Breen, there wasn't much sign of God here in this hellhole.

We stopped for a moment on the climb up towards Mary's place, to catch our breath in the smoky air. A gap in a missing warehouse wall framed the city in a landscape painting, where the end of the building had been blown away some time ago. It was a stunning sight. Huge fires burned on in factories and warehouses all along the docks and on into the city. Smaller trails of smoke filled the spaces in between. The sea breeze blew them all in towards the city centre where more fires smouldered in the distance. It looked like the end, or at very best, the beginning of the end.

A dread crept into my lower stomach and turned in on itself, so that I could barely move when Tom called me to walk on.

Billy. Why hadn't I heard from Billy? Had something bad happened to him?

I fought back the rising panic and hurried after Tom.

The inside of Mary's flat was like a haven, a reminder of how the world was before. Normal things in their place. Pictures on the wall. No soot, damp, broken glass or bits of timber or plaster blasted from their place. Ceiling intact. Normal.

Tom crashed on to the settee and was already asleep as I pulled a blanket over him to keep him warm.

CHAPTER FIVE

No one was allowed down Billy's street. A UXB had fallen near his house and buried itself in a neighbour's garden. Mum said that it had had the good sense not to go off and allowed time for the whole street to be evacuated. Word was that it was too dangerous to try to defuse it at the moment. Bombs like that had been made in a munitions factory somewhere in Germany – though the lads joked that this one had probably been made in Czechoslovakia where it had been sabotaged as there was still a lot of opposition to Hitler – and I was going to make some of our own. Return to Sender. The thought of that made me feel better as I made my way over to the church hall, where I guessed I'd find Billy.

The streets were filling with a strange collection of people, their grimy faces set hard against the dull light. Wearing grey-black clothes and faces to match, wrapped in whatever came to hand to keep out the cold, their eyes betrayed them. Eyes white against the blackness, filled with fear of the present and dread of the future. Eyes that had seen destruction and were now haunted by the unknown, the coming night, the terror from the sky... The bitter memory of the cold and ice of last winter gave no comfort and sent a chill into the very heart of those homeless, those with no one to help them repair their lost roofs and empty window frames.

I passed through them as though I were invisible. I was one with them, one *of* them, like a lost tribe of Israel, cursed to wander through a broken landscape in search of the Promised Land. A woman I recognised from our street passed by. Then another. Where were they all going?

"Out, out of this cursed city. They'll be back tonight and we're getting out. Nowhere is safe. And the cold is going to get worse."

I stopped and looked at the long line of people. This was happening in our town and our city. This is what war does to a civilian population. Tom's words were repeating in my brain like a mantra.

"*We can never let this beat us. We can never let them beat us.*"

My hands shook as I gathered my coat tight around me and walked on towards the church hall.

The scene at the hall was chaotic. Volunteers were trying to put some order on who was there, who was missing, and who had left to get out of the city before nightfall. They were giving out blankets, cups of black tea, soup and old clothes. In the midst of them I saw Billy's mother, Bess. I ran over to her.

"Mrs Newsome, how are you?" I asked. "Have you seen Billy about?"

"God bless you, lass," she said. "He's in the church with Father Breen. They're training extra fire-watchers on account of the hundreds sleeping in the crypt tonight. How are your mother and father bearing up? I heard your place was badly hit last night."

"Thanks, Mrs Newsome. We're doing fine."

It was only when I said it that it struck me that we were going to be all right. My brothers would see to that. I needed to find Billy.

He was down in the basement of the church, the crypt, originally built to bury the dead. I had only ever been there once before, to collect some storage boxes for the fete. It gave me the creeps. I remembered the old church furniture piled high in the stagnant air, and a sense of some spirit, good or bad, hovering there. I'd felt relieved to climb back up the stairs into the dull light of the church.

Now I found myself descending those stairs again, into the bowels of the church, oil lamps lighting the way. The room had been cleared of furniture and was filled with blankets, bedding and mattresses. Hearing muffled voices, I made my way into a narrow corridor that opened into a vast space whose length disappeared into the darkness. Someone was laying an electric cable to bring light to that dark space. It was half-filled with bedding. I saw Billy talking with Father Breen, Mr Watts and some other men I didn't know.

Father Breen seemed genuinely pleased to see me.

"Well Maggie, did your mother send you over to help?" he asked. "Isn't she the plucky woman to have such a family gathered about her?"

"Thanks, Father. Billy, your mother is looking for you."

"Tell her I'll be there in a minute. Thanks, Maggie."

Outside in the cold, windswept yard, I waited for him with hunger on my lips and a growing madness in my heart. The world had gone completely cuckoo and me with it. Hitler was trying to blow us off the face of the earth, and he was doing a bloody good job. Then Billy appeared, his smile a steady beacon. He wrapped his arms around me, drew me into his chest and kissed my forehead. I felt my legs go from under me. Somewhere in the hidden depths, a dam broke.

"Hush now, hush. What's with all these tears?" he asked. "Has someone been hurt?"

I sobbed for a moment longer, then planted my feet on the gravel and kissed him hard.

"Wow, Jesus, Mags, what the hell? Take it easy!"

He kissed me gently and I surrendered myself to him.

"You're gorgeous, you know that?" he said.

He brushed his hand across my face, fixed me with those blue eyes and smiled.

"We'll always be together us, no matter what, hey?"

"I love you, Billy Newsome. No matter what Hitler tries to do to us, he can never take that away."

Billy put his finger on my lips and kissed me again. The world stopped spinning out of control and a feeling almost like happiness took hold of me.

We went into the hall for something to eat and I worked there for the next couple of hours, bringing food and blankets to the new arrivals. Tom was right. The only way to cope with what was happening was to keep on doing what we could.

"Don't let the bastards get to you," I said to myself.

"I beg your pardon, Madam, let us not have language like that in here if you don't mind. We still have our standards, you know."

I waved my apologies to the old woman sat next to me. She was holding a standard lamp with a pink shade and white lace trim. Her purple dress was dirty and torn at the shoulder. Her angry face glared at me from under a feathered hat. It was time to go home.

The afternoon sun shone through dark clouds, heavy with foreboding. Smoke was rising from bombsites all across the city. Storm clouds gathered, their purple bulk filled the estuary and blocked out the sea. It was a miracle. There would be no Jerry tonight.

Black rain, sent by the God of Sky, Odin, was set to chill the soul of the city. He will pour water on the smouldering fires, and fill the bottoms of bomb craters. Damp rain will seep into the bedrooms, halls and kitchens of the poor. With luck, he will blanket the docks with a woolly fog. We should be safe for one night. Christmas was coming early.

"Home she comes when the work is done. Aren't you the smart lady!"

I knew Mum was glad to see me as she was almost back to her cheery self. The kitchen had been cleared of rubble, cleaned, and the roof wore a temporary cover that the boys had worked on all day. Now they were hungry. Food was ready and things were sort of back to normal.

"There's a hell of a storm coming in," remarked Tom. "There'll be no Jerry tonight."

He was getting ready to go back out on fire-watch, as were all the boys.

"This is going to be the best Christmas present ever," he went on. "I don't think they'll be back until the end of the week. It's going to be stormy right through to Boxing Day and beyond. Jerry loves Christmas, you know."

I looked at Tom and the faces of my other brothers, Pat and Peter, who both reflected his excitement. Dad was scratching his head again and looking unconvinced.

"Well, bombs or no bombs, we all have to eat. Make way for my best war stew. Plaster, shrapnel and roof-slate soup – with splinters added for taste."

Somehow Mum had produced a great winter stew with real meat and vegetables. I believe that it was her own way of giving two fingers to Hitler and the Luftwaffe.

With handshakes, back slaps and punches to the shoulder, the boys headed out to the docks on fire-watch. It was starting all over again. I felt the bottom of my stomach drop. That's what war does. It won't go away just because I wish it to. I suddenly remembered that tomorrow was Christmas Eve. I looked at my hand and my fingers were shaking. It really is a terrible thing to be afraid all the time.

Now that I'd decided to work in the munitions factory I felt better for it. I was going to give Hitler and his gang a taste of their own medicine. There would be no more tears. It was our turn to strike back.

CHAPTER SIX

The storm swept through from the west and brought misery and joy in equal measure. Heavy rain dampened the fires that burned across the city. Water poured through broken roofs into broken lives without discrimination, into bedrooms and down stairs into good sitting rooms and back kitchens. It flowed into people's homes, bringing wet and cold misery to add to their soot-filled world. The temporary roof that Tom, Pat and Peter had somehow managed to repair kept most of the rain out. A few pots and pans, strategically placed on the top of the stairs, did the rest.

Not everyone was lucky enough to have an army of young men at hand to set to and repair the roof over their head. The reality was that very few young men were home for Christmas. Many of the local boys were at sea, running the gauntlet of the North Atlantic. Four of my brothers were out there, and were about to be joined by the other three, and the love of my life, later in the week. What were the odds that eight of them would survive out in that cold, cruel battlefield? Tom and Pat had both been torpedoed and their ships lost. They'd been lucky to survive. It seemed to be getting worse, but you weren't allowed to say that, of course.

I told myself to get over the dress. In the grand scheme of things, what did it matter? But I had dreamed of wearing that dress. Thinking about it now, I suppose it was a way of transporting myself to another world, out of the depression of war.

It was visible on the expressions of people in the street. The tense strain contorted the faces, furrowed the brows, black-circled the eyes. A constant fear of the present and worry about the future was all around us. It wasn't helped by the lack of shelter, food, money and clothes. Pins, needles and buttons? None to be had. Fresh food? Grow your own. Sugar, tea, meat? Rationed. Torn dress? Make do and mend.

It would be ridiculous to actually wear the dress in the middle of all this. It would be sinful to flaunt it in the face of such mass destruction. It was stupid to want it in the first place. But want it I did, and I nearly paid the ultimate price for it. Thinking about it was probably what kept me sane. I was done with crying for the loss of it. It was Hitler's doing and I would make him pay.

These were the thoughts that kept me company as I travelled on the 'Simonswood' tram out to Kirkby that Christmas Eve. The munitions factory was newly built and housed in numerous buildings spread over a vast site. I didn't know too much about it. I had heard that the work was dangerous, and that was enough for me. If they want to bomb us, then I'm happy to make bombs to bomb them. And I will be helping to win the war.

"You'll be on three shifts of eight hours each," said the manager at my interview. "You must work when you are assigned. No stopping the work here. It's top secret, as you know. You mustn't talk outside about what we do here. Training starts on Friday, on the job. Welcome aboard. Sign here."

It was as simple as that. Sitting on the return tram, I felt that I would be doing something positive to get back at Jerry. The rain was crying tears down the outside of the window. When I stared at my reflection in the glass, I struggled to recognise the hard face that stared back.

"Some people are happy enough to dodge the bombs, but why bother when you have the chance to surround yourself with them day and night – and get paid for the pleasure? Where exactly is Simonswood anyway?"

"It's just a cover name, Mum, a townland, to keep the location secret from Jerry."

"Well, you could have fooled me, so I guess that'll fool Jerry!"

That was all she said, so I took it that she was not completely against me working in Kirkby. The fact that we had been bombed night after night, and that Hitler had the audacity to damage her own home probably shaded it.

"Father Breen said that you were a great help to him yesterday and such a nice girl. 'Everyone likes her,' he said. I've invited Bess and that lad of hers to come around for dinner after Mass tomorrow, seeing as they're still out of their house because of that bomb that's ticking in the garden next door."

I coughed and spluttered into my cup of tea.

"He's turned into a fine lad," she went on. "Helped us downstairs the other night after the bomb. He's joining Tom's crew on Friday. He's a radio officer, you know."

"Yes, I know. I'm going round to the hall to help with the teas. You do know, I suppose, that we're friends?"

"We all need friends, Maggie, especially in these strange times. It's good to have friends."

This was Mum's way of telling me that she approved of Billy and me. She spoke for Dad too, as he would never say anything on such matters. And she had invited Billy and his Mum to Christmas dinner! Strange indeed, but what a lovely gesture. I hugged her my thanks, and meant it when I said that she was the best. Then I was gone, leaving her to pluck the turkey that had just arrived, in the middle of the mayhem, from Uncle Peter in Ireland. Another mad thing in a crazy world.

The church hall was now a full-blown shelter, with nearly three hundred people living there and sleeping down in the crypt. Many of Billy's neighbours were staying there, hoping to return to their homes for Christmas, but the main priority for the city was to clear the streets and get the water, gas and sewerage back working as soon as possible. The bomb in their street would have to wait. We set about decorating the hall with the bunting from the summer fete, adding some tinsel and a Christmas tree that someone had salvaged from the rubble of their home. I felt a sort of happiness again that I was able to do something to help.

It felt as if Billy and I had left our younger lives behind. We were adults now and didn't have to hide our friendship. He was a bit anxious about my brothers, especially Tom, who would be First Mate on his ship. It was scheduled to leave at the weekend.

"Mary and her husband Johnny will be there as well," I told him. "There's safety in numbers. Just don't tell them that you're a Liverpool fan and you'll survive."

I wasn't joking.

The school had been turned into a mortuary as the hospitals were full. Billy told me that there were over fifty bodies in there. They were set to be buried in a mass grave on Boxing Day. Adults and children, families and soldiers, bodies and body parts, all victims of war... They were laid out in a line covered in blankets, waiting for the brief church service, followed by the final journey to the graveyard. Josie Morris and her family were there – what was left of them, that is. People on fire-watch and huddled in shelters. Those manning the anti-aircraft guns, or at the base of the searchlights, or guiding the sweep of the steel cables of the barrage balloons. Ambulance drivers, doctors, nurses and dockers. Ordinary people asleep in their beds. What was left of them.

I had to see for myself.

I brought in a vase of holy water for Father Breen, who was in there with some of the families. He was surprised to see me, and glad of the holy water at the same time.

It was a terrible sight. People were searching for lost family and friends. Their expressions equally appalled and relieved that each green-grey, dusty body under the sheet was not that of their loved one. Same age and sex, but someone else's tragedy. Move on. The atmosphere in the room was oppressive. The quiet sobbing of the women, and some men, bending over a succession of bodies, looking for the dreaded familiar face, or lock of hair, or tattered clothes. The wild eyes of parents looking for their lost children. The panic of young men or women looking for their loved ones, pain etched in their faces, hardly daring to breathe.

Here death, next door life. Who decides? Is this the work of God? Or the devil? Or just the evil of Hitler and of mankind? Who would do such a thing? I wondered why the pilots and bombing crew hated us so much. Did they have fathers and mothers and family to love and to return home to? Did they follow orders without thinking? Or did they believe that they were doing a good thing, dropping bombs on the enemy? But to achieve what? What did Josie Morris do that was different to what I did? Why her and not me? Who decides who lives and who dies?

I remembered what Tom had said, and turned away. I returned to the hall next door.

"Love, could you fetch me something to drink like a good pet?" asked an old man.

It felt good to do something positive for the living.

CHAPTER SEVEN

Christmas Day 1940 dawned to a bleak and bleary world. The rain had abated, leaving behind a high wind that blew in from the sea, bringing with it the roar of the tide in the estuary. Father Christmas had somehow managed to avoid the bombs and the ack ack guns, had negotiated the search lights and barrage balloons, and found his way through the broken streets and battered homes that now made up our world. In communal shelters, as well as shelters dug into back gardens of roofless houses, and temporary shelters in schools and churches, very young children awoke to the excitement of Christmas morning. Mothers, thinking of their older sons and daughters away in Wales, prayed that they would be taken care of by their adopted families.

Father Breen said an early Mass in the hall for those too ill or injured to move into the church, after which I helped to serve a special breakfast of ham and eggs on toast. Father Breen told me that the eggs had been sent in from the farms of North Wales as a gesture of solidarity after the bombings. I'd left Mum fussing in the kitchen where she had managed to get her hands on fresh vegetables and potatoes.

"No help needed here, Maggie," she'd said. "Father Breen is looking for you as soon as possible. We'll be over later for Mass. Merry Christmas."

You just never knew when she was being ironic, but I think that on this occasion, preparing and cooking the meal she had planned for months, she was determined to have the best day possible, in

47

spite of the bombings. You could almost say she was happy in that steaming hot space, with the patched-up ceiling and the back door held ajar with a heavy stone, with pots and pans rattling on the stove, and her sons turning in after a quiet night on fire-watch at the docks.

I had a special present for Billy – a silver locket with our two photographs, taken the day we had ventured into the city to see *Gone with the Wind*. It was on a silver chain that would enable him to keep me close to his heart, even when he was far away. A solid reminder of our love for each other; that I was always with him no matter where in the world his ship took him.

I didn't want to give it to him until we were on our own. Later.

So I busied myself being useful, helping to bring food and drinks to those unable to fend for themselves. I was feeling happy with myself on this Christmas morning, with songs of peace on earth and goodwill to all men floating about.

There is something terrible about being dislocated that strikes to the very core of our being. I could see it in the taut faces, the deep-ringed, shallow eyes that stared back at me when I handed them a cuppa, having lived through a restless night of fitful sleep.

"Ta-ra, love."

Billy was with his mother, surrounded by many of their neighbours. There was no news of the bomb.

My Mum arrived.

"I hear that they're shooting looters on sight down in the city," she said. "I hope that doesn't drive them all up to our place."

Billy turned to his mother.

"Don't worry Mum," he said. "They'll have that bomb cleared in a few days and you'll be right as rain. Besides, the street is blocked off and no one can enter."

My Mum had an opinion on that, of course.

"There'll be precious few on watch today," she said.

Billy and I exchanged glances.

"Billy and I will go up there this morning after Mass and find out what's going on if you like, Mrs Newsome?" I said.

"You're a kind one, Maggie," she replied, "and brave too, from what I hear. God bless you both."

So it came to pass that Christmas week, with the city lying battered and bruised, the docks bombed and battered, and our town bruised and broken, that Billy and I became a public item, an official couple. We became an item of considerable interest in the church hall where eyes followed our every movement, both separate and together. Love in the middle of all this? Priceless.

The Mass seemed to drag on, a celebration of a new life born one thousand, nine hundred and forty years ago. Praying to God for peace on earth, I closed my eyes only to see the face of Josie Morris. She was lying on her back under a sheet in the cold schoolroom next door. Suddenly, in my mind, her eyes shot open, and I must have jumped in my seat, because Mary caught me by the hand and steadied me. I looked across the hall to where Tom was sitting with the men, at his strong serious face, and thought how lucky it was that Billy was going on Tom's ship. There wasn't a braver person in the whole of Merseyside. And calm. And a great brother. Mary squeezed my hand and managed a discreet smile, telling me once again in code that everything would be fine. It would all work out in the end.

Afterwards, I walked with Billy up to his road. The wind was howling in the few scrawny trees that waved their branches about in a crazy dance. A high wind screeched through the rafters in windowless homes. At the entry to his road, we were surprised to find the barrier still up, but abandoned by its human sentry. A sign that read, *'Danger! UXB – Do Not Enter'* flapped madly about. The place was deserted.

We were about to turn and walk back down to my house when suddenly, out of the corner of my eye, I saw something move.

Somebody had just run out of the entry between two terraces and ducked back in again. Billy had seen it too.

"Hey! What do you think you're doing in there?" he called. "It's dangerous. There's an unexploded bomb... Hey!"

Whoever it was ran out of sight.

"Stay here, Mags!"

Billy ducked under the barrier and ran down the centre of the street. The wind swallowed my words whole as I screamed out his name. There was nothing for it but to follow. I ran as fast as I could, but with every forward step I took, the wind held me, and pushed me back towards safety.

Billy was back, panting.

"No sign. I'm going to check the house. Maggie, I told you to wait at the barrier. It's too dangerous for you here."

The air was filled with dust and bits of paper flying about. I covered my mouth with my handkerchief.

"I'm coming with you," I said.

I gave him a look that let him know I was deadly serious.

He grabbed my hand and started back towards the end of the street. We were about to pass his house when I pulled him back.

"Billy, you must check it for your Mum. I'll come with you. It will only take a minute."

Billy stopped in the street.

"Just for a minute then," he said, "and you stay in the front of the house."

Billy forced the front door to close behind us, shutting out the wind and keeping in the cold and damp. He disappeared upstairs. I walked through the downstairs rooms, the sound of my steps drowned out by the background of wild noises outside. Billy came back, taking the bottom half of the stairs in a jump, with the news that the house was secure.

"The bomb may have been encased in concrete, but I'm not sure," he said.

He grabbed my arm.

"Come on. Let's get out of here."

I planted my feet on the lino and stopped him in his tracks. The wind roared and whistled outside, rattled on the windows and hammered at the door.

"The bomb, Maggie. Come on. We have to go."

I pulled his head down and kissed him.

"Happy Christmas."

I was holding his present that I had carefully wrapped and tied with a ribbon. He looked at me with his wild eyes, pleading with me to get out of the house.

"Open it, Billy. If that bomb was going to explode, it would have done so long ago."

Billy held the locket and opened it, looked at the two pictures inside and smiled. He bent his head and our lips met in the narrow hallway. The world stopped spinning and the howling wind was silenced in the sweet nectar of that moment. Billy wrapped his arms around me and kissed me again. His embrace held me clear of all danger, and pushed away all the madness of the world that was not us.

The noise of breaking glass broke the spell. Suddenly the wind was inside, pouring through the house, sending swirls of dust into the air. Billy shouted to me to go out into the street and wait for him. He grabbed an old walking stick of his father's that they'd always kept in the hall umbrella stand. I grabbed a broken umbrella and followed into the back kitchen. There was nothing broken there. We went on into the scullery. Outside in the back yard, the white faces of two men were startled to see us, and ran away immediately.

Billy blocked up the broken door, and I sat and watched him work. I could have sat there for hours, but it was time to go. I thought of the ticking bomb just a few feet from us. Maybe it was a dud, maybe not. There was no way of knowing until it would be too late. But we had to report that all was well to Mrs Newsome. So all had to be well.

Tick-tock, tick-tock, tick-tock.

It was time for dinner.

CHAPTER EIGHT

Dinner was bleak in most houses on Christmas Day that year. Food was in short supply and expensive. Even with double rations from the war office, most people had to do with a chicken or less. Luxuries such as fruit and spices were nowhere to be found. Vegetables were scarce and overpriced.

Thanks to Uncle Peter and the British postal service, our dinner was in a class of its own. Our plates were piled high with turkey, potatoes, cabbage and carrots. Half our family were away at sea and half at home. That was better than most, because Tom wasn't due to be home until the New Year – that is, until his ship was caught by a U-boat's torpedo out in the Atlantic. So much for Tom's belief that the ocean was huge and he wouldn't get caught. Or maybe he knew all along how dangerous it was out there and didn't want to alarm Mum.

It was all clatter and noise with plates steaming, pots popping their lids and the tantalising smell of roast turkey that filled the house. Billy was introduced to all the family who shook his hand in the firm belief that he was a fellow Evertonian. Mary gave him a hug and planted a kiss on his forehead, much to the surprise of her husband Johnny and all the boys. Billy's Mum Bess kept saying, "I'm so proud of my two sons. They're all I've left. You know what I mean, Mrs Brady, what with your army of young men. And such fine young men they are."

It was a very emotional time for the mothers. Mum nodded and said nothing. Dad carved the turkey and the room fell silent as we said the grace. Then it was pass the plate, pass the gravy and pass the steaming pot of vegetables. For that brief afternoon, the war seemed a very long way away. It could have been someone else's war, a trick of the mind to make me believe that this was a normal Christmas, and John, Luke, Liam and Matt, who were away at sea, had only flying fish and bad weather to worry about.

I'd been dreaming of flying fish for months, ever since Peter told me about them when he returned from a long trip to the Pacific Ocean. He had seen them with his own eyes. Fish that could fly? I was sure he was pulling my leg, but I asked Mary and she got me a book in the library that had a picture of one in mid-air. But in my dreams, these fish turned into dive-bombing planes that swooped at the ship, machine-gunned the deck and dropped their bombs. The dream usually ended when the ship exploded, broke up and sank. Planes that appear out of the ocean... There are times when I think that I might be going mad.

I looked at the faces of my brothers Tom, Pat and Peter, my sister Mary and her husband and soon-to-be father Johnny, and my own parents. Dad was tapping the top of his head with his fingers, which he did when he was happy. Mum and Billy's Mum Bess were flushed with the success of the meal. I sneaked a look at Billy sitting on the far side of Mary. He was drinking it all in, smiling from ear to ear.

"I see they bombed Anfield again the other night. Took out a searchlight and part of the stand. Probably improved the pitch."

Everyone laughed. Except Bess.

"My Billy is going to play for them after the war," she said. "They have him signed and all."

There was laughter, as everyone thought it was a joke, followed by silence in the room.

"Billy, are you going to play for Liverpool? Not Everton?"

Tom had known that Billy was a footballer. All heads turned to Billy.

"Who knows what will happen after the war?" he said. "They came after me and I've always wanted to play for them."

The boys stared with their mouths open.

"Well, someone has to play for them. Otherwise we wouldn't be able to hammer them. I say fair play to ye, Billy!"

Dad had uttered one of his rare gems. Everyone else took a moment to let the matter sink in. In our house, football was almost as serious as war. Then Tom laughed and the tension was broken.

"We'll just have to convert you, that's all. When all this is over you'll have to come with us to Goodison and you'll see the light."

We sat into the twilight until it was time for the boys to go. We were as close a family as existed in this terrible time. I almost allowed myself believe that things would work out fine; that we had experienced the worst that could be thrown at us. We were survivors who would somehow come through and win in the end.

If only I could have captured that moment in a jar and screwed the lid on tight. I would have poked a few holes in the lid to let the air in, and keep everyone safe. Then I would never let the moment escape, turning the jar round and round forever. Safe.

If only.

CHAPTER NINE

Boxing Day. Mary told me that in times past it was the day that the servants in the big house were allowed go home with boxes of presents for their families on the first working day after Christmas and as a result it became known as Boxing Day. Today, as we buried our dead, we were giving it a whole different meaning.

Boxing Day was always called Saint Stephen's Day in our house. That was from when my parents were children growing up in Ireland. Saint Stephen was martyred having been betrayed by a wren. The legend goes that Saint Stephen was in hiding from his enemies because he argued that God was not only in the temple, but was everywhere. He had a public debate with the Jewish high priests, in front of the Sanhedrin, the Jewish court, and gave loads of examples from the bible, and argued well, and won the case. The high priests were fuming at being humiliated in public by Stephen and had him tried for blasphemy. That's why he went into hiding. The story goes that the singing of a wren in a nearby tree attracted them to him. He ended up being stoned to death outside the gates of Jerusalem. The first martyr.

In my father's home town, Boxing Day was also known as 'The Day of the Wren,' when straw boys or Mummers would tie a fake wren on to a pole, dress themselves up in straw and go from house to house singing and collecting money for the poor to 'bury the wren.'

Some things are just weird, I thought. If God is everywhere and in every time then he must have watched Stephen being stoned to death, and did nothing about it. What sort of God would do that? What sort of God would allow hundreds and thousands of innocent people get blitzed in their own backyard, or blown to bits in their beds or in communal shelters? Hundreds had died caught out in the open, some even at the anchored base of the cables of barrage balloons. Whether God is everywhere or not, death certainly is.

Tom says that you can't blame God for the cruelty of men. Fair enough, Tom, but the Jews stoned Stephen to death, and Hitler hated the Jews, and one of his bombers dropped a bomb on Josie Morris and her family... What did Josie ever do to Hitler?

Billy jumped me from behind as I walked with these thoughts up from the church to the cemetery, in the misty morning light. The wind had finally stopped hollering, and was replaced by a dreary, breathless calm that was even more unnerving. A murky fog rolled in from the sea. It picked its way slowly and carefully around empty bomb craters, and through windowless houses, poking its nose into everyone's business. It turned the cemetery into somewhere halfway between heaven and hell, a floating world of diggings, surrounded by crowds of headstones. A mass grave, a tearing of the earth that was over one hundred yards long and wide enough for two coffins to lie end-to-end, was filling up with boxes of various shapes and sizes. Josie Morris and her family. Other bodies that remained unidentified. And body parts. Funerals from all over Liverpool.

"That was a great day yesterday," Billy whispered in my ear. "Best Christmas ever!"

This wasn't the time. I shrugged my disapproval.

"Thanks for the present," he went on. "Very salubrious. I'll wear it always."

I turned and gave him the look. He stopped smiling and quietly slipped his hand into mine. We stood in the midst of the crowds that poured into the cemetery, occupying every place between graves and around headstones. An eerie silence filled the floating space, shut off from the rest of the world, on all sides, by a wall of white cloud.

"I'm in the departure lounge now, little Maggie. It won't be long before my ship calls me home."

I didn't know then what my grandfather was talking about, but laughed as you do when you are seven at what seemed to be a joke and everyone else was laughing too. I remember the faraway look in his eyes as he laughed, his pipe bouncing in the corner of his mouth so that the smoke came out in a big puff. He started coughing and couldn't stop. I was afraid he would never stop. Afterwards, he wiped away the tears with his brown handkerchief and laughed and bounced me on his knee. I always loved the smell of that pipe smoke. The sweetness of it tickled my throat, and filled my head with a feeling of somewhere far, far away.

I started to count the coffins stretched out side by side, but my eyes went blurred after I reached fifty-two. I tried to focus and get back the count, but fog was settling in the huge, sunken space. It filled the vast grave, spilled up over the edge and poured out around our feet. Then the prayers began. Father Breen and a Protestant minister led the *Our Father*.

The comforting prayers rolled on over the murky gravestones. Even though I had heard them thousands of times, it felt like I was hearing these words for the first time. If this was God's will, then I was finished with Him. *Thy will be done on earth...* How could this be God's will? And as for forgiving *those who trespass against us*, how could we do that? Forgive Hitler and his henchmen that bombed us night after night? Forgive the filthy U-boats that killed with cold, calculating torpedoes from their sneaky underwater hiding places? If I were led into temptation to kill them myself, then I could live with myself for doing that. Whatever way I could help to do that was fine by me.

The final line of the prayer sounded a call to action. *Deliver us from evil.* Hitler and his filthy mob were evil. Deliver us from them? That sounded fine to me, but I didn't see any evidence of that happening around here. How could Father Breen and the Minister stand there and read that prayer telling us we must forgive? And everyone else joining in...

"Come on, let's get you out of here. You're shivering with the cold."

Billy wrapped his coat around me, put his arm around my shoulders and squeezed and held me tight. A sort of madness that was creeping up on me disappeared. I was glad that I was starting in the munitions factory the very next day. We made the sign of the cross and turned our backs on the dead space. As I walked away, a feeling of loss descended on me, a feeling that somehow there was less to me now than there was before. It was as though some piece of me was left floating in that misty air around the coffins – hovering, waiting for the clunk of spade and the thump of clay. Caught in that wispy place between heaven and hell.

The person I had become was like a stranger that you would not welcome into your life, or into your home. We passed Josie Morris's house, or the empty space that had been her house, on the way back from the cemetery. Fog lingered among the bricks of the broken walls, and around bits of burned timbers gathered about the chimney stack. It peeped through the empty window frame of the house next door.

I shivered again and Billy drew me close. A cold had gripped my soul and held it like ice, even as I sat in the steamy heat of our back kitchen. Not even the clamour of voices, nourished with hot turkey soup, could loosen the chill that had settled like winter into the cavities of my heart.

CHAPTER TEN

No shadow of bombers' wings blocked the stars that lit up the sky above the pitch black night. The moon was in hiding, nowhere to be seen. There had been no air raid sirens all week, not since before Christmas. Tom had been right, as usual. Mum was already up, fussing about breakfast and packed lunches for us all. I had spent the night trying to sleep, seeing flying fish turning into enemy aircraft, and eventually gave up. I lay in the dark thinking about Billy going to sea, and I probably wouldn't see him for a month or more. Dad sat munching his breakfast. He had spent the whole of Boxing Day down at the docks overseeing the clearing work after the 'Christmas Blitz' as the newspapers were calling the bombings.

"Tom, Pat and Peter are shipping out," he said. "John and Matt's convoy will be here later today, please God. With a bit of luck, they may be on shore leave from tomorrow. That lad of yours is a fine footballer. I watched him in the final of the Youth's Cup."

That was high praise from Dad. He was a volunteer steward up at the ground, and often watched the youth team play. Billy's team had beaten ours in the final that summer before the war, the week before I met him at the fete. He loved his football, did Dad.

"Maggie, eat your breakfast or you'll miss your tram," said Mum. "There's a war on, you know. Dad, don't forget your lunch. It will be a while before you get to eat turkey again."

It was her way of telling us both that she was proud of us. Not the words, just the way she said them.

I was whooshed out the door into the polar air that had come south for Christmas. The stars startled me for a moment, they looked so close. You could reach out and almost touch them. So this was what the world was like while I slept in my bed, or in the shelter. A world that was tilted much closer to the heavens, straining to hear the whisperings in the dark between the gods. These stars would vanish like ghosts in the pale light of dawn but not for hours yet, still staring wide-eyed at the world in darkness, mad in a restless sleep.

The tram emptied at the factory gate. Everyone passed through and climbed on to various buses. Reporting to the office as instructed, I was surprised to be told to go into a room and take off all my outer clothes, jewellery, hairpins and shoes. I had to put on a pair of overalls and tie up my hair with a headscarf. The overalls were baggy and the boots plain. My clothes were placed in a bag and hung up in the changing area. I was taken by train to a section where gun shells were unloaded from a railway car and brought into the factory for filling with TNT.

A woman called Molly sat in a crane. My job was to loop a rope around the individual shell, which was then lifted off the train and on to a bench with rollers. Then the heavy shells were rolled on into the factory by another woman called Tess. It was physical, dirty work and I loved it, in spite of the cold. I felt like kissing each shell that winked at me as it swung past in the white light of the electric lamp. Molly expertly manoeuvred it. I was then able to release the rope and guide the shell into the queue that had formed on the rollers. Tess moved them on to the next woman, Jane, who moved them around a corner and out of sight into the factory. Somewhere deep inside, TNT was melted and the shells were filled. I was at the start of a long trail that sent our best wishes to Hitler. I was feeling pleased with myself for taking the chance to start a new job. I was happy to give up my machine job in Littlewoods, where they were sorry to lose me, *but come back anytime*, they said.

The eight-hour shift passed quickly. My turkey sandwiches made me a hit with the girls at lunch break. Good old Uncle Peter.

At two o'clock, the next shift arrived. We took the transport back to the main gate. Inside the changing rooms, there was no sign of the bag with my clothes and shoes. I hunted up and down and eventually found the bag on the floor in the corner with my clothes, but no shoes. My lovely new slingbacks – gone!

The supervisor raised an eyebrow as if to say, 'What do you expect bringing such a pair as those to work?' To me, they were my lucky shoes. I wanted to search all the other bags. She was having none of that and threw me out. The tram was waiting so I had to hop on in my bare feet, and grit my teeth against the cold.

Mum burst out laughing when she saw me hobble up the front steps and into the house.

"Well, I know that your country needs you, but I didn't think that included your shoes and all," she said.

She poured hot water into a basin, placed it on the floor of the back kitchen and told me to sit and bathe my feet. A steaming mug of turkey soup warmed my hands. The hot water stung my feet. The shame of losing my shoes stung my eyes. The soup stung my tongue. Then the clock in the kitchen chimed three o'clock, and that stung me into action.

The afternoon was smudged with dirty clouds that ran in from the sea, bringing drizzle in the dusky light. Cycling into the wind was hard and I was sweating and panting when I arrived at the shore. The Home Guard on watch looking out to sea questioned me and then let me stand on the roof of the bunker when I told them that all my brothers and my boyfriend were out there.

The sea was filled with row after row of ships, right out to the horizon. The convoy had arrived, having survived the storms and icy waters of the North Atlantic. It had dodged the deadly strike of the U-boat and the peril of the dive-bomber. It was bringing vital supplies from America. Food, war material – and vital people too. I hadn't seen John and Matt since November. They were probably waiting for the other ships to leave.

Tom and Billy's ship, the *Cumbria* was a large cargo vessel that could also carry a small number of passengers. Ships were ploughing down the Queen's Channel and on into the bay, heading for the assembly point off Anglesey. This much I knew from listening to Billy. You couldn't get a word out of Tom. He'd just laugh and say something like, "Oh, it's great to be at sea. No awkward questions to dodge!"

That's because they weren't supposed to talk about it. Official secrets and all that. *Loose lips sink ships.*

I stared for an hour until dusk turned to dark and the chill wind turned nasty. I couldn't recognise any ships and I hadn't seen the *Cumbria*, or at least I don't think it had passed by while I was there. I must have missed it, and it was gone. The captain from the watch came up.

"Missie, it's best you get back home now," he said. "You'll no be seein' nothin' up here now as there's no moon tonight."

I looked at him. He was a well-meaning man who knew my father. A chill wind had numbed my feet and burned my eyes so that they watered. I felt a trickle run slowly down my cheek. I couldn't move. I would have stayed there forever, but he gently took my arm and walked me to my bike.

"You take care, Missie. This is no place to be on a night like this."

All I could hear was the rumble of the sea and the wind whistling about. The ships had been swallowed whole into the blackness of night, and the world was turning upside down with no stars to watch over us. I felt a sharp pain in my forehead and a stabbing at my heart. Billy was gone.

I have no recollection of the journey home.

CHAPTER ELEVEN

April 1941

The cream always rises. That's what Mum says, and she should know. She'd spent her childhood milking cows and turning a heavy churn by hand to make butter, the slap and slush inside the wooden barrel as it churned, the hard metal handle jerking her hand and vibrating her arm up to her shoulder. I tried it when we visited Uncle Peter for the funeral, and I soon realised, it's not as easy as it looks.

The British and Irish Steam Packet Company ship *Leinster* was the most modern on the Liverpool-to-Dublin route. Walking up the gangplank in Alexandria Dock, carrying a borrowed suitcase that Father Breen had lent Mum, was like walking into a dream. Then we went down into the bowels of the ship to where Mum had a bunk in a cabin. We slipped out of the dock in the gathering darkness. The city lay coiled and tense beside us. Tired eyes peeled, raised faces scanned the dark sky, waiting for the raid that may or may not come. Up on deck, I watched miles of docks slip by, out past Bootle and on towards the mouth of the estuary. Out where the soldiers in the bunkers on Our Shore were watching, as I had often stood and watched too. Now it was my turn to wave from the deck, but they didn't wave back.

I thought of the Saturday in September 1939, the day before the war had started, when I'd stood with Billy and watched the *Athenia* sail down this same stretch of the Mersey. It was carrying all those waving women and children, and I had envied them, wanted to be with them. They were torpedoed the very next afternoon out in the Atlantic, the first day of the war. The *Athenia* was the first ship of many hundreds to suffer this fate.

A year later, last September, Friday 13th to be exact, we watched and waved as the *City of Benares* sailed away with more than ninety children on board. They waved back mad with excitement or sadness. They were being evacuated to Canada as part of the new government scheme, to send the children of poor families to follow in the footsteps of the rich, whose children were already in the best schools in America. Then came the shocking news that it had been torpedoed and sunk in the Atlantic. Seventy-seven children either drowned or died of exposure in the lifeboats, one of which was mistakenly missed in the rescue and spent eight days at sea.

In between those two disasters, a defeat turned into a victory by Churchill with the rescue of hundreds of thousands from Dunkirk. Two weeks after that, the sinking of the *Lancastria* with over six thousand and maybe eight thousand drowned, but we weren't supposed to know that.

There was not a word from Churchill about that, but I'd heard my brothers argue in the back kitchen about how bad it had been, and how many had drowned. The official figure was never given. The rumour around the docks was that between eight and ten thousand were on board when it was bombed off France. Fewer than two thousand were rescued. It sank in less than thirty minutes. There wasn't a word about it in the press. Tom had a soft spot for that boat, as he'd started his life at sea on it. At that time it used to ply between Liverpool and New York as a passenger ship, long before there was any talk of war.

I sat up on the *Leinster's* deck, watching the curve of the half-moon slide across the sky. I was far too excited to sleep. The ship was huge and seemed full this Friday night. People settled on chairs and stretched out on long seats in the restaurant area that was closed. The whole ship had lights out, but still had emergency lights, so that I could move around inside and just about see where I was going. It being April, the weather was good and the night was clear. I was wrapped up well and sheltered from the wind as we headed out to sea. It was lovely on deck, watching the stars with the moon peeping out shyly in a beautiful crescent that sat on the Welsh Hills. The ship rocked gently, then rolled forward and down, then back up in a way that made the moon appear to move up and down. We went down, the moon went up, we came up, the moon went down. Out of synchronisation with the world, lucky moon.

It was as close as I could ever feel to being at sea with Billy. He was out here too somewhere, on the same water. I let my mind sail further out around Ireland and on into the vast rolling waves of the cold Atlantic, beyond Iceland and on towards Halifax in Canada. Thousands of miles of ocean. He could be looking right now at the same shape of moon. I closed my eyes and felt I could stretch out my hand and he could stretch out his, and somehow we would feel each other's presence. We were connected by this liquid stream that slapped and slushed the side of the *Leinster*, and simultaneously wrapped around the *Cumbria*, as it made its way in convoy through the dark night.

The soft glow of the lights of Dublin should be over the horizon, if it was true what Tom had said. Was the Luftwaffe able to fly up the Irish coast, swing right with Dublin off their port wing, and head straight in for Liverpool? Dad had heard that it was Belfast's turn to suffer a massive raid earlier this week. As usual, the details were sketchy, with the papers playing down everything, so that Jerry wouldn't know how hard we had been hit. Liverpool was never mentioned in the Pathé News. I knew this was part of the propaganda war. Still, it was hard to watch the images of the East End of London, and listen to Lord Haw Haw mocking us, and have neither sight nor sound of the terrible beating our city was taking.

The story of Coventry was told everywhere, and even the King visited. But never a mention of our suffering. It was as if we didn't exist, didn't matter. When I said this to Tom, he sat and looked me straight in the eye.

"Mags," he said, "we are the most important port in Britain. We matter. If we're beaten, Britain is beaten. We can't let Jerry know he's hurting us."

Sometimes Tom sounded exactly like Churchill.

Dad heard on the docks that fire engines from Dundalk, Drogheda and Dublin had gone north to Belfast to help put out the fires. At least that was something.

I must have fallen asleep because I heard the voice of Lord Haw Haw saying '*Easter Eggs for Belfast*' and laughing, and when I sat up it was freezing. The grey light of dawn was spreading slowly across the low bank of clouds that sat on the horizon, back-lighting them with the promise of a new day. Up at the bow, it was extraordinary to see the thin line of Ireland float out of the sea. Mum was up and dressed, and I could feel her excitement as she held my hand.

When the sun hit the Wicklow Mountains it looked as if somebody had struck a match and lit bonfires to celebrate the return of their lost daughter. Mum pointed out the landmarks of Dublin and Wicklow as we sailed past the Kish Lightship. It marked the position of a sandbank, near where the ship that had the same name as ours had been torpedoed by a U-boat at the end of the First World War, when more than five hundred passengers were drowned. I hadn't known about that, and it shook me to think that the Germans had sunk a passenger ship in the Irish Sea and hundreds drowned. I had never heard Mum talk so much without a hint of irony. I scanned the horizon for any sign of the enemy, but there was none, only a flock of seagulls screeching their welcome, as we sailed on into Dublin Bay.

At the train station we had to wait and I bought a bar of chocolate in a kiosk. I gasped with pleasure when the delicious flavour hit the back of my tongue. The newspaper stand proclaimed the headline *Belfast Blitzed: 500 Dead, Hundreds Injured.* The newspapers carried the story of firefighters from Éire rushing to Belfast to help put out the fires. Death. Destruction. Refugees. Protests.

A train from Belfast announced its arrival on the next platform with a screech of brakes. Steam hissed from hidden compartments under wheels and rose in clouds around the legs of the Irish Red Cross workers who were waiting to meet the refugees. One thing that immediately struck me, as they poured off the train, was the number of young children, hundreds of them, their faces still greyish-green from dust and rubble. There was not a smile among them, just a look of panic and fear. I had seen that same look on the people of our own town as they shuffled along the road escaping the terrors that the sky brought night after night. Back in Liverpool, it was mainly adults and babies. The children were away in Wales.

A queue formed along the platform as I stood watching. I saw mothers dressed in worn clothes, shepherding their children about them, clutching to their bosoms babies wrapped in tattered, dusty rags. One woman refused to give up her baby, clasping her precious bundle to her chest and soothing it with an incessant shake, a madness in her eyes. The baby was dead. This was more of Hitler's evil. Not even Ireland was safe from his bases in Northern France and Norway. Nowhere was safe.

Everyone wore black for the funeral. Uncle Peter's black hat was round with a stiff wide brim and a black feather in it for luck. It fluttered in the smoke which rose from the pipe that he sucked and blew, his long, black moustache camouflaging his tiny mouth. I could see why he was known as Peter Pipe in Kilkevin.

There were four Peter O'Byrnes in Kilkevin. They all lived on what was called Byrnes Lane, because six families of Byrnes lived on the lane, not all directly related, as I was told a number of times. I had been named after my Aunty Maggie, but I never saw her alive. She was bumped down the stairs in a plain oak coffin, with strong men puffing and blowing at the weight of her. The coffin got caught in the turn at the bottom of the stairs. They had to lift her back up and over the banisters with cries of 'Hold, hold!' and 'I've got her now,' and 'Easy does it.'

I held my breath, terrified they would let her fall, and the coffin break open and Aunty Maggie stare up at me with that dead stare that I have seen too many times now, but they somehow managed. She was lifted through the kitchen with its big range glowing in the darkened room. They placed the coffin on stools in the centre of the parlour with a candlestick at each end and a crucifix at the top. Holy water, a bible and her prayer book were set up on a small table with a white linen cloth draped over the sides. It reminded me of the cloths that Billy used to drape on the altar before Mass.

Then, to my horror, the coffin lid was opened. And there was Aunty Maggie – looking not too bad dead, as a lot of people said. They shook Uncle Peter's hand, Mum's hand, and then my own, saying, "Sorry for your trouble, Miss." They blessed themselves and said a prayer. After a while, somebody started the rosary. I was feeling a bit panicky and hot, and had to get outside for some fresh air. Well, that's what Mum called it, as she didn't allow smoking in the house.

"House rules!" she'd snap.

She made them up as she went along, but no one dared break them.

Out in the yard groups of people stood about, keeping a respectful distance and nodding in my direction as one of the chief mourners. In fact, I knew Aunty Maggie O'Byrne only in legend. It was repeated to me often that she was a direct descendant of Fiach McHugh O'Byrne himself, rebel chief of the O'Byrne clan, who had ruled Wicklow at the time of Queen Elizabeth the First, the Virgin Queen, ruler of England and Ireland.

I was looking for a light, so I approached a group of lads around my own age. There was a scramble in pockets and a lighter produced. I lit my Dunhill, drew in a drag, inhaled and blew the smoke out through my nose, just like in the films. It might have looked sexy in the cinema, but in a farmhouse yard off Byrnes Lane, under the mountain in South West Wicklow, well, it was questionable. A red-haired, red-faced boy spoke.

"Sorry for your troubles, Miss Maggie. I'm Patrick O'Byrne from across the field."

He pointed in the direction of the mountain further on down the lane.

"Thanks, Patrick. Are we related too?"

"No, Miss. I don't believe so, unless you go way back to the chief."

He had an easy way about him and seemed comfortable talking to me. The other lads held back. They stood with their eyes fixed on their boots if they had them, or seemed to have a morbid fascination with their toes if they didn't, as they scrabbled about in the dusty yard. Only on occasion did they glance up, but they were listening to every word.

"I'd like you to meet my sisters if you don't mind," Patrick said. "They're over here."

He guided me around the corner of the whitewashed farmhouse. A large group of girls stood gathered under the gable wall. Eight in total, ranging in steps of stairs from my age and younger.

"Mary, Veronica, Anne, Elizabeth, Maureen, Martha, Bridget and little Nora."

Nora was hiding behind the skirt of the eldest, Mary. I hunched down to her.

"Hello, Nora. Pleased to meet you. I have a sister Mary too."

That broke the awkwardness. They gathered around and all started talking at once. Patrick stepped back. I could see immediately that it was a very kind thought to bring me around to the girls. I

smiled my thanks and he returned to his friends. Mary lifted Nora
on to her hip, shushed the younger ones and kept them all in line.

"Well, you certainly have a lot of girls in your house," I said.
"Your Mummy must be lucky to have you all to help her."

"Mammy's in heaven," Nora replied.

"Oh, Nora. I'm so sorry."

When Mum had told me that Aunty Maggie was dying, and that she
was going to return to Ireland for the first time since she'd left as a
girl, even younger than I was, I hadn't felt anything. But when she
asked me to go with her, my heart soared at the thought of it, the
adventure of it. I worked all over Easter to get the few days off.

The night before we were due to travel, the news came through
of Aunty Maggie's passing. I felt nothing. No sadness, only
disappointment that the trip was off, quickly followed by joy that
we would travel to the funeral. There is definitely something wrong
with me.

And now, when little Nora, whom I had just met and knew
nothing about, except that she had a very nice brother Patrick and
was being raised by her eldest sister Mary... When little Nora told
me that her mother was dead, I had to fight back the tears.

Mary touched my arm.

"Would you like to come over for a cup of tea?" she asked. "It's
time for us to go and the break might do you good. Patrick will walk
you back later. This wake will go on all night."

I smiled, stubbed out my cigarette and walked beside Mary. Then
Nora reached out to me and I took her in my arms and carried her
over the rutted lane. Her fingers clung around my neck and her head
rested on my shoulder. The girls gathered around chattering at once,
their voices filling the evening air that hung about the hedgerows.
Apple trees and cherry blossoms quivered in the breeze, and a steady
stream was falling like confetti or light snow, through which I
walked as in a dream.

I had to duck my head as I entered the house. Then the lamps were lit and the curtains still open. I got up and instinctively closed them. Maureen and Martha somehow managed to drop a large pot on to the flagstones of the kitchen floor. They were bringing it to the well to fetch in the water for the evening. I found myself under the kitchen table and banged my knee on the thick crossbeam that ran the length of it. Veronica or Elizabeth, I'm not sure which, screamed. The whole thing ended with nervous laughter on my part and open mouths on theirs, as I brushed off the dust that had gathered on my black dress.

"Well, it's hard indeed to get the little ones to settle with all this racket."

Mary gave her sisters a look I'd seen from Mum on so many occasions.

"Oh, I'm so sorry Mary, it's all my fault," I said. "I gave them a fright and they dropped the pot and you've all been so kind to me. I should go and let you get settled for the night."

"You'll do no such thing, Miss Maggie," Mary replied. "Tea will be ready in a minute."

She gave another look and the girls sprang into action. In a short while, the kettle was singing on the range and a half slice of buttered bread was passed around for each of us. A prayer was said before anyone took a bite and the *Our Father* sounded so different here in the soft twilight of a farmhouse that had known its own sadness. Not a sign of the enemy in sight, no mass graves to ponder, just the personal sadness of a family in mourning, of a mother gone, of a hole in the centre of the home that Mary was trying to fill. After prayer came the soft sound of munching, the sweet taste of real butter and freshly baked bread. Curious eyes peeped down from between the banisters of the stairs in the corner of the kitchen.

"All right, you two. Come on down – for five minutes only."

There was giggling on the stairs as Nora and Bridget slid down on their bottoms. Nora sat on Mary's lap, Bridget on Veronica's, and their sleepy eyes sparkled in the firelight.

Later, when the house had really settled down, and the edge of the moon could be seen over the mountain's black bulk, Mary and Veronica sat outside with me on the gate. We all smoked our own thoughts. I told them about my father and brothers and my two sisters, one a nun whom I hadn't seen for years and couldn't even remember her face.

Talking about Liverpool and the war made me realise how terrible it really was. It's not like I can't see that when I'm living it, but when the hard words came out of my mouth, it became something simultaneously attached to me and detached from me. It became more real and present and dangerous in the telling, like a story that only comes alive when other people hear it. Then it became even more real for me. All the emotions that I'd kept hidden in shelters deep underground came out into the blinding white light and the world was revealed for what it was.

I decided that I shouldn't talk too much about it to these kind girls who had so recently suffered their own personal tragedy. The passing of Aunty Maggie must have brought home to them the raw emotion of loss, making them relive the hurt of that terrible time all over again, just as Nora's words did to me earlier.

"I can't imagine how you're all coping with the loss of your mother," I said to them.

"How were you to know, Maggie? It seems to me that you've had a much more difficult time. Our loss is behind us, and our family all about us, while yours is scattered in danger on oceans around the world. Da says the Emergency has been good for Ireland. It's helped food prices to rise, which has given us a better living. We'll be all right here, *le cúnamh Dé.* Ah, here's Patrick to walk you back."

It was strange, but in the few hours since we met, I felt like I had a new family here in Kilkevin. Not Uncle Peter, but the O'Byrnes across the field, who I suddenly cared for as my own. I hugged them goodbye, whispered my thanks and turned down the lane with Patrick walking beside me. The distant sound of music was carried over the field on the breeze.

"They'll be at that a while yet, Miss Maggie."

"Please call me Maggie, Patrick, or I'll start calling you Master Patrick and we'll see how you like that," I said.

"Your Aunt Maggie was a terror for the dance Miss, I mean, Maggie. She was a champion all over Ireland and was a famous dance teacher as well, but you already know that, I'm sure."

I didn't know anything about Aunty Maggie, but I resolved to change that in the morning. I would have a good chat with Mum.

"Patrick, do you believe that there is something after you die? I mean, what's the point to all this death?"

Patrick stopped in his tracks and was silent.

It was a question I had often put to Billy, as we sat on the sands out on the shore, watching seagulls duck and dive for food in the estuary. A crab had become dislodged from his hiding place. He had been caught in the open trying to scuttle sideways to some safe place. The gulls ducked in and out, but the crab's armour protected him. His red claw snapped the air, defending himself from the aerial bombardment which grew fiercer by the minute. The gulls fought with each other for the right to attack the crab, who was halfway to the water at this point. Their screeches pierced the clear morning air with the rattle of death.

Billy wanted to chase away the birds, but I held his arm and urged him to sit and watch the battle. Some of the gulls were waiting on the wet sands to attack the crab from the rear, while others skipped out of reach of the snapping claw. If they had worked together as a team the end was inevitable, but the gulls were driven by self-interest. The crab managed to reach the shoreline and was almost there when a lucky strike or dive stopped him in his tracks. The arm was dropped and the gulls were all over it. The end came in seconds.

"Gulls have to eat too," I said.

Billy gave me a look. He had changed since going to sea, had become more quiet and thoughtful. Like Tom, he never spoke of what it was like out there. I was curious and had often asked Tom, and all my brothers, for details, but they never said anything beyond the usual banal answer.

"Ah, it's all about surviving out there, but it ain't half bad sis, so don't worry."

That made me worry.

"Was it very bad? You don't have to answer, but I have to ask. You know I have to ask."

"It was bad at times, but you really don't want to hear about those times," said Billy. "Mostly it's boring, just watching signals from the command ship and passing on the information. We're on a radio blackout because that would give away our position. It's like a deadly game of hide-and-seek. And the wolf pack is getting smarter."

"I do want to hear about the bad times, Billy. I need to know. Otherwise I just imagine them and that's worse. I can't get them out of my mind."

"You remember the *Athenia* that we saw leaving port that Saturday at the start of the war? The one that was sunk by a U-boat the very next day? One of the sailors who was rescued is now part of our crew. He told me that the ship was torpedoed north-west of Ireland on that Sunday evening of the Third of September, the first day of the war. The torpedo hit the boiler room and killed a lot of crew members in there and on the aft stairwell, but the ship stayed afloat until the following morning.

"To make matters worse, a lot of people were also killed during the rescue. A Norwegian tanker, the *Knute Nelson*, was one of the ships that responded to the distress signal and picked up many of the survivors and dropped them off in Galway. One of the lifeboats was caught in the propellers due to a misunderstanding on the bridge. One lifeboat had been emptied and another had come alongside behind it, but for some reason the bridge gave the order to go full steam ahead. The mooring ropes snapped and they were thrown back into the exposed propeller, because of the rough sea, and about fifty people were killed. Sometimes bad things happen at sea, but not very often."

He gave me a reassuring hug and a smile.

I thought of the happy passengers waving like mad, and me wishing to be on board. Once again it confirmed to me that nowhere was safe anymore. I suspected that Billy was thinking of them too because he was silent for a long time.

"You know that we travel in convoy, which means that we all have to go at the speed of the slowest vessel," he said eventually. "We have to keep our discipline and stay in position no matter what. It's just seeing the explosion and the yellow-and-red flame that leaps up, and then the fire... Watching the ship sinking stern first, because that's where the engine room is. Watching the crew jumping into the freezing sea, and the convoy moving slowly on, and knowing there's no hope for any of them. Waiting for the next explosion – and it could be you. In the dark I hear their distress signal and report it to the bridge, and then there's silence."

I reached out and held his hand. I rubbed his back and his shoulders. He was crying, quietly. I was sorry I had pushed for this, but I needed to know what he was facing, so that I could face it too.

Every day.

Patrick was quiet for a long time, and I was afraid that the question had really upset him.

"It's all about what you believe," he said. "Heaven, hell and purgatory. I believe Mammy's in heaven. She deserves to be there more than anyone I know. Da talks to her in the night."

We walked on in silence.

"Well Miss, there's a right session going on inside."

Patrick stopped in the yard.

"Maybe I'll see you in the morning."

"Patrick, thanks for taking such care of me earlier and bringing me over to your sisters."

"Sure they were dying to meet you. We all were."

I breathed in the air of the yard, and the lane, and the surrounding fields that ran off to the black mountain. Above us, the sky was clear of the threat of bombers. There were no barrage balloons, searchlights or ack ack guns firing into the darkness. No smelly, crowded shelters, or lines of barbed wire, or making bombs to be fired at the enemy. No threat of invasion. A bird sang in the hedgerow, a twittering, cheery, chirpy whistling. It had been a long time since I'd heard a bird sing.

Inside, the music had a swing to it that I never noticed before. We used to call it 'diddley-eye' when we heard Irish music played. But it was different here, raw, almost feral. Two couples danced on the floor in the centre of the kitchen and everyone else gathered around. The couples flew across the confined space, round and round in each other's arms. A group of musicians sat in a corner by the fire, playing a squeezebox, a tin whistle and fiddle. With the uplifting sound of the clatter of shoes on the flagstones, and the snap of people clapping in the air, I felt the hairs on the back of my neck stand on end. My foot started tapping and I had to stop myself from clapping along. It didn't feel appropriate while Aunty Maggie lay in a coffin in the next room.

At the end of the dance there was a burst of general applause. I squeezed past into the parlour where Mum and a group of neighbours were sitting with Aunty Maggie, who was looking pretty good dead in the candlelight.

I sat in the darkened room long into the night, listening to tales of happy memories from years ago, from my mother's childhood growing up here in this house. Tales of Irish dancing and music floated about like ghosts. And there were hard tales of emigration. Liverpool or New York, where so-and-so went, people I'd never heard of.

I must have fallen asleep, because when I woke, there was a man in the room talking in whispers to Mum. She laughed at whatever was said and rested her hand on his shoulder, in a familiar way. She took it away when she saw me wake up, but not before I noticed.

"Maggie, love, this is Peter O'Byrne from across the field. You met his family earlier, I believe."

I rubbed my eyes.

"Hello."

"Well Maggie, I can see that you have your mother's good looks," he said.

I sat up.

"Your family have been very kind to me."

Mum got up quickly and stood by the coffin.

"Peter and I grew up here together," she said. "We were best friends, you know."

He looked at her and smiled.

"Ah, she broke my heart when she left, Maggie," he said.

I didn't reply. Who was this man? And why was Mum acting strange? Then he leaned towards me and said, "I'm sorry things are hard in Liverpool. War is a dreadful thing."

I had to bite my tongue to prevent myself snapping back, "And you would know, I suppose?"

I got up then and left the room without a word. I moved quickly through the crowded house, up the narrow stairs and into the bed that Aunty Maggie had been taken out of earlier in the evening. I tossed myself into a fitful sleep full of danger from above and below. My dreams were filled with the scream and roar of bombs and torpedoes, ships sinking in choppy seas, the stamp of dancing feet on stone, and the wide eyes of children standing on station platforms with no place to go.

CHAPTER TWELVE

Waking up in the strange light of a room with a smell of mothballs all around unnerved me. Sitting up in bed, I banged my head off the sloping ceiling and gave out a short gasp, then realised where I was. The memory of the previous night came flooding back. I jumped out of bed into the early chill of a late April morning. I threw open the tiny window and let the scents of the countryside sweep around the attic space.

Climbing down the steep flight of stairs with a sharp turn at the bottom, I could appreciate even more the manoeuvrings of the coffin in that narrow space yesterday evening. The smell of a cooked breakfast wafted up to greet me. I bounced down the last step, swung off the banister, and landed with a slap of feet against stone tiles in the middle of the kitchen. Uncle Peter jumped in his seat as he sat smoking his pipe into the hearth. Mum was cooking breakfast on the range while carrying on a conversation with a group of women who were sitting in the parlour with Aunty Maggie. From the conversation, and the sight of the black circles around their eyes, they must have been there all night.

Something about Mum was different. She looked younger than she did at home, and her step was quicker and lighter, or so it seemed to me. In between the banter, she was singing. It was a song about the Vale of Avoca where the waters meet. I had only ever heard her hum it to herself about the house at home.

Uncle Peter spoke through a cloud of smoke.

"Ah, that's lovely. That was her favourite Thomas Moore song, you know. She'd have loved to hear you singing that. Young Maggie, sure you're the spit of your mother. Will you go out to the henhouse and collect the eggs for breakfast? The basket is at the door beside the churn."

I picked up the basket and left the house. Outside a voice called from the farmyard gate.

"Good morning, Miss Maggie."

"Patrick, I told you, just call me Maggie."

"Good morning, Maggie. Are you off to get the eggs?"

"I am. Do you want to come with me? I've never collected eggs before."

Patrick jumped over the gate. I noticed that when he moved, it was if he floated over the rough ground.

"You look pleased with yourself, if you don't mind me saying so," I said.

"You've made a big impression in my house, if you don't mind *me* saying so, with my sisters – and my father too."

"But not with you?"

Patrick smiled.

"With all of us. Da says you're the cut of your mother at your age. They were great friends, you know. Before she left."

"So I believe. Is this the hen house?"

Patrick opened the door and we went into the darkened coop. The hens were nesting in boxes of straw all around the walls. He put his hand in under the first hen who squawked and moved off her egg.

"Go ahead, Maggie. They don't bite – much."

I hesitated and saw the laughter in his eyes. I plunged my hand in under a hen and felt the delicate, warm shell. It was a miracle of life there before my eyes. Life and death in a perfect sphere.

Shafts of light that entered through the high windows caught specks of straw dust that hung in the disturbed air of the hen house as I continued with my task of collecting eggs. I breathed in the musty air. When I turned, Patrick was standing close. I needed to get out of that enclosed space, so I gave him a shove towards the door.

"They'll be waiting for these back at the house," I said. "Some people stayed up all night."

"Hey, Maggie, you have a strong arm there – if you don't mind me saying so."

It was the first time I had touched a boy other than my brothers, and Billy, and it felt like an electric shock went up my arm. Patrick almost dropped the basket of eggs.

Outside I breathed in the fresh morning air.

"It's the bombs," I told him. "I used to work on an assembly line, making bombs."

"Bombs! Used to?"

"Yes. I've been promoted twice and now I'm in charge of Dispatch. There's over a hundred of us in the department and our job is to send bombs and shells, all shiny and new, to wherever they're needed. And they're badly needed, in lots of places."

We were back at the farmhouse door. I was surprised when Patrick came in without knocking or being given leave to enter. He made himself at home and busied about, helping with the breakfast things, while Mum cooked the eggs. She was singing that song about love and death again.

She stopped when the eggs were done, and the crowd was called in from the other room. The talk fell silent as grace was said with bowed heads. Then came the cup of tea and the wonderful taste of fresh food, butter and the eggs like we never got any more in Bootle. Patrick joined in with the breakfast in a polite, neighbourly way.

The funeral itself was remarkable. A large crowd gathered in their hundreds, in the house and around the yard. When the priest came in, the atmosphere changed. He said prayers at the coffin and scattered incense. The lid was closed on Aunty Maggie – who was still looking pretty good dead.

I stared at the coffin, and a sense of finality hit me. Dead is dead in Ireland same as in Bootle. There is no coming back from that. In the yard, horses shook their heads and black feathers waved in the air. The crowd was silent. Men stood with their caps removed as a mark of respect. The only sound was a sharp strike of metal on stone, as the horses' hooves scratched the surface of the stony yard, like bulls about to charge.

A horse-drawn hearse made its way slowly away from the farmhouse. We followed on in a horse and cart, bumping up the rutted lane. Everyone else trailed in behind, walking a good country mile to the church. There was an even bigger crowd waiting at the whitewashed chapel, which called a single sad toll from its bell tower. Children stood on top of a low wall that ran the length of the church grounds to keep the unholy out. Everywhere was a great silence, broken at regular intervals by the sharp call of the bell. The adults stood quietly waiting, the men, bared heads bowed, holding their caps in their hands. Then the neighbours carried the coffin into the church. I recognised one of the carriers as Peter O'Byrne, from across the field, with a flame of red hair that seemed to catch fire in the morning light.

The funeral Mass was full of old-fashioned hymns. The service ended with Irish music rising into the high arches of the parish church, amid the incense and the prayers. The coffin was carried out into the blinding light, as a lonely peal of the church bell rang crisp and clear in the spring air. Suddenly, an explosion of sound made me jump. A lone piper released a melancholic series of blasts towards the heavens, a signal to the gods that we were on our way. He bellowed out a slow tune and the coffin was carried out behind him, everyone flowing out of the church and around to the cemetery for the burial ceremony in full view of the mountain.

Uncle Peter looked a lot older in the April sunshine. His pipe was nowhere to be seen. The crowd mumbled a decade of the rosary. It was only when everyone in the cemetery had shaken our hands again, and said how sorry they were for our loss, and Uncle Peter and the neighbours led by Peter O'Byrne had filled in the grave, only then was it time to leave.

Patrick and Mary were standing at a respectful distance. It seemed natural to fall in beside them. Mum walked behind us with their father, and they spoke quietly together with his head bent towards her upturned face. Uncle Peter and Aunty Maggie had never had children. I know that Mum worried about who would look after Uncle Peter. Perhaps that was what she and Peter O'Byrne were talking about.

Mary wiped away a tear from her red-rimmed eyes. Patrick put his arm around her and she managed a smile.

"Did I hear people calling you Red Pat, or was that to someone else?" I asked.

Mary lifted her chin and smiled again.

"Everyone around here calls him Red Pat, except Da, who doesn't like it because he's called Red Peter," she said.

I glanced back at Red Peter again. He was supporting Mum's arm as they walked along. The way that he looked at her, and the tender way that she looked back at him made me mad, or was I imagining it?

We followed the crowd around the side of the church and into the parish hall. Inside, there was a long narrow room with a stage at one end. Three rows of tables and chairs ran the length of the hall. A section was reserved for the family at the stage end. A number of cousins on Aunty Maggie's side, who Mum said weren't real cousins, were already seated. I found myself sitting between Mum and one of these cousins, Mary O'Toole, who gave a running commentary on everything and everyone in the room.

"Oh, the wan there, she's the divil and she ran off on her husband, Big Jack Furlong, the wan they call The Bull. Ran off on him, would you believe, with that slip of a lad from over at Blackditch, you know the mother, the wan with the gimpish eye, we always used to call her Witch Kearney... Oh, there's no luck to be had having truck with that family, I can tell you. Them Kearneys was always trouble, mark my words..."

I wouldn't mind but she was talking to Mum across my face. I was trying to eat a ham sandwich that had arrived on a large plate. When I bit into it, the flavour was of a lost kingdom from before the war. It tasted of peace and a land of plenty, of green grass and blue skies. The one-way conversation was still in full flow.

"... and then that mountain goat with the buck teeth had the audacity to ask me out on a date to the dance, and then turned up smelling of sour milk and God knows what else, and he rocking back and forth on his big farmer's heels, and the red face of him as he hands me a bunch of weeds he called flowers, so I told him where to get off with himself and afterwards..."

I had to get out. Smoking was a great excuse to use at a time of crisis. Listening to Mary O'Toole – who was no oil painting herself, as Mum remarked to me later – bad-mouth everyone and anyone, brought on as great a crisis as you could get at a funeral. Mum was well able for her, of course.

"I know, Mary," she said. "What makes me sick to my stomach is those who never stop griping no matter what, and always know what's best for everyone else, and will make sure to tell you for your own good of course, and never have a good word for anyone, they're the ones to keep your eye on."

That, as Mum said later, went straight over Mary's head. Mum said if we tied her to a steel cable and asked her any question at all, she would make the best barrage balloon ever, she carried so much hot air about her.

When I got up, cousin Mary slid across to divulge more state secrets into Mum's ear. I excused myself and went outside.

Mary and Patrick were standing talking to a group of lads, one of whom was speaking.

"… so I bought them two calves last August at the Tinahely Fair and…"

The conversation stopped when I approached. Mary introduced me to the locals; John Joe called Pike who had just been speaking; and two other Patricks, Patrick Murphy called Spud and Patrick Byrne called Flash on account of him being such a fast footballer; and his brother Seamus called Horse, maybe because he was built like a tank; and his sister Maura who was younger and said nothing.

"A lot of Patricks," I said. "I can see why they have to call you Red Pat. Do the girls get nicknames as well?"

"None, Miss Maggie, that we could repeat in mixed company. Haha!"

It was Seamus called Horse who laughed at his own joke. He complemented this gem of wisdom with an exaggerated wink at me, which made his face look very horse-like. I could see that it wasn't because he was built like a tank that he got his equine name.

"And how are things in England, Miss Maggie? We hear it's very bad in London and Coventry. And now Belfast."

"Very bad is right," I replied. "We're surviving and things will get better, but to be honest, it's easier not to talk about it."

I could see the looks of relief on their faces.

"You will, I suppose, be coming to the dance tonight, Miss Maggie? It's in honour of your Aunt Maggie and it promises to be mighty. They're coming in from all over the place."

Horse had spoken again, no winks this time.

I turned to Mary and she read the confusion on my face.

"You should be ashamed of yourself, Horse, to say such a thing to somebody in mourning. Come on Maggie, let's walk."

Mary linked my arm and we set off on the gravelled walk that led to the back of the church, leaving the boys to stare after us, mouths open probably. The path led back to the cemetery, and we strolled in the breezy air. I smoked and Mary declined at first, but took a cigarette when we were out of sight of the boys.

She stopped in front of a grave with newly picked flowers, blessed herself and said a prayer. I looked at the rising ground that ran to the base of the mountain and then took off like a plane and flew to a great height that disappeared into the fluffy white clouds. Occasionally, a sight of the great bulk beyond filtered through like a glimpse of another world, dark and purple like the colours of Lent. It was a place probably inhabited by gods who played games for sport with people's lives. A restlessness stirred in me and I felt the pull of home. It was time to get back to Liverpool.

Mary was standing beside me quietly crying. I looked and saw that it was the grave of her mother. I put my arm around her and her gentle shaking became a sob. She gulped in a breath of air to try to hold it in, but the pain burst out of her. I could feel her go weak with my arm holding her. She still managed to slide down, and pulled me with her, so that we both ended up on our knees on the soft turf. She buried her head into me, and I held her there. I could feel her pain coming from that deep place within, one that had never seen the light of day.

Afterwards we sat on the low wall and even the threat of a shower of rain didn't break the spell that connected me, Mary and her mother.

"I'm sorry Maggie, I've never done that before," she said. "It's just that Mam and Aunt Maggie were such good friends and Aunt Maggie – we called her Aunt even though she wasn't – I hope you don't mind – Aunt Maggie used to come over and help Mammy, and then Mam…. and now Aunt Maggie… I've no one left now to tell me things and show me how to raise the family. Nora and

Bridget are just babies really, always asking where Mammy has gone."

"She's gone to a good place and I'm sure she's looking down on you right now and watching over the family," I said. "You're doing a great job with the girls... and Patrick, well, he can take care of himself."

Mary smiled at that and her serious face turned brighter.

"What's to become of us all?"

The question hung in the air between us. I was afraid to think of the future, only the present like Tom said to do, and not ask too many 'loose questions' as he called them.

"Aunt Maggie is... was... a special woman, Maggie. She was loved by everyone, always had a welcome smile and a good word for us. She was generous and fun too. She was a great dancer in her day and taught the lot of us, you know. The dance tonight is in her honour. But you don't have to go if you don't feel like it. Talk to your own mam. See what she thinks."

She jumped down off the wall. It was time to go back. When we returned to the hall, the loud clatter of sound hit me like a slap in the face. To my great disappointment, all the ham sandwiches were gone.

CHAPTER THIRTEEN

There is something disturbing about throwing a dance to celebrate a person's death, even if the deceased was a dancer her whole life. Death is nothing to celebrate. I thought it was in bad taste, this business of having a *céilí* at a time of mourning. Not that anybody would pay heed to me. I believe that you should celebrate life with those you love while you are still alive. But in Ireland, a dance was to be held that very night in celebration of Aunty Maggie while she was still 'looking pretty good dead' in the graveyard.

It wasn't enough to be lying in a cold grave beside a white church, surrounded by an expanse of boggy fields that spread out at the feet of a purple-and-yellow mountain. It wasn't enough that the great mountain soared above the orange and flame-red clouds and caught the dying light of the sun in a kind of spontaneous combustion. No, there had to be a dance.

It wasn't a dance in the usual sense, with a band on stage and modern swing music to set your heart pounding and your feet tapping. Nothing like that. This was a *céilí*, a community event. The older generation sat on tiered benches on a balcony at the end of the hall opposite the stage, in bright light, and the young sat on their knees or tumbled about between rows of laughing, chattering people. Opposite them on stage, a group of musicians were in full flow with Irish dance music setting feet tapping, hands clapping and hearts racing.

In between, the hall was heaving. A crowd stood around the outside of the dancers, clapping. It was like nothing I had ever seen before, nothing I could have imagined. A different world, as Mum reminded me at every opportunity. This was the world of my mother as a child, and as a girl, before she packed her few things and left it for the great city of Liverpool, like thousands of Irish before her and since. She carried the memories, sounds and smells of Byrne's Lane in her bag, as she walked the damp cobblestones of Liverpool for the first time.

She had dismissed my objections to the dance out of hand.

"This is how it is here, Maggie. If you don't go it would be the talk of the place, but I can make an excuse that you are overcome by the excitement of it all."

She gave me the look.

"And Uncle Peter, God bless him, it would kill him if you didn't go. It would be seen as a mark of disrespect to Aunty Maggie. Besides, you've made plenty of friends who'd love to see you there too."

So in the end it was decided I would go with Mary, Veronica and Patrick, who had taught me the classic céilí dance, the Walls of Limerick, before we left the farmhouse. Standing with them and listening to the chatter of their friends rising and falling to the rhythm of the alien music, I felt like a fish out of water. And there wasn't a ham sandwich in sight.

"One-two-three and one-two-three, step-two-three and one-two-three..."

First we joined hands in a line and met another line coming from the opposite direction. I danced with the person diagonally in front of me, catching hands and twisting and turning, first in one direction, then the opposite. After that we stood and let two other people dance, and then on through the line to start all over again with the next line. The music and steps repeated until I had met and danced with half the people in the room. It was a very social form of dancing, with so many shared looks, winks, nods and infectious smiles that by the end of it, even someone as grumpy as me was smiling – until I caught sight of Mum and Red Peter disappearing outside. I decided to go out for fresh air.

There was no sign of the two of them. Horse, Red Pat, Mary and Veronica followed me out. I stood and smoked for a while, and they chatted about the local gossip. Horse talked about the British bomber that had crashed that very week into a mountain, about twenty miles away to the north, killing the crew on board. He explained about different types of sheep and how much each type was worth. In the end I was glad to walk down to the graveyard with Mary and Patrick to say goodbye to Aunty Maggie for the last time.

In the gathering dusk, I thought I could make out two shadowy figures sitting on the wall at the end of the cemetery. Red Peter came forward and spoke softly to his two eldest children who had stopped in front of their mother's grave. I went on past him to where I believed Mum was sitting on the wall, but there was no one there. When I returned to the hall, she was up on the floor dancing with Uncle Peter, Cousin Mary and a lot of other cousins all called Byrne, O'Byrne, O'Toole or Hayes. When she saw me she waved and smiled.

It struck me then that, despite my earlier reservations about dancing only hours after laying a loved one to rest, these people were not denouncing death, they were celebrating life. Aunty Maggie would have been proud.

I had never really seen Mum enjoy life before, and never once witnessed her dancing at home except when the lads pulled her reluctantly around the kitchen. There was a glow on her cheeks and a light in her eye. I'm certain that it was the happiest I had ever seen her in my entire life.

CHAPTER FOURTEEN

I was glad to get on the train after an epic journey from South Wicklow in a car that had broken down twice and needed to be fed an enormous amount of water and oil. The driver employed a mixture of love and hate as he poured in the precious liquids from a series of cans that were strapped along the running board. He kicked it a few times, cursed and swung the starting handle. It kicked back and nearly broke his arm. Then a splutter and the engine coughed an apology, gasped again and finally sprang into life with a bang.

Mum never spoke a word, just hummed to herself as we drove along twisty roads that seemed to follow every riverbed in the county.

The train journey from Arklow zig-zagged its way through the rolling Wicklow countryside, with occasional glimpses of small farmhouses and hidden villages. The track continued along more defined river valleys, bursting with the freshness of late spring. A glint of dark water filtered through gaps in thick woodland, like ancient stories with their meaning half-hidden from view. Then the railway line burst out on to a coastal plain at Wicklow and travelled with the sea on one side and a soggy landscape on the other, seabirds screaming in circles above the sloblands. Mum was quiet, deep in thought, as she watched the sights slipping past.

Afterwards, the train chugged through the sleepy fishing village of Greystones, around and under the huge bulk of Bray Head with its tunnels and sudden sea views of rocky coves, where seabirds scrambled on sheer cliff-faces. Then the track opened on to the fashionable resort of Bray, which looked like Blackpool when glimpsed between the elegant houses and hotels that lined the seafront.

"Penny for your thoughts," I said.

"Now, Maggie, thoughts are dearly bought," Mum replied. "You won't get much for a penny."

She was silent again, so I watched the seascape from the dusty window seat. I felt a combination of sadness and joy. It was good to be going home, but it would have been nice to stay here in Ireland, in the hope that the war would pass around me, and over me, and somehow not touch me.

It was only when we were standing on the aft deck of the *Leinster*, with her things stored below in her cabin that a semblance of the old Mum returned. We gazed on the dark outline of the Wicklow and Dublin Mountains, which collected a vast amount of rain in their sponge-like bogs. The waters filtered through valleys and lakes into the River Liffey, which ran away to sea beneath our keel as we sailed out of port in the soft twilight, with the clouds burning red in the western sky.

Only then did she sigh. She exhaled that part of her life, her love of home, her memories and opportunities lost, into the violet air. It seemed to come from a place deep within her, somewhere I hadn't known existed, camouflaged in England by years of hard work capped with layers of irony. She turned her back on the land of her youth and, without looking back, stepped through the doorway leading to a stairwell that descended to her cabin in the bowels of the ship.

I had collected a bunch of flowers earlier in the day, along the hedgerows that bordered the farmyard. Uncle Peter had told me about the sinking of the first *SS Leinster* in the last months of the Great War in 1918. More than five hundred people were drowned, including over fifty postal workers who had been in the mailroom, when it took a direct hit. One of them was a first cousin of Uncle Peter who had gone up to Dublin to get a job in the Post Office and ended up on board sorting the mail from Kingstown to Holyhead on that fateful morning.

The first torpedo missed, but the second scored a direct hit on the mailroom. Everyone in there was killed instantly. The torpedo went right through the ship and blew a hole in the other side of the hull. The ship tried to return to Kingstown, but sank slowly in the rough sea. They started to lower the lifeboats and get the women and children off. Not satisfied with that, the commander of the U-boat fired again. The mail boat was rocked by another huge explosion that blew it apart.

Uncle Peter told me of men swimming frantically about, holding their children up in the water while the women sank first, their long dresses dragging them down like anchors. By the time the rescue boats came out from Kingstown – later renamed Dun Laoghaire – and Dublin, there was hardly anyone left to save. Of the 770 people on board, 530 drowned on a stormy October morning in 1918, within sight of the Irish coast.

Uncle Peter took his brown handkerchief from his trouser pocket and wiped his eyes. I remembered passing the lightship on our way over, the waves rolling about as if nothing bad had ever happened. The great sea cover-up.

Then Uncle Peter took up the story that Horse had mentioned to me about a British bomber which had gone off course three nights earlier and crashed into the Wicklow Mountains. The entire crew were killed instantly. Blessington Town had come to a standstill for four funerals, on the same day Aunty Maggie was buried.

Mum came back on deck. I threw the wild flowers into the air. The wind whipped them astern as we ploughed on headlong into a rising swell. The flowers remained afloat off the stern, but then got caught up in the wash behind and disappeared into the swirling water. I said a prayer to Njord, god of the sea, to take care of their souls, those five hundred and thirty men, women and children, whose watery grave was all about us.

I closed my eyes and remembered, in a flash, the sight of the *Athenia* sailing proudly out of Liverpool on that fateful Saturday afternoon, the last day of peace. A feeling of dread gathered about my heart. I didn't go below with Mum, preferring to stay on deck with the stars and my thoughts for company, while the ship sailed on into the gathering darkness, under the relative safety of the Irish flag.

I must have fallen asleep and dreamed that the ferryman Charon was looking for payment from me to carry us across the River Styx, that I had always pronounced as 'Stynks' at school. It's the swamp that divides the living from the dead, Earth from Hades. I was in dread, as I had no money, and neither had the four young crew of the bomber that had followed me over to Ireland and ended their short lives, smashed to pieces on a bleak Wicklow hillside.

As Billy said, sometimes bad things just happen. Those young men, who'd set off on a bombing raid on Germany, and somehow ended up in a graveyard in Blessington in Wicklow, seemed real in my dream. Together we were about to face the daunting prospect of wandering the earth as spirits for one hundred years without peace or rest, not even in death.

Out of the misty swamp, a ghost ship appeared, carrying hundreds on board. Men, women, children, soldiers, nurses and postmen sorting through tonnes of letters and parcels, working to deliver the mail on time. I woke to the chill of a damp dawn in the misty waters off Liverpool. I was glad to leave that nightmare behind me in the Irish Sea. Ahead lay the reality of the struggle to survive on a daily basis on shore, a different kind of nightmare from which there was no escape. Billy was somewhere out on the waters that connected us, probably scanning the moonlit darkness for any sign of a deadly foe. This was a picnic in comparison.

The city lay sleeping and there were no fires burning, a sign that no raids had taken place in the last few days. Since the attack on London after Christmas, the Luftwaffe raids had a new pattern. They dropped thousands of incendiaries at the start of each raid. This was followed by high explosives that spread fires and killed firefighters at the same time. They had done that to us in March.

We descended the gangplank, on this last Friday in April, to the news that Churchill was coming to our city this very lunchtime.

"Things must be bad if that old dog is taking the time to come and see us, and the news from Greece and Tobruk and just about everywhere is bad, bad, bad," said Mum.

"Still, he's been right about Hitler all along, Mum," I said. "Let's get you home first. I'm going to come back down later. I know Tom would go if he was here."

"Remember to say hello to Rufus from me," she said. "I like the look of that dog. He seems to know what he's about. I reckon he's as good a bet as anybody to get us out of this mess. Or at least not to get us into a bigger one. If it were up to me, I'd put the dog in charge."

Mary stood waiting for us and her rounded figure showing under her top coat made a heartening sight. With Mary and me linked either side of Mum, we picked our way through the carters that thronged the quays. We reached the station, looking like refugees fleeing some great catastrophe, except we were going in the opposite direction. We made a strange sight, led in front by Johnny, who was carrying our case and a large bag of food that we had brought over from Ireland. Home.

Crowds lined the broken streets and cheered. They stood on mountains of bricks piled high on either side of the road and cheered for Churchill like we had just won the war. I remembered

Tom's words about how much we matter. Looking about at the grimy faces smeared with toil, I watched them light up when a black motorcar passed with Churchill in the back, smoking his cigar. I couldn't see if his dog was sitting beside him, where Mum had said he would be.

The cheering went on and on. Churchill stood up in the open-roofed car and waved. The energy from the crowd was like a blast wave that spread throughout the whole street. Within that energy, buried somewhere deep inside, was exposed a core determination that we would never give in, no matter what. Not even the knot in my stomach or the pain in my head could prevent me from feeling that I was glad to be back in Liverpool, where I belonged, and I found myself cheering along with the crowd. Then he was gone and a voice beside me broke the spell.

"It's all right for him what sleeps in a steel bunker deep underground and hasn't had his house bombed like us to speak of never givin' up. I'd give up in the morning if I could."

The woman was shaking with anger. Her face was stained with dried-up tears, and the words came from a hard mouth that snapped shut when each sentence was complete. She looked like she hadn't eaten in a while.

I offered her a sandwich that I'd been carrying in my bag. It was a fresh ham sandwich made with the food we'd brought home from Ireland. Her eyes opened wide as she tasted the first bite, then she kissed my hand. She stuffed the food into her mouth and almost choked. I had to turn and walk away.

Thinking about it afterwards, it was remarkable how Churchill could face us and draw us all together. The war was going terribly badly, although nobody would say that out loud. Dad said that when Churchill had spoken directly to the men down at the docks, he'd praised them for their role in helping to win the Battle of the Atlantic. It was as though Hitler, in bombing us into submission on his maps, succeeded in doing the exact opposite on the ground. He was bombing our cities, but in doing so was releasing a spirit in all of us, an absolute determination that he would never defeat us.

I couldn't wait to get back to work.

CHAPTER FIFTEEN

Thursday 1st May 1941

So it begins. The week that changed our lives. Forever.

Is it possible to measure love? Can it be counted and marked on a chart and placed in an underground storeroom ready for shipment? Can it be brought out blinking into the bright May sunlight when most needed at a time of crisis? What is love anyway?

War changes things and it changes people too. When Billy was home before Easter, he seemed more concerned for the safety of his mother than he did before. Maybe it was that UXB at Christmas, when they nearly lost their home, at a time when so many others in our town were killed. Yet, because of that, Billy and his Mum had Christmas dinner at our house, and that was a brilliant day.

The Army Bomb Disposal Unit went in on the Sunday after Christmas and worked on it for hours. I saw the look of relief on that young soldier's tense face. He looked almost as young as Billy. When he saw me, he smiled and waved. The lorry started forward and his smile and those white, wide-open eyes were gone, never to be seen again. He was driven away, behind the bomb, to somewhere out beyond Our Shore for its safe detonation.

I went up with Billy's mum Bess when she was given the all-clear. She said that she was too nervous to go on her own in case the looters had come back. I sat on the stairs while she went through the house, room by room. She climbed down past me into the back kitchen and examined where the intruders had tried to break in. I could see that she was shaken by the whole experience and she had asked me to stay the night for company. My brothers Matt and John were home, so Mum had given me the all-clear, but I had to be back for breakfast before going off to work.

I slept in Billy's bed that night and fell asleep with the taste of his lips on my mouth and the smell of him all around. I tried to focus on the memory of Christmas Day here in this house, but that was soon replaced by the pain of him being away in the mid-Atlantic. The lurch of the boat moved in rhythm with my body as I tossed myself to sleep.

I felt most at home when I was at work. There was something about being part of the fight against this thing so evil that calmed me, and banished that feeling of hopelessness. Tom was right.

"Take it one day at a time. Do what you can in the moment and don't think too much about the bigger picture. Draw strength from those around you."

He should have been a preacher, Mum said.

When I first joined the factory, on the day after Boxing Day last Christmas, there were about two hundred of us. Now there were over twenty thousand women, and some men, working on a site that stretched over ten square miles. Much of it was underground, linked by a network of railways and roads. Work never stopped, even during an air raid, unless it was right overhead. My job was to send the finished bombs and shells to wherever they were needed, and get them there in the right number and at the right time. Lives depended on it.

It sounded simple enough, except there was a war on and that complicated things. The railway would get bombed and shipment would be delayed. Another way had to be found, with the minimum of delay. Sometimes telephone lines went down, ships got caught up in bad weather, or there was a raid on. I'd just turned eighteen, but they thought I was nineteen. I could calculate in my head faster than they could on paper, and remember everything to the last detail about the shipment.

On this Thursday morning of the first day of May, I was on site at five for a briefing and in position at five-thirty to ensure a smooth swap-over at six. It had been a quiet week as far as Jerry was concerned. The nights were getting shorter, the weather improving and food rationing was becoming more severe. Mum said that the rationing was far worse because of the longer days. She couldn't wait for winter to come.

We had a newly arrived ship in the docks, the *SS Malakand*. It was waiting to be loaded with a cargo of bombs and shells bound for Egypt. That's all I knew and needed to know. It was in the Huskisson Number Two dock, the middle of the three docks where Dad was based, and we could use the railway to transport the cargo. Munitions were badly needed in the Middle East and this order was a priority. I liked things brief and to the point. It would take a couple of days to load the full shipment of over one thousand tonnes of high explosives, over eighty-thousand shells and a couple of thousand bombs. That would keep us all busy and focused for the rest of the week.

Billy had shocked me when he told me that if your ship was sunk and you ended up in a life-raft, you were considered off-duty. Your pay was stopped from that moment, until you were rescued, returned home and assigned to a new ship. I was thinking of Tom the morning before Christmas after our home had been bombed, after Josie Morris and her family had been blown to smithereens. Having heard me moaning and groaning over my dress, Tom had taken me down to the docks to knock some sense into me. He never uttered a word of complaint. Off-duty officially and with no pay, yet he volunteered to go on fire-watch in the docks, with the Luftwaffe making a bloody mess of the city, the docks and our town too.

I couldn't get over the way Tom handled himself. I often thought of those few days during Christmas week, and in a crazy way they seemed to be happier times than now. Billy was afraid that something bad was going to happen, but as I said to him, bad things happen all the time, so it's best not to think about it. I don't believe that Billy was too impressed with my logic from the look on his face.

"Right so. I won't worry about anything serious happening to you or Mum, because bad things happen all the time... and that makes it normal. Is that what you're saying?"

"Billy, you know what I mean. We're made of tough stuff."

"We are made of flesh and blood, Mags. We may be tough on the outside, but we're soft inside."

I could have killed him for saying that and leaving me with those words to ponder on our last night. He had taken me to the Rialto on a proper date. He'd even worn his uniform. God, he looked so handsome in that uniform. We danced for a while, but the energy was sucked out of the room by a blast wave from a bomb that exploded in the next road. We walked home in silence, hand-in-hand through the pitch-black streets. I could sense his dark thoughts embark at the docks and sail out beyond the narrow channel in the estuary. My own fears moved quietly through the waves beyond the Mersey shoreline, out towards the end of our world that scrambled over the Welsh hills and on into the great western ocean.

The logistical operation of loading shells and bombs on to the train, and transporting them to the dock was my department's responsibility. It required meticulous planning, gentle lifting, secure storing and timely transportation. I travelled on the train down to the dock to see the loading operation for myself, and to calculate how long each round journey would take.

It was the first time I had travelled through the city on the railway. The scars of war were everywhere to be seen. Gaps in streets, gaps in buildings. The city lay pockmarked in the aftermath of a gigantic chickenpox. Smouldering factories and damaged churches and schools were scattered across the blackened landscape. In between, life went on. Shops, offices, banks, cinemas and public buildings were open for business. Trams, buses, lorries and trains were on the move. The line from the factory ran down to the Overhead Railway, the Docker's Umbrella which connected the docks that ran for miles along the banks of the Mersey. At the river, hundreds of carters steered their carts loaded with cotton or timber under the steel frames of the railway, their dray horses walking on towards delivery yards to connect with the factories and mills of Lancashire and beyond. On the river, ferries chugged their way across from Birkenhead to the Pier Head, pushing bravely against the tide.

The Huskisson Dock consisted of a set of three docks that ran perpendicular to the river. It stretched from below the Overhead Railway to where all three opened on to the main dock that was connected to the Mersey by a series of barriers that could be opened or closed depending on the tide. The *SS Malakand* occupied the middle dock. It sat low and small in the water, its one central black funnel standing erect and ready for action. It was flanked by a bridge and crew area. There were two masts and two holds, one fore and one aft.

The loading operation was already underway as I watched. My orders were to get the job done as swiftly as possible and have the ship fully loaded within three days, ready to sail on full tide on Sunday morning. The dock was lined by ancient warehouses filled with everything from timber and tobacco to cotton and steel. It was no exaggeration to say that hundreds of workers were busy loading and unloading supplies that were essential to the war effort.

Standing on the platform of the Overhead Railway with my father by my side, it was possible to see the huge operation that was the Merseyside docks system. Below us, the munitions train was systematically being stripped of its shells and bombs as they were loaded into the hold of the ship. Out on the river, warships and merchant ships of every shape and size were either on the move, tied up at anchor, or in for repairs in docks stretched all along both sides of the estuary. A line of barrage balloons was overseeing the whole operation from on high, glinting silver in the morning light.

"It's a fine sight, Maggie," said Dad. "We'll soon have all those twenty-five pounders loaded and on their way to where they're badly needed. You just keep 'em coming as fast as you can."

"Mum says that if the country was run half as well as the docks, we'd win the war in no time. I can see what she means."

"We all do our bit. I hear the bomb girls are doing great work up your way. Just on the QT, I also hear Tom's convoy has started for home and should be here next week."

Dad tapped the side of his nose as he said that. He was watching me for a reaction, but I pretended it was of only passing interest to me.

"We'll have a train here every four hours if you can handle that."

"That and a lot more."

Dad lifted his cap, scratched his head and laughed.

"That Billy lad is a good footballer with real potential," he said. "Liverpool, though! We'll have to see about that. Tell your mother I'll be late tonight. It looks like we'll be working well into the evening. Matt and John are coming down on fire-watch after tea. They can bring me something to eat."

I had never seen Dad at work before. He was a different person and I could see where the boys got their positive attitude. Dad reminded me of Tom in the calm way he went about his business. I knew that he was in charge, but everyone was getting on with their tasks and he just nodded or waved a hand from our elevated position to the crane operators, the dockers on the quayside, or on the ship.

I had to shade my eyes from the glare of the morning light that caught the silver of the barrage balloons. They shone like a collection of giant mirrors in a cloudless sky.

"It's going to be a warm one for sure, but a blow is coming in later tonight," said Dad. "Don't forget the clock is going forward two hours this weekend. That's two hours less sleep on Saturday night. Your mother says it'll help the rationing no end."

I laughed for the first time since returning from Ireland.

"I need to get back. We'll have a train for you every four hours, last one at four this afternoon."

As we watched, a new barrage balloon was launched from a base on the opposite side of the dock. It floated into the air on the sea breeze, rolling from side to side like a giant egg on a string let loose from an alien world. Seagulls circled about its bulk like tiny fighter-planes in defensive formation about the mother ship. It reminded me of a time long before the war when Dad had taken me to the park to play. We had sat on a bench eating our sandwiches, watching a couple try to fly a kite. Every time she launched it, it flipped. The man tried to run, but he was too slow, and the kite crashed into the grass every time. Then Dad ran with it and it flew to the sky. The couple thanked him and waved at me. I remember being proud of my Dad. I remember the look on their faces. I remember feeling happy.

Across the dock, the team unwound the steel cable and the oblong shape rose into the air. It was placed in position directly over the Huskisson Dock, directly overhead the *SS Malakand*.

All hail to the giant gods of air

Keep us safe in thy godly care

I have crazy thoughts sometimes, but slowly and surely I am learning to keep them to myself.

I turned at the red-bricked station wall to say something, but Dad was already down on the dock below, talking to the men as they loaded the ship with its deadly cargo. Somewhere out beyond the horizon, dark clouds were gathering.

CHAPTER SIXTEEN

If you were ever able to step outside the front door of your life and look in through the window, you might be surprised at what you would see. Rooms stained with worry and dread. Rooms that carry constant pain in a deep hollow hidden away under a stair, a pain that catches your breath with every sudden movement of the day. A house with the roof slightly askew, living with the daily possibility of death from the air. A house filled with a strong feeling of dread that something terrible is going to happen, even though something terrible *is* happening almost every day. But that's not it. A house filled with an air of belief that it has an important contribution to make. A house filled to the rooftop with the chatter of voices, echoing like ghosts in the rafters of your life.

Sometimes it is better to stay inside a fool's paradise. When I returned from Ireland it was with a clarity of vision that I had only glimpsed in snatches before I'd set out. The sea air had blown away the cobwebs that had clouded my sight. It was as plain to me as the nose on my face that we were in a desperate way.

The first bombs of the week fell on Wallasey at the western tip of the opposite shore. Sirens wailed in the gathering gloom, and echoed over and back across the river. Thousands of people scurried into air raid shelters on city streets, huddled under archways and bridges, or streamed into basements and cellars, large and small. Many scrambled into Anderson Shelters dug into back gardens, or hid under stairs of homes without shelters, where children were bundled by their mothers acting as father and mother, protector and

111

nourisher. The heavy thump of ack ack guns added to the drama as searchlights swept the sky. It was like the opening scene of the film at the Broadway Cinema, from where I was returning with Mary having watched '*Third Finger, Left Hand.*' We'd laughed our socks off at the romantic comedy in which a career woman, played by Myrna Loy, invented a husband, then ended up having to pretend Melvyn Douglas was her husband, with hilarious consequences. We were still laughing arm-in-arm up the road, when the sirens announced the arrival of the Luftwaffe in our skies.

At first, the dull thud of explosions sounded far away, but the steady growl of their engines grew in anger with every passing second. Then suddenly it was upon us, and we could hear the clatter of incendiary bombs hitting the roofs of buildings, smashing the tiles. All around us, we could see the dull yellow glow that started a small fire which in turn became a much larger conflagration, with a sulphurous devil at the heart of it, spitting venomous flames. Fire-watchers and firemen ran here and there, trying to put out fires before they had a chance to catch hold. Incendiaries fell on the roofs of houses, churches, schools, factories and shops, like angry meteors sent from the gods.

We avoided the hoses and broken tiles that lay strewn on the streets of the town and quickly made our way up home. Looking back from the front steps of the house, it looked like the docks were the main target. A yellow glow was visible in the darkness. I shivered. Matt, John and Dad were down there.

The night was shattered with the scream of high explosive bombs. A series of blasts followed from the direction we had just come. We scrambled as fast as we could through the house, out into the shelter and closed the door. The ground was shaking and we were too. Mum was praying and we joined in. It was the rosary, the great prayer to Our Lady, Mother of Jesus.

Holy Mary, Mother of God,
Pray for us sinners,

Now, and at the hour of our death.

Amen.

While it passed the time, I thought that praying about the hour of your death while the angel of death hovered overhead was tempting fate for sure, but this wasn't the time to start that particular conversation.

Mary sat on the bench, her fists clenched. I reckoned she was thinking about Johnny, somewhere halfway to Canada, passing Tom and Billy's ship in the opposite direction, in the white darkness that passed for night up there near the Arctic Circle. She had once shown me a library book about that part of the world, with pictures of polar bears standing looking across a sea filled with chunks of ice. I shivered.

The all-clear sounded. When we stepped outside, it was raining. Once again the gods of sky had saved us from the enemy. Dad had been right about the weather. He arrived home just as Mum made a pot of tea.

"There isn't a man in the whole of Ireland, England, Scotland and Wales that can smell a cut of bread and a cup of tea better than this one," she said. "What time of the night do you call this to be coming home from work?"

We could see that she was glad to have him home in one piece.

"They hit the road bridge over the canal down on Stanley Road, and a pub near the Broadway picture house," he said. "They seem to have dug most people out. Thank God for this murky weather. But they'll be back tomorrow night as sure as ducks are ducks. Mark my words. Their work isn't half done yet."

"Did they hit the docks?"

"Both sides of the river, but nothing too bad. The ack ack guns did a great job. The flak forced them so high they dropped their bombs mainly on to houses. This is the first time they've ever bombed us with a full moon. They might have been able to fly up the river by the brighter light, but it meant we could see them too. They didn't get any ships tonight."

Dad was the best, as he must have seen I was worried about the *Malakand*. We had succeeded in loading just under half the cargo of tank shells, gun shells and bombs for the tanks and soldiers and RAF fighting in Egypt and across North Africa. This was a vital supply and I was going to be in work at five in the morning to check that the railway was open. Nothing would stop this shipment if I could help it.

"Matt and John are staying below just in case Jerry comes back, but this won't blow over till morning," Dad said. "Make the most of it, because the weather is set to be fine for the rest of the week."

"Here, stop your gabble and eat your supper before it becomes your breakfast." Mum was in top form. "Father Breen will have a few more to fit in tomorrow. The crypt will soon be standing room only."

I looked at the hard face of my mother and saw in a flash her laughing eyes and dancing feet on our last night in Ireland. She was at home there in another world, where people died naturally in their beds and the whole community spent days and nights celebrating the event. A place where the birds sang in the perfumed air of the soft evening light. I thought of Mary and her sisters and Red Pat and Horse and little Nora and Bridget, and I was suddenly back in the graveyard in the failing light. Red Peter was there at the back wall with someone who turned out to be a ghost from a previous life that vanished in the gloaming.

CHAPTER SEVENTEEN

Friday 2nd May 1941

The weather front had blown through, leaving fresh, clear air in its wake. If I reached out my hand from the Huskisson Station, it appeared that I could touch the opposite bank of the Mersey. Thin wisps of black smoke escaped from various buildings along the margins of the river, rising through the clouds of barrage balloons to the shocking blue sky beyond.

The railway had survived intact. Our train was on its way at first light from the siding where we had stored it overnight. It arrived at the Huskisson Number Two dock at a quarter past six. Our target for the day was to beat the thirty thousand shells that had been loaded yesterday. With a clear run, we would load thirty-five thousand shells today and finish the job by tomorrow lunchtime.

Dad was optimistic.

"You get them here and we'll load them," he said. "It's going to be a warm one."

He took off his cap, scratched his head and slowly put it back on.

"There's a full moon tonight. If Jerry sends his Junkers back then he must be getting desperate, but we'll be ready for him."

I put my hand on his arm.

"Mum told me to remind you that if you don't come home before dark there'll be no dinner for you tonight."

Dad laughed.

"That woman's bark is much sharper than her bite. I had great peace and quiet while she was away. Don't you worry about me. The boys will be down later and will bring me some food. They're not back to sea till Sunday. Now off you go and keep 'em shells comin'."

I spent the day checking load after trainload of munitions. My shift finished at two o'clock, but I stayed until after five. Then I went to see Billy's mum Bess, but she wasn't home, so I wandered over to the church hall. Mum, Bess and many of the other women in the Women's Voluntary Service, the WVS, were preparing meals for the three hundred homeless men, women and children who were living in the hall and sleeping in the crypt.

Father Breen was floating about organising more bedding and tending to the sick, reassuring those who were nervous or worried. He stopped when he saw me.

"Maggie my dear, you are so kind to come over and you working all day you-know-where."

He tapped the side of his nose.

"Thanks Father. I'm afraid I don't hold with turning the other cheek."

"Even Jesus drove those market sellers and moneylenders from the Temple, Maggie. You have the right to act to defend yourself, your country and your religion. We are like shepherds and these good people are like sheep, lost and in need of protection from the forces of evil."

"But you know the bit that says, 'Forgive us our trespasses as we forgive those who trespass against us…' I've been having trouble with that part for a long time now."

Father Breen raised his dark eyes to heaven and laughed.

"We'll worry about that when all this is over, Maggie. In the meantime, there's another part that says 'Love thine neighbour' and that's what you are doing here Maggie, and in your work that helps to protect us from the aggressor. Rest assured, you are doing God's work. People have to eat and sleep, and we all have the right to live in peace."

I looked at him through different eyes, not as a priest on the altar each Sunday morning Mass, but as a man, and a tired and worn man at that. He looked like he'd had little sleep.

"Were you up last night Father with the bombing? You look worn out. If you want to lie down and have a rest, I'll make sure everything is done just the way you like it."

Father Breen laughed again.

"You make us all ashamed, Maggie. To see a slip of a girl like you, who was up half the night yourself and spent all day, if I'm not mistaken, moving things around this city at great risk to your own life, all in the service of your country, and now to be worrying about me! Mark my words, Maggie. So long as there are people like you about we will never be conquered. And God is on our side."

"I heard that Jerry modelled his SS on the Jesuits, Father. Perhaps Hitler thinks God is on his side too?"

When I saw the look on Father Breen's face, I was sorry that I hadn't taken Tom's advice and kept my big mouth shut. Sometimes I say things that I regret later, but this question had been bothering me for a long time, so perhaps it was good to put it out there and take the consequences.

"Make no mistake, Maggie, Satan is alive and working with the evil forces that would try to destroy us." Father Breen's eye had started to twitch. "He is alive in the planning and in the execution, on the U-boats, and in the bombers and the bombs that we know are real and deadly to us. He is working through the evil ambitions that Hitler has to destroy us, and everything that we stand for. Hitler turned his back on Christ as a young man."

The pulse above Father Breen's left eye was jumping up and down, contorting his face and adding to the earnestness in his voice. I was trying to think of a way to get myself out of this hole I was digging when we were interrupted by Mr Watts, our local air raid warden. He grabbed Father Breen's arm amid talk of fire buckets, stirrup pumps, church roofs and bell towers.

I looked about, but no one was staring. To my relief, it appeared that our conversation was lost in the general clamour of the hall. The women of the WVS were serving a type of fish stew that was made from an assortment of fish landed at the docks, and a selection of scarce vegetables from local allotments. To hungry people, it smelled and tasted like manna from heaven. It was hot and nourishing, if fairly tasteless, and not one drop was wasted or left at the end of the meal.

As I gathered up the dishes, I chatted to mothers with their babies, and to old people huddled in twos and threes. There was a tension throughout the hall as some of them joked about the last supper, but not within Father Breen's hearing. Someone had spooked them with a story that Lord Haw Haw had said Liverpool was in for it.

"The Liver Birds had better fly," he was reported to have said, or words to that effect.

I remembered what he had said about Belfast before Easter and a dull pain began to circulate in my lower stomach. The infants in the hall had that same look as the children on the platform in Dublin, a look no child should have. Fear.

Then someone started playing the piano and a group gathered around. The singing started and the whole hall joined in. I couldn't help but smile at the transformation on the faces of the children and the old folks singing along with the chorus. A group of women gathered in a circle and danced and sang. The world seemed to stop spinning quite so fast, and laughter was heard bouncing off the walls.

Roll out the barrel…

But the cheering and clapping were soon interrupted by the fire warden announcing that the hall had to be cleared in the next ten minutes, in case of an early raid. The crowd gathered what little they had about them and headed down to the crypt, where another piano had been set up to continue the sing-song. It was good to sing and be happy, even for those few short minutes when you forgot who and where you were.

As I walked home with Mum, she had a faraway look and was whistling, which she didn't usually do. She was probably thinking of Ireland. I was thinking of Billy and Tom. I imagined them somewhere out in the rolling waves that broke the surface of the sea into a series of white-topped hills and deep black troughs that went down like dark thoughts without end.

Light filtered through the shocking orange sunset as the sun sank behind the lines of cloud in the west. It signalled that the edge of night was fast approaching. Overhead, the blue sky darkened to magenta. No birds flew in the soft orange light carried on the warm breeze in from the sea. Even the seagulls had abandoned us and headed up the coast to safer ground, out beyond where fires were set on the sands, during the raids, to confuse the bombers. The trick sometimes worked in the black of night, but in the light of a full moon, with the estuary glinting silver against the dark land, it would be nothing more than a distraction. That's what Dad had said to me this morning.

"Get your mother, yourself and Mary into the Anderson Shelter as soon as darkness comes," he said, "and stay there no matter what."

I nodded and told him not to worry about us. Sometimes it's scary being treated like an adult when you feel like a child inside. I tried not to show it, not even in my eyes, or with a quiver in my voice. At times like that I thought of what Tom would do or say if he was here. I was glad Billy was on the same ship as him. Tom would watch out for him for sure.

Mum was keen to get home and feed the boys before they went down to the docks. I was suddenly starving as I realised I hadn't eaten a morsel since morning. Mary was sitting on the steps outside the house. Her great bulging stomach was a wonder to see. I loved having Mary around again. You can't beat a sister for having someone to talk to and confide in. Someone to trust with your life. You can rely on a sister never to tell you a lie, never to let you down. Her Johnny had sailed on a convoy heading to Halifax in Canada, and wouldn't be back for the birth. Mum had insisted she move in with us until the baby arrived.

Matt and John had spent the day down on their ships. They were getting them ready to set sail, overseeing the loading of cargo, food and water. They ate under the watchful eye of Mum who had silently prepared a parcel of food for Dad.

"We saw a lot of people leaving the city this evening," said Matt. "There could be a big night ahead. Will you be all right here?"

John took after Dad as a man of few words. He looked up from his plate at the serious face of his younger brother.

"You can't hold back the tide, Matt. What will be will be."

"The targets will be down at the docks if they come," said Matt. "They can hardly mistake us up here for what we are. Houses and nothing much else. What do you think, Ma?"

"I'm not your Ma! I've told you a hundred times not to call me that. Sometimes it's better not to think too much on things you can have no control over. Better to die happy in ignorance for your country than to die miserable and informed. A much more fulfilling death, boys. But there'll be no dying tonight in this family, over my dead body!"

Mary looked startled. She had been out of the house way too long, and had forgotten the routine. I smiled at the way Mum wound up the boys.

"That's a bit harsh, Ma."

"I'm not your Ma!"

Mum let loose with Sting and clipped Matt on the side of the ear.

"Ow! I hope none of those German bombers have as good an aim as you or we're all in real trouble."

He grabbed Mum around the waist and skipped a few steps across the kitchen floor dragging her with him, singing that song from the *Wizard of Oz* about the yellow brick road.

Even Mum was laughing as the boys grabbed Dad's supper and headed out the door.

I sat chatting with Mary on the steps outside the front door, as a warm May breeze blew softly through the house. Mum joined us with a cuppa for each of us and one for herself. We sat there in peace, watching the light fade from the street, as if some giant God was slowly turning out the light and simultaneously turning on the darkness. I was thinking of that three-quarters-full ship down on the docks that was in reality a time-bomb. If it should take a direct hit…

I tried to stop thinking something bad was about to happen, but that was easier said than done. Mary was worried about going into labour during a raid, and besides, the hospital was as big a target as any ship.

"Christ was born in a stable," Mum said. "Don't you worry, Mary, many a child has been born in a shelter. And ours is better built than most, thanks to Liam and Tom. I have everything we'll need if it happens."

Our street and the whole town itself seemed to be wound up, coiled tight hardly daring to breathe, waiting for what was to come. There was no one about in the open. Even the breeze had disappeared and an eerie silence descended on the empty streets. We were talking in whispers when the shattering sound of an air raid siren made the three of us jump. Mary was slow to get up, and as I helped her to her feet, I saw a look of fear in her eyes.

"I think it made the baby jump too," she said. "God, I hate all this."

Mary waddled through the door and along the narrow hall, out through the back kitchen into the garden, and down into the shelter. We heard the familiar sound of the heavy thump of bombs falling in the distance. Then the guns in the park down the road opened up with a mighty roar of thunder. There was no sign of Mum.

I went back out to the front door to find her still sitting on the steps watching searchlights chase the shadows across the black sky. As we watched, a full moon rose over the rooftops opposite, bathing the scene in a silvery glow that turned the night back into twilight.

Planes buzzed like flies above the docks and circled over the city centre. Incendiaries were spitting fire like sparks from a great volcano giving sacrifice to appease the angry gods. The searchlights were weaving and criss-crossing in their quest to expose the enemy. Guns blasted off with massive shells into the night without obvious success. High-explosive bombs started to fall. The ground and the air were alive with vibrations, flashes and explosions. The madness went on and on.

I grabbed Mum's arm and tried to move her, but she resisted. I screamed at her to move. She looked at me as if I were a stranger. I managed to cajole, half-carry and half-push her in through the house and out into the shelter, where Mary asked, "What the Hell is going on?"

I sat Mum down without a word. Then I had to go back through the house to the front door to lock up. The whole sky down towards the city was alight. It was a terrible sight.

The all-clear sounded around first light. We left Mary sleeping and came out to find our house and street untouched. Fires were glowing through smoke rising from the direction of the city. The stink of burning filled the air.

The hint of a sunrise was visible through the black smoke.

It was time for breakfast. There was work to be done.

CHAPTER EIGHTEEN

Saturday 3rd May 1941

In the beginning was the darkness.

That's what I was thinking. I was sitting listening to Mum reading from her bible as I ate my breakfast.

I liked the sound of that passage from Genesis. *And darkness covered the face of the deep.* There was an order to the world before men came and messed it all up. Before the flood. Then a second chance. A new beginning. A chilling thought struck me. *Perhaps what is happening is like another flood, sent to destroy the world.* Our world, being destroyed before our very eyes.

Well, I was going to do something about that. Time to enter the real world.

Having been cleared of a UXB, the line was declared safe and we were underway by ten o'clock. The first train had to proceed at a snail's pace with every yard of the line checked by a man on foot in front of us. Dad, flanked by Matt and John on either side, were at the dock station waiting for the train. Leaving it to be loaded on to the ship, we climbed up on to the platform of the Overhead Railway, which ran parallel to the shore on an elevated track along the length of the docks, transporting thousands of Dockers to stations all along the river.

From the elevated vantage point, I could see that the city had taken a heavy pounding. Fires were still burning along the river and especially towards the city centre, where numerous trails of smoke smudged the clear morning light. It was such a relief to see the three of them, their blackened faces and tired eyes a physical manifestation of the drama of the night. Dad was smiling.

"Good to see you got here in one piece. We need to get this ship loaded today and out of here as soon as we can. Jerry will be back tonight as sure as ducks are ducks."

"You all looked tired," I said. "Can't you go home and get some rest?"

"Matt and John are going to get some shut-eye. I've already had a sleep since the all-clear, so don't worry about me. Just get the rest of this down here today."

"There's a speed limit on the line, but we'll do our best."

"That's all anyone can ask, Maggie. Now, let's get to work."

It was one of those rare days in early May when you get a blast of heat sent from the gods, a teaser of the summer to come. A foretaste of the long, hot days, like those that Billy and I had spent out on Our Shore in that summer before the war. Then, the only danger coming from the sky was the gulls trying to snatch our sandwiches, while we splashed about in the golden light of a peaceful world.

Now, the Gods of Sky were playing with us today, sending trickles of sweat down the back of my neck, as I stood in the bright sunshine with my clipboard full of checked-off lines. One more trainload and we'd be finished loading the *Malakand* ahead of schedule, which was exactly what I had planned.

I travelled down the track with the driver and waved to the signalman, who waved us on every time we passed. He smiled broadly. He was enjoying his part in our effort to hit back at Hitler. Churchill had said as much to Dad and the Dockers. We are going to win the Battle of the Atlantic, and we are going to strike back in Africa. We have already started. This was a part of it. We were all helping to win the war.

Everyone bent and strained to their tasks at the Huskisson Dock. There was an energy around the ship as the cargo holds were nearly full. According to Dad, the ship was scheduled to sail with Matt and John's convoy on Sunday for Gibraltar and the Mediterranean. I loved to hear the names of those exotic places which we weren't allowed to say out loud. Just a hushed chat between a father and daughter. The last train would be on its way mid-afternoon.

As we stood there on the raised station platform, a German Messerschmitt was suddenly spotted flying low straight up the river, below the height of the barrage balloons. Three more flew by in tight formation, then spread out and weaved their way up the river, as the guns on the embankment opened fire. In broad daylight! Even Dad was taken by surprise.

They disappeared out of sight in towards the city where more guns were heard firing.

"The cheeky buggers!"

Dad's mouth had fallen open and his eyes were staring back up the river.

"Quick! Get down!" he shouted. "They're coming back."

The first fighter plane was veering in and out along the margin of the docks. It suddenly opened fire, and the rattle of its machine gun could be heard getting closer by the second. We lay flat against the wall of the station. The planes sprayed the warehouses and quays, and some of the boats, before two spitfires appeared and started to give chase. The whole episode had taken less than a minute. Seeing those planes at close quarters for the first time was a revelation. Those monsters of the air streaked above our heads before disappearing over Wallasey and out over the Irish Sea.

Dad was back up giving the order to resume operations. All along the docks you could see the cranes move as one. The train was empty. It was time to leave. A massive knot was tying itself up in my stomach. I felt empty and sick at the same time. Dad put his strong arms around me, and then held me at arm's length and looked into my eyes.

"Get Mum and Mary into the shelter as soon as you get home," he said. "I don't like the look of this. Did you see what they were doing? Taking pictures, that's what. They'll be back later as sure as ducks are ducks."

"What about you? Will you be home for dinner?"

"We need all hands on deck here tonight, lass. The boys are coming back down. They'll bring me some food. Tell your mother. I know she'll understand."

Dad laughed at that and it seemed to go very deep. The laugh started somewhere in the belly, and rumbled like a lump of molten lava bubbling in those chambers in the sides of volcanoes I used to copy from my geography book in school. Then another rumble, and it exploded out of him like it was the best joke in the world, ever.

The evening sun glowed red in the western sky, bathing the city in pale orange light. Swallows appeared flying low between the buildings, feeding on the swarms of midges that hung in the stifling air. I hadn't seen swallows since Ireland, where they darted between the trees and buildings of Uncle Peter's farm, and had taken up residence on every available nook and cranny in his overgrown barn. Hot air rose from the pavement. It was a sweltering evening with a high, clear blue sky that was visible if you looked straight up between two buildings, standing in the shadows out of the sun.

The order had come through earlier, just as the last train was already on its way. Signal on red. Tommy, the signalman, filled us in. The operation would be delayed till morning. Harbour Master's orders. There was nothing for it but to comply. The train was parked in a siding as far from anyone or anything as possible. The siding was next to the signal box. We would finish the job first thing in the morning, still ahead of schedule. A trickle of sweat ran down the back of my neck as I raised my head and scanned the sky for enemy activity. There was nothing for it but to leave two fire-watchers on the train and head off to the church hall.

I sat with some new arrivals from the bombing last night. Their story was one so often heard. Incendiaries followed by high explosives. They were lucky. A bomb had demolished their house, but they were in the communal shelter built at the end of the street, where part of the roof collapsed, killing a family of five. They had no place left to go and came to the church in desperation, the clothes they were standing in their only possessions. Father Breen was on the move as usual, tending to the frightened and the sick, reassuring everyone with his friendly smile and welcoming words. He was also helping the volunteers and making sure there was enough food and water and tea to go around. He even found time to join in the singing. If there had been water near, I imagined he could very likely have walked across it, if he had needed to. He gave me a warm greeting and was gone, whisked away to another meeting – with Mr Watts and the fire-watchers, I presumed.

Mum was busy serving food. I carried some plates to the elderly who were delighted to have a chance of a chat, as they munched their way through a watery stew of vegetables with a hint of meat.

Afterwards I accompanied them into the church. Father Breen was standing at the back near the door and had a look of concern on his face as he nodded to Mr Watts who was pointing to something up in the bell tower. A steady stream of people, old and young, grandparents and mothers with babies, wound their way down the stairs, lit by a single electric bulb, into the crypt below. It was a depressing sight to see so many forced underground, like an ancient people fleeing the demon that they could not see, but feared would come with the night. Billy's mother Bess was among them.

"I don't feel safe in me own bed and no one to keep me company," she said. "I'm going to sleep over 'ere tonight."

I felt an anger rising in me like the filling of a shell. I wished I had a job tonight firing those big guns hunkered down in the park at the end of our street. I couldn't pray. I could not ask forgiveness. What sort of God would allow this to happen to us here in our own town? I left the church without blessing myself.

I hurried home as fast as I could. When I stopped to look again, all the swallows had vanished, leaving the sky empty, waiting for the arrival of the full moon.

Mary had introduced me to Shakespeare some months earlier. We would read a play, then she would talk about it for hours. Sometimes it was like a secret code that we would quote to each other. I enjoyed playing the character of Lady Macbeth. I thought of her as a female version of Hitler, who would stop at nothing, not even the killing of children, to get what she wanted. She had blood on her hands. Literally.

"Out, damned spot! Out, I say!"

I quoted that line when I was washing up after dinner. Mary was drying and trying not to drop the dinner plates, she was laughing so much. Then she came back at me.

"She's not really a female Hitler," she argued. "He will keep killing men, women and children without remorse. Lady Macbeth was driven mad by guilt. Hitler is just mad. Pure evil."

Mum didn't tolerate any mention of witches and would quickly put a stop to it all.

"Double, double, toil and trouble;

Fire burn and cauldron bubble."

That was Mary and me dancing about the kitchen table, pretending to mix the spell, chanting, me skipping, and Mary waddling around as best she could.

"Eye of newt and…"

"No more talk of the power of the devil in this house. Enough! You know I hate that terrible play. It's evil from start to finish."

Mum shot us a look and we both knew that it was curtains.

This evening of all evenings, though, I couldn't get those witches out of my mind.

'Where shall we three meet again in thunder, lightning, or in rain? When the hurlyburly's done, when the battle's lost and won.'

I wondered if the battle would ever be won. I thought of Billy and Tom, and the daily and nightly danger that they faced on their homeward journey. The sight of those German planes flying in broad daylight up the Mersey had been a real shock. *When will we three meet again?* It was impossible to clear my mind. *Something evil this way comes.*

Mary was quiet at dinner that evening. I knew she was thinking of Johnny out at sea, in the same danger as Billy and Tom. Afterwards, the three of us sat out on the front steps with the evening heat rising from the concrete beneath us. I lit a cigarette and blew smoke rings into the air. Mary was uncomfortable in the heat, and left us to walk up and down the road before returning to sit by our side. Mum was as quiet as a church mouse. I wondered what she was thinking. We sat there for a long time into the dusk, with Mary restless. Then the air raid siren shook the still air.

We hurried as fast as Mary could through the house and out into the shelter. Mum had a supper packed out there against the heat. Mary was complaining of swollen ankles, so I put her legs up on the bed with a pillow under them. It was then we realised that Mum was missing again. I scrambled out of the shelter and ran through the house, with the urgent scream of the siren beating in my breast.

Mum was sitting on the steps, watching the sky fill with planes. The moon was up and they were visible in the silver light like moths flitting around a light bulb. Then the guns opened fire from the park at the bottom of our road. The air was filled with the boom and the vibration of the blasts, as they fired off their shells in quick succession.

"Mum! Quick! Come inside. They're right overhead! The sky is full of them. Have you gone crazy?"

I had to drag her up and push her through the house and into the shelter. Then I rushed back through the house again. When I looked down towards the docks, I saw a sight that stunned me. The sky was charged with bombs falling, searchlights frantically searching, and ack ack bombs exploding. I knew they were incendiaries that were falling, and that Dad, Matt and John were directly under that onslaught. My thoughts froze with a vision of the ship sitting in the dock with the firestorm raining down upon it, a vaporous downpour sent from hell. I locked the front door and raced back through the house, trying to fight the rising panic that was twisting my gut, forcing my heart into my mouth. Mary was very uncomfortable and was unable to lie still. She whispered to me.

"Maggie, what kind of parent would bring a child into this world? What future would there be for such a little life?"

"Hush, Mary. Everything will work out fine, you just wait and see."

The vibrations of falling bombs grew stronger and the noise level was increasing. Suddenly, there was an almighty explosion and we all jumped. Mary rolled under the bed, on to the mattress we had placed there for just such a time as this.

"Jesus, Mary and Joseph, have mercy on our souls."

Mum was praying for all three of us and the baby in one frightened breath. More shattering explosions followed and something heavy pounded on to the roof of the shelter. The ground shook and the air was filled with dust. Mum panicked, pulled out the gas masks and told us to put them on. Mary squeezed my hand hard and I held her gaze. Moments later, she pulled the mask off her face and gasped. She squeezed my hand again and it struck me that I was an idiot. It wasn't just the shelling outside that made her face contort in fear. She was in labour.

Mum was better for having something to do. The sound of the explosions seemed to fade a little into the distance as she busied herself getting sheets and blankets that we had stored earlier in the week, and put on the kettle to boil some water. It felt that the world was spinning out of control. An hour or two passed. Mum was looking worried, and signalled to me that she wanted a quiet word. It was for me to get Nurse Reynolds, the midwife.

"It's breech," she whispered. "Tell her it's urgent. She's over at the church crypt. Don't panic. Sometimes the baby will move around itself, but if she can come it would be better."

I had to push hard against the door as there was something heavy blocking the entrance. I managed to open it sufficiently and cleared the steps of rubble that had fallen into the garden. In the light of my blackout torch, it was clear that we'd had a near miss.

It was a terrible sight that met me on our front steps. The whole of Bootle, right down to the docks and on into the city was on fire. Up at the top of our road, near the railway, the opposite side of our street was also aflame. I ran as fast as I could in the flickering light from the burning houses. There was a fire crew connecting their hoses at the junction of the park. They looked at me in amazement. I shouted 'Midwife!' to Mr Watts, who had grabbed my arm. He nodded and released me, and left to deal with the fires. I scrambled on through the smoke.

Father Breen was standing with a group of fire-watchers on the steps of the church. He ran out to meet me and led me into the church porch. Someone went to fetch Nurse Reynolds, who was down in the crypt tending to babies. Father Breen looked different in his tin hat and uniform, not like a priest at all, but a man like Dad, doing his best in a terrible time.

"Be careful, Maggie," he said. "This raid is bad. They've been dropping thousands of incendiaries all across the city. We had to put out fires in the roof on and off, but so far we're winning the battle. It's gone quiet now, but you need to hurry home. How is Mary holding up?"

"The baby is breech, Mum says. Nurse Reynolds will know what to do. Please God everything will be okay, Father. Say a prayer for us."

"I've been non-stop praying and fighting fires this past night, Maggie. Tell your mother we're all praying for a safe birth. Here's Nurse Reynolds. Be off now and may God go with you."

"God bless you too Father. God must be very proud of you."

I was glad afterwards that I said that.

Nurse Reynolds wrapped her shawl about herself like a shield, took one glance at the sky and plunged on into the moonlit night. I grabbed her bag and she nodded in thanks, and we shuffled on through the smoke-filled streets as fast as we could. We passed fire-fighters and fire-watchers as they scrambled to get the raging fires under control. There was a huge glow in the sky from down at the docks and from the direction of the city. We hurried on through the wretched air and reached our house without further incident.

Mum was so relieved to see Nurse Reynolds it unnerved me. Something must have gone badly wrong with the labour. Nurse Reynolds gave a knowing nod, threw off her shawl and coat and examined Mary.

"Umm. That's all right, dear. You just try to relax and we'll have everything right in jig time."

She fussed over Mary. I felt that I was in the way, so I slipped into the house and out on to our front steps again. The drone of heavy bombers sounded in the distance, blown in on the sea breeze. The ack ack fired from the park at the end of the street, as searchlights swept the arc of sky above. The drone grew to a growl, and then I saw them in the clear light of the moon. I caught my breath and my heart froze.

The sky was full of planes, as far into the distance as I could see. There were hundreds of German bombers – heading straight for us! I expected them to turn and follow the river into the city, but instead they flew straight on. I saw the first bombs falling in the silver light, black and terrible, bringing terror to those below. I was rooted to the spot for what felt like an age, but was probably just a few seconds. I could see what Hitler planned to do. He was going to blast our town out of existence, just like he did all those years ago in Guernica.

I ran through the house as the first explosions shook the ground, and through the garden, with the bombers directly overhead. I dived through the door of the shelter and locked it shut behind me. Bombs were exploding all around us. The ground shook. The noise was overwhelming.

Mum stared at me, her eyes wide open. I blessed myself.

"Jesus, Mary and Joseph, keep us safe this night."

I repeated it over and over like a mantra, and Mum joined in. Nurse Reynolds had done some manipulation, and maybe the vibration from the bombs helped, but the baby was now fine. Mary was sweating as her contractions came hard and fast. The roaring of bombs drowned out any cries that came from her lips. It seemed that the whole world had gone mad. This was surely the end. We would all be blown to smithereens.

"Jesus, Mary and Joseph, keep us safe this night."

"They say you don't hear the one with your name on it," Nurse Reynolds commented. "After I was told that, I never was afraid of the noise no more."

Mum handed her a cup of tea she had been brewing as bits of rock and stone hit the door of the shelter and the ground vibrated like the world was ending. And it was.

The noise of explosions merged into a rush of air that filled the shelter. Thankfully, Tom and Liam had done such a good job when they built it. I closed my eyes and concentrated on the picture of Billy and Tom, arm-in-arm, with their ship sailing up the channel and on towards the city, a great crowd cheering. My reverie was broken by a cry from Mary and there was a pause, then a little cry like a sound that does not belong to this world.

Nurse Reynolds and Mum were washing and cleaning, and saying, "There, there," and then Mum cried, "Oh my God, it's a boy!"

I caught a glimpse of Mary, looking very pale, with strands of her hair stuck to her forehead. She was smiling, and tears were flowing at the same time. Then I caught sight of a long red-and-white body like that of a skinned rabbit, and a mop of black hair, and it crying. Nurse Reynolds wrapped him in a white baby blanket and placed him on his side beside Mary. His thumb found his mouth and he started sucking. It was the most magnificent thing. Mary had a boy!

The bombs were still falling, but not as near as before. Nurse Reynolds tended to Mary and then Mum got some water and baptised the baby.

"I baptise you in the name of the Father..."

"His name is William," Mary interjected.

"I baptise you, William, in the name of the Father and of the Son and of the Holy Ghost."

She made the sign of the cross over the baby's forehead and poured some water over his head, at which point he started to cry. Mum hushed him on her shoulder and hummed him a lullaby. He seemed to connect with the sound and went quiet. His thumb found his mouth again.

"He's maybe looking for the comfort of the breast."

Nurse Reynolds was a very knowledgeable midwife, a wise woman who had brought half the population of our town into this world.

Just then the all-clear sounded. I left Mary to her maternal duties and pushed my way out into the back garden, which was strewn with rubble. The first light of dawn was struggling through the dense air. I could make out that our house had been spared, but there was a gap like a pulled tooth in the terrace a few doors down. It was possibly Mrs Waldron's house, but I knew she was away with her daughter Kate, so that was something. The back lane was chock full of rubble. I grabbed my bicycle and wheeled it out through the house.

From my vantage point on the steps outside the front door, it looked like the whole world was on fire. Thick black smoke filled the air. It snatched at my throat. It was difficult to breathe without feeling I was going to choke. I hurried on through our town with a damp headscarf wrapped around my face. I passed through the clusters of rescue workers and firemen attending to the blazing buildings, and the bombed-out buildings. I dodged to the side of the bomb craters, and was diverted around the UXB's. Down at the docks, fires were burning out of control. A strange tightness gripped my chest. I caught sight of the flames leaping from burning warehouses all along the margin of the river.

The ship will never survive this, and Dad and Matt and John are too close.

I was turned back by another UXB. I cycled hard up towards the siding where we had left the train overnight. The city was unrecognisable. I lost my way amid the rubble and stench of utter devastation. Two men carried a piano out from the ruins of a house and left it in the road. When I asked them where the railway siding was, they pointed on up the street and went back inside.

At the end of the road, the houses were reduced to piles of rubble. I suddenly saw the train, or what was left of it – four carriages out of ten. Tommy, the signalman, came towards me through the smoke.

"Keep back, Maggie. It's not safe," he said. "We managed to save some of the carriages by uncoupling them, but the fires caught hold and the last carriage exploded, so the best we could do was save these. Then the others started to explode. It was touch-and-go for a while, but we unhitched them and made it down here before the other five carriages went up with a massive bang. I haven't been able to find the two men who were on fire-watch, but I think they made it out."

"Are you telling me that our train did all this damage to the street?"

"The fires were burning everywhere and we did our best to put them out," he said. "There were too many incendiaries. They kept falling faster than we could get to them. The fire started at the back of the train and we managed to uncouple the front section. It was too dangerous to save the others. We had to move the front of the train down here. Then the big explosion blew me off my feet. The fires were everywhere."

I could see it all. The train on fire. Tommy and the men racing to put it out. Realising they were fighting a losing battle. Making the decision to save as much of the munitions as possible. The three of them running down between the carriages of the train with the threat of an explosion any second. The turning of winches and pulling of pins. Moving the unhitched carriages forward as far as they could. Then the back carriage exploding. The whole world lighting up with a flash, a roar and a blast wave knocking them over, taking the roof off the terrace of houses. Fires burned everywhere.

"Are you all right?" I asked him. "I'll move the shells as soon as I'm able. I need to get to the Huskisson Dock. You're very brave."

"I don't feel brave, Maggie, just exhausted."

"I'll get someone down here to watch the train and relieve you as soon as I can."

I freewheeled back down towards the city centre. The air was filled with a pungent smell from thick black smoke. The heart of the city was on fire. Fire crews were on ladders, pouring water through the broken windows and on to the empty roof space of Lewis's department store, where the roof menagerie used to be. I remembered being up there with Mum when I was much younger, petting guinea pigs and hamsters, and wanting to take them home. Now there was a black hole with smoke pouring from it. The animals were blown to kingdom come.

With Double Summer Time coming in overnight, it was already after eight o'clock. There was no let-up in the fires. The firemen, who must have been exhausted, took it in turns to stop and grab a cup of tea and a sandwich, then returned to tackle the flames. The Overhead Railway had taken a direct hit in more than one place, and was shut down. The city centre was burning out of control. The whole world was in chaos. Hitler was doing a pretty good job trying to break us.

The streets around the docks were cordoned off because of the fires burning out of control in the warehouses along the quays. When I mentioned the ship's name I was brought to the Chief Fire Officer immediately.

"Well, Maggie, such a young person to be in charge of a dangerous cargo," he said. "The dock is on fire at the moment. You can't go out there. It's far too risky."

"Chief, my father and two brothers are in that dock," I said. "What's going to become of the ship? Is it in danger?"

"Maggie, the ship has been in danger all night. The barrage balloon overhead caught fire at the height of the raid, and fell burning on to the ship. The brave lads on fire-watch managed to get it out in time to stop it spreading to the ship's hold.

"As of now, the warehouses in Huskisson Dock are ablaze and out of control. The firemen requested to tow the ship out into the river, but the Harbour Master refused permission, for fear it could blow out there and block the channel. That could put the whole port out of action. They're trying to sink her in the dock. A group of volunteers are attempting to cut a hole in the hull and scuttle her on the spot, while the fire-fighters battle the blaze. That's the only way we will save the cargo and prevent a massive explosion."

I closed my eyes and could picture the whole scene. The ship filled with high explosive shells that I was responsible for putting there. Dad and the boys trying to cut open a hole in the steel hull, using cutting equipment that could set off an explosion at any time. The ship ablaze at the bow in the bright yellow light. Blinding smoke. A river of fire flowing like molten lava from the warehouse, out across the quay, pouring over the side and on to the ship.

Firemen, four on each hose, pouring water into the very heart of the fire, their burnished faces glowing in the white light. It was hopeless.

"We've evacuated everyone within half a mile of the dock. It should be enough."

I looked at the taut face of the fire chief. For a fleeting moment, I thought I saw a flicker of fear in his eyes, then it was gone.

"If the ship blows, it could be the largest explosion this city has ever seen," he said.

I stared straight ahead, remembering the loading of the ship with bombs and shells bound for Egypt.

"Over one thousand tonnes of high explosives," I whispered.

"A thousand tonnes?"

"Yes, just under one thousand and fifty tonnes, all high explosives. Can't you order the men out?"

It was a couple of minutes before nine o'clock. Sunday morning. The blast wave sent the church bells swinging in their high towers above a city at war, ringing out a warning that was already too late. A ball of fire jumped hundreds of feet into the air, its red, angry flame mixing with thick black smoke, like a thin curtain that could not contain the fierce light behind. Then a noise hit like a roaring wind, as debris flew everywhere. The chief grabbed me and we took shelter behind a nearby fire engine, as the shrapnel splattered all around us. Chunks of metal, white hot, fell upon the stricken city.

I grabbed on to something and closed my eyes.

I could see the fire shoot out like a flamethrower and jump into the rigging of the ship. Dad, Matt and John looking up and seeing their own death, realising that it was a lost cause. Firemen screaming over the roar to get out quick. Then a mad scramble up the deck and along the quay, with their boots melting in the heat. The fire engine turning out the gate and on to Regent Road. Then it blew.

"Maggie! Maggie!"

The chief was holding me because my legs didn't want to work. Someone grabbed me and carried me to a First Aid station that was set up nearby. The face of the chief appeared again.

"Maggie, I have to leave you here, but I'll be back to check up on you."

He left to organise the exhausted crews to fight the biggest fire that Liverpool had ever seen.

CHAPTER NINETEEN

Sunday 4th May 1941

I have always believed that if someone close to you dies, some pain in the heart, or a blank moment in the brain would disturb the rhythm of the day, like the sudden flight of birds taken fright in the rushes. Birds that you knew were near, but could not see. Then afterwards, looking back, you would pinpoint that moment. It would become a permanent mark in your lived memory of time and place. The only flaw in this theory was that it had never been tested.

At the First Aid station I was handed a cup of sweet tea and a sandwich. It tasted like sawdust, but it probably did me some good, as I hadn't eaten since Saturday night. The nurse was treating someone who had been dug from the rubble of a basement, and was waiting for an ambulance to move her to hospital. I felt embarrassed to be taking up her time and was about to leave when she stopped me and urged me to sit.

I could see beyond her to the burning centre of the city on one side, and the whole dock alight on the other. My legs still felt like jelly.

A new patient was carried in with a bloodied bandage crudely wound around his head. His helmet was badly dinted, his uniform scorched and covered in dust. The two ambulance men were gone, leaving him sitting opposite me, looking at me through his one visible eye.

"Are you badly hurt?" I asked. "What happened to you?"

"Well, Miss, I think, what with that huge blast shaking up the whole place, I think that a wall decided it had had enough of this lot, and fell down on top of me. I was busy pouring water on the fire up at the hospital at the time, but luckily, I heard it coming at the last minute, and nearly managed to jump clear. Once they clean up the gash in my forehead I'll be back out in a jiffy. The rest is bumps and bruises."

"Is the hospital on fire too? Which hospital?"

"Mill Street. 'Twas badly bombed, Miss. A lot of patients and staff have been killed and injured. The mother and babies ward is gone. Even the operating room in the basement has been destroyed. We're still fighting the fires and digging through rubble, but the whole hospital is in ruins. So many mothers and babies... all dead. We don't know how many yet, but it could be a hundred or more."

The air between us suddenly became very heavy. I was thinking of Mary, up at home with her new baby boy William, and all those mothers and their babies killed in a place that should have been one of safety. Only for Nurse Reynolds, we might have had to get an ambulance for Mary, and she and her baby would have been killed.

"A lot of shelters has been hit as well, Miss. There's thousands dead and thousands more injured, mark my words."

"You sir, talk too much. Lie down here and I'll take a look at you."

The nurse removed his bandage. The whole side of his face was smashed, especially around his eye. I stood up and my legs were shaking, but I couldn't stay a moment longer. I thanked the nurse and went out to the corner of the road, where my bicycle was parked. Holding on to the handlebars for support, I could see on towards the docks. The fire was bigger than anything I had ever imagined possible.

I stood looking into the gates of hell. Angry red and yellow flames burst out in a mad fireball that carried on up and up into the air, fifty times higher than the Overhead Railway, which was eaten by the flames and the smoke. The firemen looked like tiny figures from a toy game, their hoses like strands of wool, crossing and criss-crossing along Regent Road. There was no sign of Huskisson Dock. It was swallowed whole somewhere inside that monster that snarled and snapped at the miniature creatures who dared approach it. Thick black smoke obliterated the sky. The stench of burning oil and rubber was everywhere, growing stronger by the minute. The sea air was full of dust and ash. It went swirling about the streets, covering the ground in a thick coat of smouldering grey that smothered my throat.

I felt an overwhelming urge to get home. Dad and the boys would be up there by now, if they weren't helping to fight the fire. I tried to telephone the factory, but all the lines were down. Someone said that the Central Telephone Exchange had taken a direct hit. I needed to get out to the factory to give a report. That would be expected. That was what I had to do. *Keep calm and carry on.*

Cycling away from the docks as fast as my shaky legs would go, I could see the extent of the devastation on almost every street along the journey. This time we really had been blitzed. We had come through a terrible night of fires and more fires, explosions and more explosions. The very people putting out the fires were themselves bombed and blown to kingdom come. Docks, warehouses, offices, banks, churches, schools, ships, hospitals, the canal and the railway had all been targeted. Dad was right. "As sure as ducks are ducks" was his way of saying it. Hitler was trying to destroy Liverpool. And our town. And everyone in it.

Up off Breck Road I met an ARP officer who had stationed himself beside the train in the railway siding. Standing in the signalbox, with a clear view of the city, he had it on best authority what had been bombed.

"Look, Lewis's and Blackler's department stores, the Head Post Office, the India buildings, Littlewoods building in Hanover Street, the whole area around Wolstenholme Square, and Leyton Paper Mills... They're all up in flames."

He was pointing to each huge fire that we could see through the gap where a factory had once stood. I added in my tuppence halfpenny worth:

"And I saw Lord Street. It was an inferno, going on and on as far as the smoke would let me see. And the Custom House and the Museum and Library where my sister works. And the docks. All along the river, as far as I could see, is on fire."

"They dropped a load of parachute mines last night when the incendiaries had done their work. They dropped tens of thousands of those infernal devils."

"I heard that they bombed Mill Street Hospital."

"And a shelter at Addison Street School."

"Then the ship went up."

I stopped and remembered to breathe.

"I have to go. I'll send someone to take control of the train as soon as I can."

I have always found it the same. Things are far worse as soon as you talk about them. It is as if in the telling they become real. Like telling a story from the inside out. I set off again to catch the tram for the factory. I had to make my report.

It was late afternoon before I got home. The loss of the shipment both on the *Malakand* and at the railway siding was a setback, but the wheels were already turning to organise a replacement ship. We had plenty of stock in underground storage. We would start moving it as soon as it was deemed safe, but for the moment the city was in lockdown and another clear, moonlit night was forecast.

I cycled home past streams of people leaving Bootle, carrying their belongings on their backs or in their arms. There were more people on buses and trams. War weary, some homeless, all frightened, they were heading out for the night to the safety of the countryside. Some would return in the morning to carry on the business of the city. Thousands on the move.

Mary was sitting in the back kitchen with William nestled in her arms when I got home. The colour had returned to her face, but dirty, dried tear marks ran down her cheeks. Mum had gone around to thank Nurse Reynolds at the church hall and hadn't come back.

"Oh, Maggie, I have a very bad feeling!" she cried. "After that explosion shook the house and the fire at the dock… I've never seen anything like it. Where are Dad and Matt and John? Have you seen them? What am I to do to keep little Billy safe? Is there anywhere safe, Maggie?"

I put my arm around her, but I could see that it was shaking. Her words put flesh on the bare skeleton that was my thoughts. Should she leave now while there was still time? But where would she go with a one-day-old baby? The shelter was as safe a place as anywhere.

"The city has been badly hit," I told her. "Everyone who can is fighting fires and digging people out of rubble. We probably won't see Dad for a day or two. John and Matt are shipping out today or tomorrow. They'll have been called aboard because of the bombing. I wonder what's keeping Mum."

"I hope and pray that you're right, Maggie. Here, hold Billy for a minute while I go to the toilet."

Mary placed the baby in my lap.

"Billy? Are you calling him Billy?"

I smiled and Mary smiled back.

"Don't be nervous of him. Put your hands here and here."

She disappeared, leaving me looking into the squashed-up face of the sleeping infant. He looked grumpy. He raised his clenched fists to his face, opened his eyes and blinked. He looked at me in surprise, yawned, blinked again and started to whimper. I hushed him and bounced him on my knee. He smiled a quick smile that turned to a yelp. He gave me another look as if to say, 'You'd better take good care of me.' Then he started a screechy kind of cry to let me know he wasn't too impressed.

I lifted him and gave his back a gentle rub. He promptly threw up on my shoulder and gurgled a laugh. I sat him on my lap. He smiled again, wriggled, and I felt the strength in him. It was almost miraculous to see the freshness of this new life shining at me through those bright eyes. Today of all days.

I was relieved to hand Billy back. He slotted into the crook of Mary's arm and settled down to sleep. I went to see what was keeping Mum.

It didn't take long to discover what it was. The church tower, which yesterday had stood pointing to the heavens, was now a crumbling ruin, with curls of black smoke seeping out of the rubble. The roof had fallen on the main part of the church, with only a few rafters left open to the sky. The hall next door looked untouched. The rescue services were digging in the area that must have been the entrance to the crypt. It was completely blocked with bricks and timbers, slates and lumps of concrete and metal. There was a sweet, sticky smell of burning brick and timber in the air. Mr Watts was directing operations. When he saw me, he came over and asked how Mary was.

"She's fine, thanks, Mr Watts. A healthy baby boy. What's happened to all the people in the crypt? Are they all dead?"

I could see he was calculating if I had anyone down there belonging to me.

"We managed to get most people out through the escape hatches we had installed in the very event of something like this happening," he said. "The first bomb came through the roof and into the stairwell of the crypt. It exploded in the outer room. Anyone in that space had no chance.

"Then a second bomb hit the bell tower and that collapsed into the crater left by the first bomb. We'll keep digging as long as there's any hope. These miners arrived by train from Wales this afternoon to help in the rescue. They've been dispersed across the city. There's a crew here and one up at the prison. They're making some headway. We'll be able to pull the bell out soon.

"Your mother is next door in the hall if you're looking for her. There's nothing you can do here."

"You should get some rest, Mr Watts," I said. "I can take over here for a while if you like."

Mr Watts laughed.

"Maggie, I'm fine, thanks. I heard that ship of yours go up this morning. According to these lads, the anchor was fired over a mile-and-a-half through the air and landed, still smouldering, on the road in front of the hospital on Oriel Road. That's what they're saying anyway."

He nodded in the direction of the miners who were busy bending to their gruesome task.

Could it be possible that parts of the ship had been blown on to the streets of our town? It was nearly two miles from the dock to the hospital. If the ship's anchor had been blown that distance… A shiver ran down my spine and I felt my legs go like jelly again. I needed to see Mum.

I found her organising the evacuation of the survivors to some church hall up the coast, near Southport. They sat in an orderly line that snaked around the hall, their few belongings gathered about them. Women with young children and babies, the elderly and the infirm. Buses arrived and the hall slowly emptied. I helped carry what meagre things people had salvaged from the ruins of their lives. When it came down to it, human life was all about survival. Blackened, anxious faces peered at the sky, through the dusty windows of the buses, as they set off in the late afternoon sunshine.

Inside the hall, the WVS volunteers were locking down the centre and removing the food supplies and drinks that had been stored there. Mum was sitting with a group of women who were checking lists of names. When she finished, we walked outside together and sat on the steps in the warm sunshine. We could hear digging in the church and the lilt of Welsh voices carried on the soft breeze. She turned to me and took my hand.

"Maggie, there's no easy way to say this," she said. "Father Breen, Bess and over thirty others were in the outer room below the steps, or standing on the steps, when the bomb exploded. They're all gone. I'm sorry, Maggie. The miners will keep digging, because that's what has to be done, but I don't believe there's a chance of finding any of them alive."

The heat of the day closed in around me, turning the air dark and oppressive. There are times in your life when you are unable to speak.

"Father Breen and Bess…do you mean Billy's Bess? Is Billy's mum dead? No, that can't be true. There must be a mistake. I'll go up to the house and bring her down here to show you."

Mum caught me by the shoulders and held me tight. I looked into her eyes and I knew that it was true. They would have checked the list and therefore knew who was in the outer room of the crypt when the bombs struck. I closed my eyes and saw the bell falling and the tower crumbling into the space now covering the steps. That was where they were standing, keeping an eye on the roof for incendiaries, while the WVS volunteers made cups of tea for everyone. I could see Father Breen talking to Mrs Newsome about Billy, how he would be home soon, and what a comfort it must be to have two such great sons. The noise of the sing-song drifting out from the inner room. *We're going to hang out the washing on the Siegfried Line…*

Then the crash and flash as the high explosive bomb did its work. Everyone in that part of the crypt was blown apart, so that Father Breen, Mrs Newsome and the others all became a thousand pieces of themselves, meeting thousands of pieces of each other. A moment later the falling blocks and bricks and timbers, and the giant bell, all came tumbling down on to the inferno. The force of the explosion collapsed the link corridor. That saved all the people in the main section of the crypt, where the roof didn't collapse. The dust-filled air stopped the screaming, and everything settled into silence, with gas masks hastily pulled on in the pitch dark.

I broke free from Mum and ran out into the street. I ran and ran, up towards the railway, away from the docks, and the city, and the terrible destruction and broken lives that lay in pieces in our town.

Please God, do not do this. Don't take Billy's mum who has been through so much, and always with a helping hand and a good word. Please God, let me find her safe at home, where she'll look in surprise at my anxious face, and smile, and ask me in for a cuppa.

I found myself in Billy's street and outside Billy's door. I stopped on the road and looked at the house. It was intact. Not even a tile missing from the roof, as far as I could see. I knocked on the door and waited, but no one came. I hammered with my fist. Still, no one came.

"Mrs. Newsome! Mrs. Newsome! Bess! Bess!"

No one came.

I sat with my back to the door for an age. I could think of nothing. I felt nothing. A crater had opened in the centre of my life and the good things had fallen in, lost forever.

The shrill notes of a siren startled me. I lifted my head out of my hands where I had been resting with my eyes closed. It was dusk, and the call of the alarm through the empty streets echoed somewhere deep inside me, stirring me into action. Home. I must get home.

CHAPTER TWENTY

Monday 5th May 1941

The all-clear sounded at dawn. Following a hasty breakfast, I cycled and walked down to the docks, through the bombed-out town that wasn't recognisable as our town any more. The sea breeze fanned the flames, sending black smoke billowing into the clear air, and carried it towards the city centre.

Fires along the docks were still burning out of control. At the centre of it all was the place where the Huskisson Dock had once been. The fire from the explosion was still burning fiercely. The roads around the docks were restricted *'for emergency personnel only,'* but I was let through to see the chief fire officer. He looked a lot worse for wear, but still managed a smile when he saw me.

There was no sign of Dad or the boys, but I knew that their ships had sailed, or were sailing this morning, so they should already be on board. The chief had no comfort for me.

"There are hundreds missing all across the city," he said. "The captain gave the order to abandon ship hours before the explosion. The firemen who were last at the ship have not been accounted for yet. There were no reports of any casualties except a couple of newlyweds whose car was flattened by a section of the ship that was blown on to the road over half a mile away. Poor sods! ...Jerry came back to finish the job last night, but our guns gave 'em hell."

I could only think of Dad and the boys. I was tempted to check with Derby House to see if Matt and John had reached their ships safely, but it was all top secret in there. Even the location deep underground was secret. If I went there I would be arrested. I knew about it from a friend of Molly's who worked in the map room. They were busy in there re-directing convoys, organising escorts and trying to win the "Battle of the Atlantic," as Churchill called it. They wouldn't know who was on board anyway.

The city stood battered and bruised in the stinking air. The blackened frames of landmark buildings gawked stark naked, like the skeletal remains of a great herd of beasts picked clean to the bone. A whole section of streets and blocks of offices, shops, cinemas and every kind of building had been wiped off the face of the earth. What was probably a square mile of the city centre was completely flattened. It was as bad as anything I had seen on *Pathé News*, only a lot worse, because it was here in our city.

Then came the biggest surprise of all. The smoke cleared for a minute and the Liver Building remained standing, with only its windows broken, in the midst of the desolation. The male bird was undamaged, watching over his part-ruined city. For some reason, the sight of the bird lifted my spirits and I could hear the voice of Tom in my ear. *We will never be beaten.*

I cycled out on to the Pier Head to see if the female bird was intact too. She was watching out to sea, watching over the ships and sailors, watching out for their safe return. It was a miracle.

The legend of the birds was given a different twist by Dad every time they were mentioned. His eyes twinkled as he reminded us that the male bird was watching to see if the pubs were open, and the female was looking out to sea, waiting for the sailors to return to port for a bit of brisk business. Mum would tut-tut, but there was laughter in her eyes. Sting never lashed out at any of the boys if they repeated it when Dad wasn't there.

There they were, both Liver Birds proudly standing tall, untouched by the devastation all around them. A miracle. Looking back along the margins of the river, it was destruction as far as the eye could see. Miles and miles of docks on fire on both sides of the estuary. Yet somehow the Liver Birds had survived untouched.

"They'll be back tonight as sure as ducks are ducks."

I cycled away from the river, out to catch the tram to the factory where it was business as best we could. I spent the day organising a replacement shipment and getting things ready to begin its transportation by road.

After my shift, it was back by tram and home along roads filled with refugees fleeing the town before the return of night. The whole city seemed to be on the move. Mary was having trouble nursing Little Billy. He still had his grumpy face on when Nurse Reynolds arrived again to see her. She said I'd saved her life by calling her out when we did, before the bomb struck the church. She chatted reassuringly with us all about where would be the safest place for Mary and baby Billy to stay. In the end it was decided to move Mary to Johnny's cousin's place, out in the country beyond Ormskirk. Mum would have to go with her for a day or two until things settled down again.

There was still no sign of Dad. Every time I thought of him, my heart sank a little lower. I remembered feeling the power of that blast wave – and I'd been a mile away. Anyone left in the dock would have had no chance. But the chief said that the captain gave the order to abandon ship hours before the explosion, so they had time to get out of there long before the massive blast, long after the all-clear sounded. Tomorrow was my day off. I had to find Dad and bring him home.

The bus left, with Mary carrying her precious bundle and Mum minding everything else. I wanted more than anything to get on that bus. I wandered over to the church. The miners had lifted the broken bell and retrieved what body parts were there. They sealed what was left with quicklime and cement to prevent disease. That was a big fear in this heat. There was no trace of Mrs Newsome. Nothing.

I sat in the ruins of that bombed-out church and wept dry tears for his mum, and for Father Breen and the thirty-seven others who were known to have died. I mourned my own loss and prayed for my own family too. Still no word of Matt or John. Dad was still missing. None of the boys were here now and Mum and Mary gone to the country. Our town and our city in ruins. Billy and Tom out somewhere on the Western Approaches, which were considered very dangerous as far as I knew. I was left alone to face the night.

I looked up at the ruined statues, the broken altar, shattered stained glass windows, scorched pews, the fallen tower and the hole where once the bell had been. If there was a God, then it ought to be ashamed of itself to allow this to happen.

The world was broken and maybe God was too. This was our flood. Our deluge from air.

Our world was drowning in fire.

CHAPTER TWENTY-ONE

Wednesday 7th May 1941

Shakespeare was a wise man. Considering Hamlet is such a doozy, he had many a wise saying. So you can be wise and do nothing until it is too late, and then the consequences are death and dead bodies all over the stage, the innocent and not-so-innocent. Such a doozy.

Mary had given me a copy of *Hamlet* to read before she went away. I was feeling sorry for Ophelia for the way that she was used as a spy by her father Polonius, the Prime Minister. But then she denied her love for Hamlet and wasn't true to her heart. She lied to him, broke his heart and sent herself mad. I felt that she deserved what she got. Mad and drowned. She came to a bad end.

There had been no sign of Dad since Sunday morning, when the dock explosion took place. The fire was still smouldering and the area closed off, while fire-fighters checked that all the shells and bombs had been destroyed, either in the explosion or in the fire that had burned for two days and nights in its wake. There were rumours all across the city, and in our town, of secret burials and mass graves, of basements being sealed and concreted over. Stories of thousands dead and the cemetery bombed. Bodies, bones and coffins strewn all over the place. No rest even in death.

I spent the day looking for Dad. Mr Watts said that the gymnasium at the Town Baths was being used as a temporary morgue. I thought I'd try the hospital and afterwards the new morgue. There was nothing at the hospital. I wasn't ready to face the morgue. I walked on into the city with the warm sun on my skin. I was shaking, or shivering, I'm not sure which.

The docks were badly hit again. Smoke was rising from fires old and new. Firemen poured water on the flames of burning ships. It seemed that every building had been targeted. Factories, warehouses, churches, schools, hospitals and shelters. The Overhead Railway had been hit again and was down in two places that I saw, looking like a slain dragon brought down to earth. Warehouses and docks smouldered all the way into the city. Houses, shops, tenements, stores, cinemas, banks and offices were damaged. Whole sections of the city were flattened into heaps of rubble.

Heavy rescue crews worked to lift the beams and concrete slabs, with no real hope of finding anyone alive underneath. A lilt of Welsh voices was sometimes carried on the light morning breeze. The lists of dead and injured at the Pier Head grew longer. A crowd was shuffling from list to list in silence. I read them all. There was no sign of Dad or the boys on the lists.

Later I found myself standing looking at the Mill Road Infirmary. It was in ruins, just as the man in the shelter had said it was. The centre of the old building was now a huge hole. Years ago it used to be a workhouse before becoming a hospital, vital in the heart of our city. An ambulance driver leaned against the front wheel, smoking. I asked her what had happened. She told me that a bomb had landed in the yard at the rear, killing many of her colleagues. Their ambulances were destroyed. Further bombs had taken out the maternity ward. One bomb went right through to the operating theatre in the basement where a surgery was taking place. They had rescued the patient, and two of the medical staff got out alive, but injured. Many patients and staff were dead.

There was an almighty hammering and clanging of drilling tools, a clunking of crowbars and more Welsh voices of miners helping to clear the rubble. Then there was a call for silence and everything stopped. The ambulance driver standing opposite me pulled the cigarette off her lower lip where it had stuck. The smoke trickled out of her mouth and up her face, like a cloud clinging to a Welsh mountainside.

A voice cried, 'Over here!' and was followed by a renewed effort to clear the rubble, brick by brick. After a minute there was a shout and another call for quiet. They must have heard something because there was a concentration on one place. Bricks, plaster and rubble were cleared by hand. I couldn't see what was happening, but the ambulance driver said that they had found one of the nurses alive and were digging her out. It was extraordinary that someone could have survived under that debris for two days, but she had.

Many streets were cordoned off, unstable buildings being the main concern. Then there was the danger of time bombs and UXB's in other places. The roads were littered with bomb craters. Bricks and rubble were scattered everywhere, and hoses like snakes rose up from the underworld. Makeshift centres had been set up on the sides of roads where there was a safe space. They were filled with groups of dusty and dirty adults, men in flat caps in spite of the heat, and women in head scarfs, carrying little or nothing except their babies. They looked through tired eyes at their children already playing on the side of the road. The older ones hunted for bits of shrapnel amid the ruins of our world.

I spent the rest of the day searching. First I went to Broadgreen Hospital, where the patients from Mill Street had been evacuated, and scoured the lists of injured and dead. Then it was on to Fazakerley Hospital and back through Walton Hospital. Dead and injured and dying lay all around, but there was no sign of Dad anywhere.

When I got home I half expected him to be waiting for me when I pushed my bike into the front hall, and left it there, as the back entry was blocked. But the echo of the front door was the only sound that greeted my 'Hello, I'm home.' I checked upstairs in his bedroom, but there was no one but myself to disturb the quiet of the house.

The evening heat filled the room and gave off a musty scent. It was like I had walked into a ghost house, a spectre of the boisterous home that was. A shiver ran down my spine and I felt a chill. An overwhelming urge to lie down on my parents' bed overcame me. I clasped both hands over my forehead and tried my best to fight the rising sense of dread.

I woke to the shrill whine of sirens in the darkness of my parents' bedroom. I ran downstairs and out on to the front steps. A silver moon turned the night air grey. The Luftwaffe was already over the river. I could clearly see them held in the searchlight, with the flak bursting orange and black around them. But on they came, straight for our town. They had returned to finish us off.

The entire skyline was filled with the black menace. I watched as the first bombs were sent spiralling down on to our town centre and the nearby docks. First the flashes and afterwards the shock wave followed by the awful noise. I was rooted to the spot, watching in horror. They had come back again and were never going to stop bombing us, unless we stopped them for good. The guns in the park down the road opened up. The searchlights over at Anfield spotted the leading planes and held them in their sights for the guns to send up their barrage of fire. Then the bombs shook the ground all through the town. The park exploded as a series of bombs ripped through it, and on up towards our road.

I sprinted through the house and out into the Anderson Shelter. I dived in under the bunk, on to the mattress beneath it where Mary had lain just two nights earlier. The whole ground shook and the noise was deafening. I was sure I was about to die – and maybe that wouldn't be so bad. Anything had to be better than this madness, night after night, hour after hour. I pulled on my gas mask, put a pillow over my head and grasped the locket with the pictures of me and Billy.

I pretended to be out on Our Shore with him that afternoon in late summer, when he had just come home from his first trip to the Mediterranean. He talked about Gibraltar, Malta and Alexandria like they were just down the road. He told me about the colony of wild apes up on the Rock of Gibraltar, and the harbour at Valetta that had to be seen to be believed. It was the scene of a famous battle between the Ottomans and the Knights of Saint John.

Billy recounted the story of the Great Siege in which the Catholic defenders, led by the French knight, La Valette, overcame the Muslim army of Sultan Suleiman the Magnificent. It was a victory of a determined few defending their home, and their way of life, against an aggressive and powerful invasion force bent on destroying their culture, religion and way of life.

Billy danced back and forth across the sands, enacting the battle for the tiny fort of Saint Elmo. After that battle was lost, he jumped up and down on the sands, relating how La Valette turned what appeared to be certain defeat into a decisive victory. Afterwards they built the magnificent city of Valetta, named after their leader, the capital of Malta. It was once again under siege from the Germans and their Italian allies.

Billy wouldn't say anything about Egypt as they had been sworn to secrecy. I wanted to know about that more than anything, but he resisted, saying, "It's just another harbour."

The ground shook all night long. I was reminded of Billy's description of the battle for Saint Elmo's Fort, with attacking forces pounding the life out of a tiny band of defenders. We would have to see this through just like they did in Malta all those years ago. A time must have come when it had seemed hopeless to them, when defeat looked imminent in the face of such an overwhelming attacking force, yet they managed to hold out for days beyond hope, and through nights of despair. They overcame the threat, repelled the invaders and somehow achieved victory. They never gave up.

CHAPTER TWENTY-TWO

Thursday 8th May 1941

Hamlet believed in fatalism. According to him, no matter what I do to change things, events will always turn out according to the great plan that God has laid out for me. That was really more like the Greek myths, where gods played with the lives of humans. I was fighting the demons who tried to convince me all night long that Hamlet was right. That no matter what I did, my destiny was already set on a particular path.

I must have dozed off in the quiet of the early morning. The all clear woke me with a start.

There comes a time in war when you are so intensely inside the battle, surrounded by death, that the world outside ceases to have any meaning except in relation to fear, loss and a primeval need to survive. I staggered out like a drunk with the sound of the all-clear wailing lament through the town. Our home was still standing, but the roof was gone. Curtains flapped about through the broken windows. The air was thick with soot. I could taste it in my throat and in the grit between my teeth.

It is impossible to describe the devastation wreaked on the town. Outside, our street was strewn with bricks and rubble thrown up by the explosions. One had landed on the houses fifty yards down from ours. There was a gap in the street where three houses in a row were flattened. Piles of rubble marked where they had stood. Another hit across the road. I guessed that the bomb had landed in someone's back garden as the houses stood in a drunken poise, twisted, leaning to one side, hung over in the early morning light. There was no one on the street. Down at the park, the soldiers looked exhausted. They perked up when they saw me picking my way through the damaged street. The only sound to break the silence was the crackle of glass under my feet.

Mr Watts had suggested to me yesterday that I use the shelter down at the Co-Op in Bootle, so that I wouldn't be alone. I had fallen asleep on my parents' bed. When I woke up, the raid had already started.

It was just as well. That shelter was in the basement. The building above it, the Co-Op, took a direct hit and collapsed. People were digging frantically into the hill of rubble that sat on top of the cellar. God knows how many were dead or trapped. I shivered, thinking of a previous hit on a shelter on Durning Road where gas and boiling water from the heating system flooded the basement and gassed or burned any victims left alive after the bomb had exploded.

On Oriel Road I could see a curl of smoke rising from the temporary morgue that had been set up in the gymnasium at the Baths. A moment later, my fears were confirmed. It was completely burned out with its roof open to the sky. No one could tell me exactly how many bodies were in there. Somebody mention a hundred and eighty, most of them unidentified, but more had been brought in last night. It was hit by incendiary bombs and the roof caught fire. The whole building was destroyed and the roof collapsed on to the corpses and the APW below. A number of fire-fighters were injured trying to save the dead. Death by bombs. Death by fire. Death from the Gods of Sky.

The soldiers up at the park said that all the roads out of town were blocked or bombed. I pushed my bicycle around the massive hole where once the bridge over the canal had stood. The road section of the bridge was missing, but it was possible to pass with care on foot. The air was thick with black smoke rising from fires still burning, soaring up to join the ceiling of black cloud that sat on the town like a shroud. The heavy rescue crews scrambled from one site to the next.

The Co-Op shelter was another disaster. The whole corner of the street had collapsed in on itself. Rescue crews were digging through a mountain of rubble, with little hope of finding anyone alive. About fifty bodies were lined up in a bombsite across the road. I could see the bodies of children and women. My hands were shaking. I clenched and unclenched my fists, and turned my face away.

Every street was broken and smashed, lives and homes shattered everywhere. Most of the town was empty, as people had left last night, and just as well. The docks were burning where I thought it wasn't possible to find anything left to burn. It was the end.

There was no way that the bombers could have mistaken our town for the docks. It was a clear moonlit night, with only a light mist rolling in from the sea. The docks were already on fire. They must have known that they were dropping their filthy bombs on people's homes. It was Guernica all over again. They were trying to bomb us out of existence. If there were no people, there could be no port, no ships, no docks, no supplies for the war. Hitler was trying to win the war by pounding us into extinction.

In the city, I watched as help came in from Manchester and all over. More miners arrived from Wales with their blackened faces, grim smiles and lilting voices.

Keep calm and carry on. In times of trouble we often turn to routine to pull us through. I had a job to do. I had to get out to the factory. I needed to do something to help put a stop to this madness. The only way to fight fire was with fire.

From the high ground at Everton I could see the whole sweep of the river, and the extent of the damage. Everywhere I looked, it was more of the same. Fire, rubble and smoking rubble. Suddenly, the black cloud cleared for a moment and I saw the Liver Bird still standing looking over the destruction of his city. I drew some solace from the fact that he was still standing and so was I. Even as I watched, there was movement on the river. The broken city struggled to carry on with the great work of the port.

Dad was probably busy somewhere helping to clear up this great disaster, or maybe he was injured and moved into a hospital somewhere across the city. Somewhere safe. I would surely know if something terrible had happened to him. Last night I must have dropped off asleep because I remembered seeing the face of Mrs Newsome come floating into my dreams. It was just her head, suspended in the black air of the church, crying for her body that was blown to smithereens. I woke suddenly in fright in the dark, with the rumble of aircraft overhead, crying for Billy's loss. How would he cope with the death of his wonderful mum?

The soldiers had said that there were thousands dead and thousands more injured. I had to get out to the factory and do my job. That's what Tom would say to do. *Keep calm and carry on.* I turned my back on the river and pointed my bike in the direction of the Simonswood tram. My mind was gripped with a determination to make more bombs and get them out to Egypt. I was going to play my part and hit back at these bombers that had trampled across people's lives, and the madman who thought he was God, who was to blame for the whole sorry mess.

Love is like breathing. It is part of my being, a connection that I can't live without, like a beating heart driven by the oxygen of love. I found it difficult to breathe at that moment. The whole world had taken a sharp intake of breath, one filled with smoke, dust and metal filings. It hurt my throat and caught in my chest. It was an ache that I carried inside, every hour of every day, like a breath held in suspense. The whole world was in suspense.

Yet love was the one belief that sustained me, carried me through and kept my faith that things would still turn out all right. It was the thought of Billy returning soon. I wanted to hold him in his pain for the loss of his mum. How would he cope with such a thing? Tom would sort out the chaos that our lives had become, and find Dad, and make some sense out of the madness. In the back of my mind, I was worried that their ship might be diverted away from Liverpool because of the damage sustained in the port.

I placed that worry in the chest that contained all my fears, and slammed the lid shut. Breathe in, breathe out. *Keep calm and carry on.* There was vital work to be done and I was determined to see it through. One step at a time. It was such a lucky thing that Billy had Tom to look out for him.

Such a lucky thing.

Water

CHAPTER ONE

Tom

The trauma specialist in the hospital in New York told me to write down things that have happened, and things that are happening. She said it might ease the pain. At that time I was finding it increasingly difficult to distinguish one bad day from another.

"Go back as far as you like - things you can remember," she said.

I had always wanted to go to sea, from as far back as I can remember. As a child, I loved the excitement that went with the start of a sea voyage. Sitting on the Da's shoulders, watching the giant liners slipping out of Prince's Dock... The sun always shone in those happy times. I remember smoke pouring from funnels, shouts and flags rising and falling with the wind and tide, passengers waving over rails, sailors pulling in gangplanks and throwing ropes through the air.

I can still hear the heavy iron chain of an anchor clanking through the hawsehole and the Overhead Railway rattling by. I see carts, carters and horses, and people pulling their coats and hats close against the wind. Then suddenly the ship's horn would sound, reverberating throughout the dock. I'd cover my ears, with my mouth closed so that my heart wouldn't jump out, as Da had said could happen. I'd feel the vibration of the sound through my teeth. Then would come the second blast, as the ship floated away like magic. I couldn't wait to grow up and go to work on one. Nowadays I'm First Mate, responsible for the ship's operations on land and at sea.

I worked for a few years on the transatlantic liners before I moved to New York for eight years. When I came back to Liverpool, I joined the Merchant Navy and worked my way up through the ranks.

The war has brought a whole new set of dangers, but after New York, life will never have the same hold on me as it did before. War is a welcome distraction from the pain of remembering. Death can happen at any time, but when the people you love are no longer around, there's not as much to live for. Hitler, and the threat to the survival of everything left in this world that I care for, is enough for the moment. Bootle and Liverpool are taking a terrible pounding from the air most nights. If there's one thing I know, it's that we won't go down without a fight. The battle at sea is every bit as hard as on land and in the sky. Britain can't survive unless we get the supplies through from America, Canada and around the world. Victory hangs in the balance.

"I know, that's a bit mixed up, I'll try to keep things simple."

There are sights no human should see, sounds no human should hear. Moments that change your life forever.

It's a thin line between life and death. Every sailor knows that at one moment they can be laughing at a joke, or bending to a task deep in the hull, or thinking about a wife or girlfriend, and the next they could be blown to bits or tossed into the oily water of a shipwreck, or, worse still, burned alive in it. Drowning is attractive by comparison. Sometimes death is seen coming straight and clear like a lookout pointing at an incoming torpedo, but that doesn't happen very often, not even in a time of war. Death can happen as easily as stepping off a sidewalk.

I have witnessed this at first hand on more than one occasion. In October 1940 I had returned from a difficult crossing of the Atlantic

Ocean. Almost half the ships in the convoy were lost. I was picking my way home in the gloom through the bombed streets of Liverpool. I heard planes pass overhead and felt the blasts from under the railway arches where I took shelter, but no bomb fell near me. It was a short raid and the all-clear sounded in jig time.

Rounding a corner, I came across a woman sitting on the footpath, cradling a man's head in her blood-soaked apron. Her screams could be heard above the wail of the air raid siren that signalled a new attack. She was wailing and pointing back at a house across the road. I went in to see if someone was injured inside. In the half-light, a man's body was standing at a hole in the wall that was the front window. It was jammed between a piano and the side wall. There was blood everywhere, and a pulse of blood was still flowing from the place where his head had been. His hand was resting on the piano and his finger was pointing out the window at his own head.

At sea, life and death are two breaths on the same wind. Off Newfoundland one wintry day, a giant wave washed three men overboard, clean off the deck of our ship. One moment they were there, then there was only the sea boiling in a raging ocean, and an empty deck. The next wave fired one of them back on board, where he grabbed a rope and clung on for dear life. When he was brought inside, stripped and wrapped in a blanket, his wide eyes were popping, staring down death. Freezing water was gathered on his beard. His skin was blue and white, his teeth chattered, unable to speak. It was not his time.

"All that is very grim. What about before the war?"

My growing up years are wrapped in a fog, like the white bank that rolled up the river from the estuary and chilled anyone who stood still for long enough. I never did. I was busy playing football in the park at the end of the road, or running errands for Mr Watts in the corner shop. On Saturdays, the Da would carry me shoulder high through the crowds outside Goodison. I was almost as high as the policeman on horseback, who blew his whistle and waved his arm.

Over the years, my brothers and sisters arrived on the step of the house, left by the stork. I had watched them standing on one leg way out on the sands. They didn't look very strong, but when they spread their wings and took off into the sky, they transformed into messengers of the gods. I was bigger, stronger and better at football than all of my brothers.

Most days were sunny and long, and winter went fast. It was after the Great War, but the Da didn't go to the front on account of being a docker, and not being allowed. When I was old enough I went during the summer holidays to work as a tea boy at the dock. I earned real money there. I loved to listen to the men's stories and, when not serving tea, I learned how to operate giant cranes. I got to watch the great ships sailing away on the river and liners gliding in from all over the world, like something alien from another planet. For me, it was one of the most beautiful and exciting sights on earth.

As sailors, when we step on board a ship, we have already accepted that the sea may take us. My brother Liam called it "an occupational hazard." He talks like that now that he's a ship's engineer. Last time he left port, it was in the calmest of weather. The sea was a shimmering lake, looking like it wouldn't harm a fly. Three days later he was in the middle of a violent storm.

"The sea boiled around us in all directions and the ship went down into the deep with the next wave towering above the deck," he told the brothers gathered around the kitchen table.

"Somehow the Old Lady pulled herself up out of the trough and struggled up and over the next crest that smashed on to the bow, poured over the gunnels and swept the deck, clean as a whistle."

Liam loved telling a story, and he was good at it too.

"The sky was filthy grey, the ocean was black and grey and the world moved only in black and white."

Liam paused and looked around the table at the upturned faces hanging on his every word.

"If you were there you would need a strong heart and a stout head and a stomach built to withstand the heavin' seas that would devour you in a flash," he went on. "When the ship ploughs through the crest of a wave, you can catch a glimpse of the raging seas that thunder all around, and the giant waves lined up like soldiers in rows charging towards you, on and on bayonets drawn. Down in the engine room, it seems that the ship could not hold together, but must break its back and the sea pour in."

Ah yes, Liam was a good man to tell a story.

At sea, if you didn't have faith and believe that your ship would get through the worst of weather, the kind that would shake its anger out only when it was good and ready, you would never have the heart to go on. Instead, you would drop down dead like the passenger on my ship, the *Lancastria*, as she was sailing into New York harbour all those years ago. Life is fickle in the hands of the gods. If you have no faith and don't believe in a god, then it comes down to skill and luck and fear. There's nothing like fear to drive a ship.

"What's it like to be in the Merchant Navy at this time of war?"

The battle at sea started on the first day of the war, Sunday the third of September 1939, and has continued every day and every night since.

Everyone sailing in a convoy knows that the wolf pack is out searching and could attack at any time. U-boats are slow under water and prefer to surface, where they are much quicker. They use the cover of darkness to get in close.

A yellow, red and white flash breaks the curtain of night. Below deck, the crew feels at first a dull thud, then the vibration of a shock wave that runs the length of the ship, followed by the sound of the shattering impact.

It's all in the hands of the gods. Nothing can prepare a crew for that moment, stumbling about in the dark with the ship listing and the convoy sailing on regardless into the black night. Orders are clear and everyone knows the drill. Sail on. Do not stop under any circumstances. If there is an escort nearby, it will concentrate on trying to get that U-boat rather than stopping and saving the crew.

The really unlucky may be carrying a cargo of iron ore or similar heavy load. That ship will go down in less than a minute. There's no time to launch the lifeboats. Just about time to curse, or recite a prayer. Old habits. The cold Atlantic will have them all for a midnight snack.

The engine room is often in the stern. If it takes a direct hit, then the ship will go down stern first in under a minute, as the boiler room floods. The icy sea will pour into the engines through the impact hole blown in the side of the ship, below the waterline, sending steam hissing and oil spewing. There is a strong chance of a second explosion if a boiler goes. Prepare to meet the gods.

The U-boat usually fires two torpedoes. If a ship is really lucky, one would miss and the other would hit the side, forward of midship. No one would be killed and there would be time to launch the lifeboats. The launching operation is difficult and dangerous on a sinking ship. The lines can get caught up if the ship lists, and a lifeboat can be thrown back against the hull or on to the deck. It has been known to twist in the air and throw the occupants into the swirling water around the propeller.

Then there is the weather, to complicate matters. The rolling waves of the great ocean will pitch a ship and increase the danger of upturning the lifeboat, and everyone in it, into a sea filled with oil. If you swallow oil it will sear your lungs, sting your mouth and burn your stomach. Sometimes that oil burns with a stink of human flesh in the choking fumes. Screams don't last long, except in memory.

If the weather is really stormy, the U-boat can't operate, which is some consolation. There are plenty of stories of times when some, or nearly all, of the crew were killed in the initial attack. The remaining crew had to deal with injured crew and terrified passengers. There was always the threat of another attack, another torpedo, or a shell from the gun mounted on the U-boat in front of the conning tower, or a bomb or machine gun fire from an enemy plane. In those cases, it was a real struggle to launch the lifeboats. A lot of ships went down with no survivors. No one talked about that.

Out in the mid-Atlantic there is an area we call the Atlantic Gap, where there is no air cover. The wolf pack is usually waiting there, spread in a wide line watching for the tell-tale sight of smoke on the horizon. Then they report and wait for the rest of the pack to arrive. They even try to sneak into the middle of the convoy under the cover of darkness, before sending their torpedoes at the largest target.

Nearer home we are faced with the dangers of the Western Approaches. The South Irish Sea was mined after Dunkirk in preparation for an invasion. As a result, all ships heading for Liverpool or Glasgow have to use the North Western Approaches, around the top of Ireland and down the Irish Sea into Liverpool. In the Western Approaches there are the added dangers of U-boats underwater and Condors in the air, usually armed with bombs that they drop from just a few hundred feet. The bomber will attack from forward or aft, giving the pilot a longer target to hit. They rarely miss, unless we get them first.

The Luftwaffe has dropped magnetic and acoustic mines into the North Channel, the area of sea between Rathlin Island at the north-east tip of Ireland and the Mull of Kintyre in Scotland. They are also found at the entrances to the ports. They wait, floating like jellyfish on the tide. The magnetic ones are attracted by the pull of the hull. The acoustic ones are detonated by the noise of the propellers.

Being in a convoy attracts the U-boats. Sailing alone, if you are fast enough to do that, attracts the Condors.

If we survive all that, we win the right to pass beyond the Bar Light Vessel that signals the approach to the estuary, and catch sight of port. Liverpool, the greatest port in the Battle of the Atlantic, with her miles and miles of docks and shipyards on both sides of the Mersey. A lifeline for Britain. We join tens of ships waiting patiently to enter the largest system of docks in the world, bringing vital supplies of food and war material from the New World. We pass tens of ships leaving to face the perils of the outbound journey. In the labyrinth of docks, dozens of ships are being loaded or unloaded, dozens more are in for repair in the dockyards across in Birkenhead. The twin spires of the Liver Building hover over the city in the smoky air.

"So what is it like for you coming in to port?"

I stand on the bridge, taking it all in. There's smoke rising from the fires and bomb damage as far as the eye can see. Barrage balloons hang in the air hundreds of feet up, like shiny ships in the smoky sky. Cranes move on the busy quays, doing the business of the port. Seagulls wheel overhead, their squawks and cat-like screeches shouting a welcome. The sounds and smells are carried on the breeze. Home.

Welcome home.

I worry, passing terraces of houses smashed in the overnight raid, their privacy exposed and gaudy in the morning sunlight. With mixed emotions, I walk into Bootle, my town. Death and destruction are everywhere, even in our street.

Home.

The house is still standing, with laughter, banter and pure love contained within its walls. The Ma issuing standing orders to all and sundry. Boys turned into men, eating breakfast and preparing to face another day of trial on land or at sea. Da, already gone to work in the docks. Mary, married and expecting a baby in late spring, or early summer. Maggie, my baby sister, growing up too fast into this world full of danger.

Home.

Sailing up the Mersey brings simultaneous feelings of relief and dread. Liverpool has taken a hell of a pounding from the air nearly every night since the Blitz started late last summer.

Sitting at the breakfast table in the heat of the kitchen, listening to a list of dead neighbours, friends-of-friends and distant relatives, I was thinking how we are all taking a hammering on land and at sea. I thought of the ship I had set sail on a month previously. It now lay six hundred fathoms at the bottom of the Atlantic, a giant coffin to eight of my crew.

Secrets. The world is full of them, buried deep under the rubble of life, hidden from family, friends and neighbours.

I have closed my mind like a door on the past and welcome the distractions of the day. Night is a different matter. It brings faces, words and deeds that roam free in the dark like troubled spirits. Dawn is full of shame and blame and memories that twist like a bayonet in the gut. War is a welcome distraction.

"What do you mean by 'distraction'?"

I have bad dreams.

I was looking into the freckled face of a seven-year-old girl who had recently lost her two front teeth. I took in the excitement in her voice, her crooked smile, as she skipped along, holding my hand, chatting non-stop, as I walked with her to the kiosk on Coney Island to get an ice-cream. There was a lisp to her speech caused by the gap in her teeth so that she made a low whistling sound inside her words.

"Oh Pops, can I have a bawoon? Pease Pops. Pease?"

Her upturned face so full of light, her red-blonde hair streaming strands down her back. Her tiny hand holding the three red balloons that struggled to escape her squeals of laughter.

Secrets.

Ma placed a bowl of steaming porridge on the table.

Voices from another world, from another time.

The whole thing is sliding under. We are all in danger of drowning.

CHAPTER TWO

December 1940

How did you feel going back to sea?

The convoy left Freetown without any escort. The weather in Sierra Leone was foul for most of our visit. The dry Harmattan winds had been blowing off the Sahara for weeks, covering everything in a layer of red sand. Even the mangrove swamps had a thick coating of dust, but at least it kept the mosquitoes at bay.

There was change in the air on the morning of the departure. The day dawned warm and sticky and the sea rolled happily by under a hot sun. My ship, the *Mistral,* carrying a cargo of pig iron and onions, sat low in the water and chugged along at eight knots. This heavy load would make us a sitting duck in an attack.

I was glad to be at sea, even without the protection of the Navy. I don't like these African ports with their overpowering stench, piles of filth and slums with rats the size of cats. Too much poverty and disease. I hate the sight of undernourished children running after me in the street, trying to sell me a pup or a baby monkey. I had to turn away from seeing their swollen bellies and runny noses and huge, white puppy eyes covered in flies. The crew were off drinking, whoring and fighting. Everywhere, people on the make or take.

Of them all, Freetown was the best. It was inhabited by a large number of the descendants of Negro slaves that had been re-settled there by the British after the abolition of slavery. They had chosen to remain on the coast and build a new life for themselves in the place that the British named Freetown, a new settlement built around the huge natural harbour. The food was said to be the best in Africa. Nevertheless, I was glad to set sail out of her beautiful harbour, leaving the chaos of the ramshackle city behind, with the warm ocean breeze on my face. It was good to be heading home.

Across the bay, the fourteen ships that made up the convoy steamed out through the white-topped waves and took up their positions in a four-four-three-three formation spread out over a couple of square miles of ocean. With no escort to protect us, we were wide open to attack, but the threat from the enemy must have been considered low.

I didn't have time to mull over that fact. From my position at the back of the convoy, I could see two ships to starboard and three lines ahead. We were all painted in battle colours of off-white, grey and duck-egg blue, covered over with red dust. The ships sat low in the white-tipped deep blue of the sea and the high blue of the bright sky. We were scheduled to sail to Gibraltar, and once there link up with a larger convoy, to reach home just after Christmas. The journey north to Liverpool would take about three weeks if everything went to plan.

It didn't.

At noon on the fourth day, a sea plane was spotted off the starboard flank of the convoy. It was too small to fly out so far in the ocean. It could only mean one thing. A German cruiser had to be about. All ships went to battle stations and full alert. Shortly afterwards, the order to scatter was given. We changed course on the heading north-northwest, which would bring us close to the Cape Verde Islands. Within an hour we were alone in the dome of sky. The rolling waves under the hull gave nowhere to hide. On board, everyone went about their business in silence. On deck, the ocean waves could be heard slapping against the hull, like the caress of an old familiar friend.

The lights of Praia were off the port bow, when the torpedo struck mid-ship. A blinding flash of yellow flame screamed into the dark night. The crew felt the shudder in the bowels of the ship as the heavy explosion ripped into the heart of the hold. Fragments of metal, timber and pig iron were fired like shrapnel in all directions. Immediately, the seawater rushed in to claim its treasure. The ship began to list and sink. Thanks be to Christ, half the hold was full of onions. I had time to gather everyone I could find alive on board, and launch one life raft into the black water.

Two of the crew had jumped overboard into the oil-filled sea and those of us on the lifeboat had a job hauling them aboard. They were choking on their own vomit and gasping for air, burning from the inside out. I knew they were done for. When I turned to look back, the ship was gone. Just eight of us remained, bobbing up and down in a sea of onions, being tossed side-wards in the crosswind. It could not have taken more than two minutes for the whole episode from violent start to final end.

We knew that the U-boat was still about and could easily sink us or bomb us out of the water. Then, only a hundred yards away, it suddenly surfaced in a rush of air and surge of water. It was alongside us within a few minutes. We were completely at its mercy.

A searchlight was trained on us and I knew that machine guns would follow our every move. A voice called from the tower above in clear English.

"What is the name of your ship? Identify yourselves. What is your tonnage and what cargo were you carrying?"

I shouted out the answers and was taken aback when they asked were we all right to reach the island. Did we need drink or food or medicine, they asked. They seemed happy with my response that we would be fine, and slipped off into the darkness. Later, when I had little to do only think about what had happened to my ship, and write my report, my pen was held suspended in space over the page. First they sank us, then they checked to see if we were all right. A U-boat captain with a decent streak in him... Extraordinary.

The sail was set with a snap and the lifeboat pointed in the direction of the lights of the city. The sea befriended us and the lifeboat was carried towards the island.

"So you ended up in the Azores on your last voyage?"

No, not the Azores. They're much further north. It was the Cape Verde islands. A couple of days spent in Praia were pleasant enough. The locals complained about the war, but were kind and looked after us well. The one thing they all mentioned was the sinking of the *City of Benares* the previous September.

With so many terrible incidents and stories of death from all over the world, it would not have surprised me if most people were hardened against the worst stories of death and destruction. In war, people are replaced by numbers. Such-and-such number of people killed, so-and-so many people injured, so many people homeless, so many missing in action. But the *City of Benares* was different. It was a story with human suffering and loss at its core. Everyone remembered that disaster. All those young children being evacuated to safety in Canada.

The vessel was the Commodore's ship of the convoy OB-213, which would have made her a prime target of the U-boat pack. The locals could recount the details in graphic detail; the sinking of the liner six hundred miles west of Donegal in rough seas and near gale force winds. The torpedo hit the stern near the third class area where the children were sleeping. In the struggle to launch the lifeboats, many capsized in the freezing ocean and others were smashed against the side of the ship as it reared up.

The lifeboats were designed to stay afloat as they carried sealed barrels of air. Most did stay afloat, but they half-filled with water in the rough seas. The children were soaked, sitting there in cold water. Some of the boats were so flooded, the children floated away.

The locals remembered the heroics of the guardians, who dived repeatedly into the freezing ocean and rescued so many children from drowning. They could recount every detail: the difficult rescue by *HMS Hurricane* later in the afternoon; searching for survivors in the dangerous sea; finding children clinging to tiny rafts and half-submerged lifeboats with less than half their occupants still alive. All others were given up as lost. Parents were told the worst news a parent could possibly hear. Then eight days later, Lifeboat 12, which had not been waterlogged, and had drifted outside the search zone, was spotted by chance by a Sunderland Flying Boat. A rescue operation followed with *HMS Anthony* picking up its forty-six occupants, including six children.

The newspapers carried the story around the world. So many children dying of exposure in the open, sodden lifeboats in the cold Atlantic. Only seven out of a hundred children on board survived. Those readers who still had a shred of decency left in them were shocked. The Germans had a lot to answer for. The people of Cape Verde were in no doubt as to where their sympathies lay. When our ship was hit, eight of my crew went down with it. Two more died in the lifeboat. It was fortunate that we had been so near the island of Santiago when the torpedo struck.

We held a short service in the cathedral in the centre of Praia. Afterwards we buried our two comrades in a graveyard on the stony hillside with a view of the bay. The remaining five crew formed a guard of honour while I read a short commendation at the graveside. These young men had given their lives in the service of the king. There was real anger at the loss and, at the same time, a wish to get back home and do our bit. We had only to wait a day in the warm sunshine before hitching a lift on a cargo ship to Gibraltar. Once there, my crew joined a large convoy of forty-two merchant ships and a mighty escort, which set sail the following day, bound for Liverpool.

The convoy was led by three sloops and six corvettes out of the safe anchorage under the Rock. Shortly afterwards we were reinforced by two more sloops, three destroyers, four corvettes and the aircraft carrier HMS *St John*. Nineteen ships in all. This time we were well protected with enough escorts to chase any U-boat and still have the convoy protected. I had befriended a young Canadian radio officer on board, and sat with him for hours in his lonely outpost at the top of the ship. I watched and listened, intrigued, as the Australian destroyer HMAS *Hawkstown Bay* chased down and depth-charged a U-boat off Cabo da Roca in Portugal, the most westerly point of mainland Europe. For once it was the Hun that was on the run. Then one of Jerry's reconnaissance planes, a Focke-Wolf, was chased and shot down by two of the American Martlet fighter planes from the *St John*.

Two days later, four of the warships went hunting a U-boat detected shadowing the convoy twenty miles off the port side. Soon after, three Martlet fighter planes took off and followed them over the western horizon. We were able to follow the action as the team sunk another U-boat. Sadly, the pilot of one of the planes was shot down and lost in action.

The next night, one of the destroyers took a direct hit from a torpedo. The ship was a burning inferno that lit the blackness with a wall of red, yellow and orange flame. Then night was turned into day as the order came through for every ship to fire star shells. They illuminated the sea that boiled and burst with water, thrown hundreds of feet in the air by the depth charges dropped by the command ship. When the U-boat surfaced it was rammed, turning it on its side, from where there was no way back. But we had casualties too. The following night, just before midnight, there was a sickening explosion as the aircraft carrier *St John* took a direct hit of a torpedo. Within an hour, she was low in the water and shortly afterwards she was gone, with the loss of over eighty lives.

"How did you feel, watching all this destruction going on around you?"

It was maddening not being able to do anything except listen in as the disasters unfolded, one after another, around us. At least this time, the odds were slightly in our favour. I could see the pasty face of the Canadian humped over the radio, following the fight, blow by blow. On deck the shouts of the sailors could be heard, then the sounds were swallowed by a fierce wind that blew in my face as I peered into the darkness, tiny lights bobbing up and down and disappearing astern.

When we reached Liverpool, the commander was hailed a hero. Five U-boats had been sunk for the loss of two merchant ships and two warships. Most of the vital supplies were saved. The cost in men and machines was terrible, but that's what war is. Terrible. What counts is survival. Coming up the Queen's Channel and looking out on the docks and the city smouldering in the aftermath of yet another night attack from the Luftwaffe, it was all about survival. The bonus for me was that I was home early for Christmas.

"And did you go straight back out to sea?"

No. I had to file a report and later was issued with a new uniform and reassigned to a ship that would sail immediately after Christmas. Later that day I was about to go on fire-watch when an early raid caught everyone by surprise and nearly killed my sister Maggie. She had been off buying a new dress and shoes that she had saved for, and had talked about for a year or more to anyone who would listen.

Jerry was determined to destroy the docks. Each raid followed the same pattern. First incendiaries, falling in thousands so that the fire-watchers on the ground were eventually overwhelmed. No sooner had we rushed to one fire point and dealt with that, than another two incendiaries burst into flames. When the fires were at their height, lighting the night sky like beacons, the heavy bombers came in waves. There was a constant danger from a high explosive bomb or a land mine. The docks were an inferno with fires blazing all along both banks of the river. When the all-clear sounded, it brought little Christmas cheer.

The following night my brothers and I were down at the docks on fire-watch. Our home was damaged by a near miss at the very start of the raid. The Ma and Da were nearly killed in their bed from the blast and the flying glass. Some of the neighbours weren't as lucky and took a direct hit. Eight of them were killed and a good few injured. Maggie's friend Billy helped Maggie and Mary get the parents down the stairs and into the shelter. The next day the weather broke and the stormy nights brought misery, but respite from the bombs.

"What was Christmas like?"

Billy and his mother Bess came to dinner on Christmas Day, because of a UXB up on their road. The Ma made an excellent meal, when you consider the state of the house, never mind the state of the world. I looked around the table at the faces of my brothers Pat and Peter, my sister Mary and her husband Johnny, and Maggie, turning into a beautiful young woman. It was good to see our parents smiling and shutting out the war for that magical day.

You couldn't really shut out the war though. It was never far away. You could see it in the faces all around. It was in the lines of worry on their foreheads or the shift in their eyes, or the little tremor in their fingers when they lit a cigarette. But for the Ma and Da, it was one day of happiness. The meal was out of this world, thanks to Uncle Peter, who sent the food from Ireland.

Maggie signed up to work in the munitions factory immediately after Christmas. I was glad to receive orders that I had been reassigned to a cargo ship, the *Cumbria*, and Billy was going to sail with me.

"How did you feel going back to sea?"

Going to sea is what I do. It's in my blood.

Years ago, I was about to set sail for the first time as a cabin boy aboard the ill-fated *RMS Lancastria*, bound for New York with one thousand three hundred passengers and three hundred crew. Not many people have heard much about what happened to that liner in the end, because of the censorship. From what I heard around the docks, it was the greatest disaster ever at sea in the entire naval history of the British Empire. More than all the deaths from the *Titanic* and *Lusitania* combined. I heard the details of the story from a survivor who had crewed with me on the *Mistral* and had survived that sinking too.

It happened after Dunkirk the previous summer, after the fall of France. Thousands of soldiers and refugees were fleeing west in front of the German advance into France. The *Lancastria* had by then been taken over by the Navy and converted to a troop carrier. It was sent as part of a small flotilla to the Bay of Biscay to evacuate everyone they could from the area off Saint-Nazaire.

The evacuation was slow because of the low tides in that part of France. The captain was given orders to ignore the safety limits on the number of passengers she could carry. His orders were to pick up as many soldiers and refugees as possible and had probably more than six thousand on board. Some say it may have been up to ten thousand, but none who counted them survived.

They had spent the previous two days loading her, ferrying them from the shallow harbour out to the ship anchored off shore. The word is that over six thousand drowned when she was bombed. She went down in under thirty minutes. The German plane that bombed her strafed the lifeboats and those in the water with machine gun fire. What kind of person would do that?

Anyway, all those years back, I was about to set sail for the first time on the *Lancastria*, which was a luxury liner at that time, sailing between Liverpool and New York. I was the bee's knees, as the Ma said, sitting on the quayside with the Da, watching the movements of ships in and out of the busy port. Da lit his pipe and smoked for a bit, watching with expert eyes the working of the port. Then he paused and held the pipe like a sextant pointing out to sea.

"You mark my words, Tom, there are some people in this world who would smile in your face and piss in your pocket, but they're not worth worrying about," he said. "Let them do their worst. They'll get their comeuppance in the end. There's no good will come of that carry-on. Don't let yourself be caught up with people like them. You can't change a bad penny just by turning it over in your pocket."

The Da took off his cap and scratched his bald head. Seagulls wheeled in from the sea and screeched above us. His eyes followed a ship as it slipped past the dock and on down the Mersey towards the open sea.

"Tom, I believe that the world is made up of three kinds of people," he said. "Some would do you a good turn and not expect anything in return. Them people are gold. Keep them close. Then there's some who are out for themselves at all costs. They'll do anything and anyone they can if it's in their interest to do so. Fair enough, I say. What you see is what you get with people like them. At least they don't pretend to be something they're not. Keep a close watch on them with your eyes open."

He sucked hard on his pipe then and had a faraway look I'd never seen before. He blew the words out through the smoke.

"But there's some who would be close, who pretend to be gold and will smile in your face, and at the same time twist a knife in your back as quick as look at you. Sometimes even within their own family. Them are the worst kind. They'd dance upon your grave if they thought no one was looking... with a spite that gathers like rust about their heart. Have no truck with them. They'll get their comeuppance in the end if ducks are ducks, mark my words."

It was the weekend that I was off to sea on my first adventure. I didn't know then what the Da was talking about. It was only years later, when I heard the story from the Ma, that I fully understood what the Da had said that day. The story goes that he had been done out of the family farm and a lot of money at home back in Ireland. It took me a long time, and many mistakes, and some considerable pain, before I began to realise what sound advice he had given me that day. Going to sea was what I did. The sea was in the blood.

The cargo ship the *Cumbria* weighed seven thousand tonnes and had been built in Glasgow in 1936. She had orders to sail on the Friday after Christmas. We set off around mid-afternoon into a cold wind and a growing swell. We slipped down the Queen's Channel and on into the Irish Sea, heading to a rendezvous point off Bangor in County Down.

Out in the bay, we passed the incoming convoy of John and Matt. I had promised Maggie that I'd keep an eye on Billy, but quickly found that he was well able to take care of himself. He had been to the Med and down as far as Alexandria. He was young and carried an air of confidence about him that was picked up by those around him. Football does that to you, if you're good enough. It can give you confidence and strength, but not cockiness. It inspires respect, especially at such times as these. The crew gave him the nickname *Striker*, and no matter how much he told them that he was a centre-half, the name stuck.

The convoy assembled over the next twenty-four hours and slowly made its way, in howling winds, around the north of Ireland, battling past the graveyard of so many ships. The weather was foul, and the rigging began to freeze in a bitterly cold northerly wind. Our convoy was protected by a team of six destroyers which ploughed its way slowly out to twenty degrees west into the teeth of a gale. Then the escort turned back, as it was believed that the U-boats couldn't operate out beyond this line.

Up in the radio hut, on the upper deck behind the bridge, at the highest point of the ship, every twist and turn and roll was exaggerated. It felt as though the ship was being tossed about like a cork in a boiling, angry sea. The roar of the icy wind filled that space between the hut and the bridge, and could be heard inside, even with the door closed. There were no windows in the radio hut, and breath hung like cigarette smoke in the freezing air. Billy busied himself identifying every ship in the convoy, listening to the messages being passed on from the centre of operations in Derby House.

The icy sea froze on the decks and in the rigging, and icicles hung down like shards of glass as the ship made slow progress into the face of a raging gale. The deck turned into an ice rink and the crew, wielding sledgehammers, fought a losing battle trying to break off the thick glacial mass. Frozen sea ice penetrated our coats, beards and gloves. Billy never complained, even when he was violently seasick. He got on with the job in between bouts of vomiting.

One after another, the storms swept in from the west. The convoy arrived in Halifax a week late, battered and bruised from the elements. It had been one of the worst crossings in living memory. The only consolation was that the U-boats couldn't attack in the rough seas. The weather for the return trip didn't promise to be much better.

Life at sea was cruel at times like this. You had to hate yourself to love it.

CHAPTER THREE

April 1941

I t was the stormiest January and February since records began.
Storm after storm ripped across the Atlantic, one lined up
behind the other like a heavenly convoy. Those of the crew
who were superstitious said that the gods were angry with the state
of the world and agitated the seas and poured rain from the heavens
above. The rest of us just got battered and wet.

In March, the weather settled down to something like normal,
which allowed the U-boats to resume their filthy work. Many ships
were lost in the mid-Atlantic Gap, the section of sea west of Iceland
where there was no air cover. Perched high on the upper deck in his
metal hut, Billy had to listen to the distress signal and hear the cries
for help and relay them to the bridge. The ship sailed on with the
convoy, leaving behind those red lights bobbing backwards in the
icy black seas, all hope of rescue gone.

By Easter we had run the gauntlet two more times and managed
to survive. We were given five days' shore leave at home while the
Cumbria underwent essential engine repairs. The news was grim
everywhere. Liverpool was taking a heavy pounding from the
Luftwaffe. So many ships were lost at sea. The war was going badly
on all fronts. Food and everything else was rationed and in short
supply. The mood on the streets was dark and ugly.

When we set sail again, I noticed a change in Billy. He was quieter and kept to himself more. He said that he was worried about his mother alone in the night. She was refusing to go to the street shelter that they had built at the end of her road.

The unofficial news from the convoys was bad. Some had lost over half of their ships in the bloodbath that was going on out here in the Atlantic. The Navy was stretched to breaking point, we could see that. Most convoys didn't have enough protection to fight off a sustained attack from a wolf pack of U-boats. They lay in wait in the safety of the mid-Atlantic Gap, beyond the reach of long-range bombers.

Everyone knew it, but no one was saying it. It was bad luck. A sailor who walks up a gangplank is giving his life to that ship. We bind our hearts and soul to a metal hull with a metal and wooden superstructure. We enter a machine world driven by furnace and piston, watched over by dials. Men work in tandem with the valves, pipes and metal galleys. Leaving harbour to sail the great oceans of the world, we face imminent peril on a daily basis.

Danger lurks everywhere, from the U-boats below, the Luftwaffe above, and mines floating like jellyfish on the tide. We live with the knowledge of the devastating nature of the sinking after a hit. Our lives are a random mix of dangerous elements with the potential for disaster never far away. That's why I never speak about it at home. They have enough to worry about with the Blitz getting worse by the day.

The crossing was hard. Five ships were lost and not a sighting of a U-boat. Everyone was relieved when Canadian planes were heard on patrol overhead. Most of the convoy was for Halifax in Newfoundland. Our ship was headed to New York, a place I knew well. Billy was astonished to catch sight of the lights of Coney Island blazing the message 'No war on here' to the world. The bright lights of the park were visible for miles as the *Cumbria* rounded the point and entered New York harbour. If the U-boats were ever able to come this far west they'd have a field day with the ships visible against the lights for miles out to sea. In my first years on the *Lancastria* I could never pass the Statue of Liberty without raising my arm in salute.

"She's a tough old girl, standing there in defiance through sun and wind and rain with her torch of liberty held as a promise pointing towards the land of her birth," said Billy, pretending to be a tour guide. "She stands as a reminder to us all just what we are fighting for."

He raised his right arm in salute as he spoke. I smiled. It was as if he had spoken my own thoughts out loud.

The ship stopped at Ellis Island, then sailed on to Manhattan Island for essential repairs to the engine, which was acting up again. We had a day's shore leave.

"After the war I'm going to bring Maggie over here," said Billy. "She has to see this. She'll love it."

We were standing in front of the Chrysler Building on East 42nd Street, amid the bustle of Manhattan. Billy shaded his eyes against the bright April sunlight that caught the crown and car radiator tops that dominate the building. It gave me a pain in my neck looking up at that gaudy building.

"You know Tom that for eleven months in 1931, it was the tallest building in the world at one thousand and forty-six feet, until they built the Empire State Building. Isn't she a thing of beauty? Did you know that they built four floors a week, can you imagine that?"

I remembered watching the progress of that building week-on-week from across the river in happier times, but I didn't say anything to Billy. I didn't want him carrying stories back home to Bootle.

Billy insisted on us taking the ferry out to the Statue of Liberty. When you have lived in a place in a previous life, been to a place many times, even one as hectic as New York, the novelty wears off. Walking the streets with Billy, watching his reactions and hearing his enthusiasm brought me back to when I saw the city for the first time. Then, a boy standing on deck, mouth open, I had watched the wonders of the New World rise up out of the ocean. Now it holds memories, locked like a tomb, that remind me of those happy years spent with the people I loved most in the world. Bright lights can deceive and blind the eyes, but not the heart.

"Do you think about the past much?"

On the ferry to the statue I was thinking of the thousands who had drowned when they sunk the great ship *Lancastria*. I had sailed on her so many times, with all her flags flying, proudly gliding past the Statue of Liberty and on into New York. I couldn't get a vision of her terrible end out of my head. Now she lies on the bottom of the Bay of Biscay, a giant coffin to unknown thousands that she had tried to save from Nazi tyranny.

The scene had been recounted to me once by an officer of the *Oronsay*, which, like the *Lancastria*, was a converted liner. Both vessels were taking part in Operation Ariel, to evacuate those left behind after the chaos of Dunkirk. The small convoy lay at anchor eleven miles off the shallow coast at Saint-Nazaire. For two days they had embarked thousands of civilian refugees and troops. They had stopped counting the number on board the *Lancastria* when they reached six thousand, but continued to embark thousands more.

The *Oronsay* had been bombed at about two o'clock in the afternoon, just as they were about to set sail for the safety of England. The bridge had taken a direct hit and immobilised the ship. The destroyer *HMS Havelock* had to stay with the *Oronsay*, so the captain of the *Lancastria* was faced with a difficult decision. Go without cover, or stay and risk being attacked. He decided against leaving without cover as he was carrying many thousands below deck. It would have been disastrous to be caught in open water by the Luftwaffe. He decided to stay.

The bombers were back just before four o'clock. They dived straight out of the afternoon sun and the ship took three fatal hits. One of the bombs went directly down the giant funnel and blew out the heart of the ship. Another struck a second fatal blow that opened a huge hole in the ship's side. She went under in less than thirty minutes.

The sea was transformed into an inferno. Those who could get off found themselves burning or suffocating in oil, or drowning in oil-filled waters. Most of the dead were trapped below deck. They stood no chance. I could feel the panic and confusion as I gripped the rail of the ferry. It was a disaster on an enormous scale. The other vessels in the flotilla did their best to pick up the survivors under a hail of machine gun fire from the planes overhead.

It was the greatest single loss of life in the history of the British Navy. That's what the officer said. My first ever ship. Gone and not a word about it. Dunkirk was disaster enough for the morale of the British people. The news of the loss was censored.

Billy was beaming from ear to ear. We were standing on the bare rock at the base of the Statue of Liberty. I braced myself for a history lesson. Instead, Billy produced two tickets that allowed us climb the internal staircase up to the windows in the crown. Billy raced up them. I followed as fast as I could. When we reached the top, I rested my hands on my knees and struggled to catch my breath.

"From here we are going to bring the light of liberty to the world," Billy declared.

He was standing again like a statue with his right arm raised. I smiled at his enthusiasm and naivety, but my heart was stopped by the size of that idea. The light of liberty was being shut out all over the world. For the first time in my life, it struck me that we might not succeed in this brutal war.

I believed for years that we needed America to help us defeat Hitler and the evil of the Third Reich. Not just helping us, but fighting together. If America really stood for freedom then it couldn't stand idly by and watch Britain being crushed by the forces of evil. The Statue of Liberty carries a light in her right hand. She tramples a shackle and chain, symbols of slavery, under her feet as she walks east, towards the Eiffel Tower that is under occupation.

"Do you think about death a lot?"

Death is an everyday thing. A ship goes down and thirty or forty, or often many more, are gone with it. Each number a statistic. Each ship a cog in a giant wheel. Each number a person with a life and a family back home going about their daily routine, under fire from the Luftwaffe, not knowing that their loved one has gone to the bottom of the ocean. Each family spends their days and nights dodging bombs and fires, scraping together an existence, only to hear by telegraph, *'Missing at sea, presumed lost.'* Then their whole world collapses, brought to its knees by those simple words.

I'll never forget the image of that woman in the street in Liverpool, holding her husband's head in her apron, looking at me with an expression of horror that no words can express. I don't like thinking about death, even though it's never far away.

America called itself 'The land of the free' and had a statue to prove it. If Britain went under, America would have to stand alone against Germany, with no land base in Europe. It was unthinkable. I repeated to myself the mantra, *'One step at a time, one day at a time.'*

"America will have to come in and help us win this war, Tom," said Billy. "A country that can build such a city can do anything. We have to stop those bastards before they kill us all!"

He was so excited, his energy was infectious. I smiled. For a Liverpool footballer, Billy was all right.

CHAPTER FOUR

September 1929

We met in the autumn of 1929, on a crossing of the *Lancastria* from Liverpool to New York. The weather was stormy in the mid-Atlantic as it often is, sending passengers to their cabins. Most of them stayed there for two days, not even surfacing to take meals.

I was assigned to Second Class, changing bed linen in the cabins, because so many were sick from the rough seas. When I rounded a corner, I saw her on her hands and knees, retching into the channel at the side of the deck. Her hair had fallen forward into the vomit that slopped from side to side with the roll of the ship. I dropped the soiled bed-linen that I was carrying down to the laundry store. When I returned to help her, she was gone. I found her sitting on a bench out on the side deck. Her body was bent double, her head low between her knees.

"Are you all right, Miss?" I asked. "You can't be out here. The sea is too rough."

I had to shout as the wind whisked the words out of my mouth and threw them overboard into the white and grey of the wild ocean. She never lifted her head.

With a groan, she rolled on to her side. I caught a glimpse of her face through the sticky strands of hair that stuck to her scalp. There was shocking purple and blue puffy flesh around her eyes and mouth. She was shivering from the cold or sickness, or both.

"Miss, come in and lie down. I've changed the sheets and blankets. You'll be much safer inside."

I shook her gently on the shoulder. She screamed, jumped up and backed away from me. Her reaction startled me.

"Katie, are ye all right? Is this fella botherin' ye?"

A young lad tried to grab me by the jacket, but he stumbled and fell as the deck swayed first up and back, and then sideways and down. I managed to grab Katie and pull her away from the rails, just as a wave broke over the bow of the ship. The shock of the cold spray was like a sudden slap, gone in a second. I lifted her and carried her inside. She suddenly went taut and threw up all over my hands and arm, and on to my trousers and shoes.

"What cabin are you in?" I asked. "You need to lie down."

I found out later in the voyage that the young lad was her brother, taking her to a new life in America. Away from some brute, by the looks of things, someone who took pleasure inflicting pain and suffering on a young woman. Even with the bruising and the sickness, it would take a blind man not to see how beautiful she was.

Later in the voyage, when the sun came back out and the wind dropped, I met them sitting in the sun, out of the breeze, near the swimming pool. Her bonnet was pulled forward to hide her face and her hair fell across the worst eye. She didn't look up when I said hello, but her brother introduced himself as Larry.

"Thanks for looking out for us," he said. "That was pure madness, what with the sickness and all. Have we much further to go? We'll be glad to get back on dry land again."

Now that I had a chance to look closer at him, Larry couldn't have been much more than fifteen or sixteen. As it turned out, he was fifteen, and Kathleen was seventeen back then, the same age as me. I caught a glimpse of her damaged face through the filter of her hair. She glanced at me for a split second, then turned away.

"I hope you're feeling better," I said.

Larry had gone to the Second Class dining salon, where they were holding a dance.

Kathleen shook her head, like the past was stuck in there and all this was just a dream. Her eyes darted from me to the deck, to the rail and on to the smooth rolling sea stretched in all directions. Landfall was still two days away. There was no dry land anywhere to be seen. The world was made up of water and sky. Many times afterwards, she told me that's what she was thinking at that moment, a world of water and sky with the land all gone.

We met up in Brooklyn, where her Uncle Frank on her mother's side had a butcher's shop. Larry was going to work there and learn the trade. They had an apartment over the shop that froze them in the winter and cooked them alive in summer. They didn't complain because they had food on the table, when so many others were starving after the Great Crash. Construction was down and unemployment was rife. Kathleen said that the Great Depression washed over the world like a massive wave that had come in and forgot to go back out.

She had a great way of saying things like that, but not in the beginning. Not a word was spoken to me in the beginning.

The *Lancastria* was sent for a major refit and as a result, I had a month's shore leave. Uncle Frank let me bunk down in a store room at the back of the shop. I was up every morning to help haul in the carcasses, carry out the bones and offal and generally help for an hour or two, depending on how busy things were.

Persistence and perspiration pay off in the end. That was a great saying of the Ma, who usually added something like, 'Even the dogs in the street know that.' The local priest in Brooklyn, Father Doyle, was Irish. He organised a dance every Friday night in the Church Hall. I went there with Larry the first weekend. Larry talked so much about it afterwards that when we said that we were going out to Coney Island on the Sunday after Mass, Kathleen joined us without a word. When we got off the bus, she refused to go on the Cyclone or anything else. Larry got mad.

"Katie, why come all this way if you're not going on the rollercoaster?" he asked. "What's the point?"

Kathleen turned and walked away towards the boardwalk. I gave Larry a couple of dollars and instructions to meet up at the bus station at five o'clock, and ran after her. I found her leaning over the railings, gazing out to sea. It was cooler at the beach and she shivered beside me. I offered her my jacket, but she refused. We walked most of the afternoon. I talked and she said nothing. I bought her a hotdog and twisty chips, which she took without a smile or a word.

It wasn't until the following week, when the purple rings around her eyes turned pale yellow and green, that a bit of a thaw set in. Larry had gone off with Uncle Frank to watch the Brooklyn Dodgers up in Ebbets Field. Kathleen slipped her arm through mine as we sat on the bus for Coney Island.

We sauntered along the boardwalk with the screech of gulls rising above the monotonous pounding of the shore. The hiss of waves, sucked backwards into the ocean, created an orchestra of sound. Sitting on the sand, she began to talk of the beatings, the abuse and the brute that she had left behind in England. She spat phlegm out of her mouth. I listened with clenched fists.

"Tell me about Kathleen. What was she like?"

Larry had told me most of their story during those first few days in Brooklyn. Kathleen was the only girl in a family of five boys. Her four older brothers looked out for her after their father died suddenly of complications from a burst appendix, leaving his pregnant wife to mourn and give birth to Larry within two days of his death.

There was never enough money until the boys went down the mine. Shortly after that, their mother died of galloping consumption. Kathleen was sent to her aunt in the country, who had a small shop in a village. The aunt married her off at sixteen to a local farmer, who cared more for his scrawny cattle than he did for any person, living or dead.

"So she's a married woman?"

She was when I met her. Uncle Frank locked up the shop and went home every evening at six. He was very proud of his newly built house in Queens, and rightly so. He was moving up in the world that was America, even with the Crash. His money was in bricks and mortar, he would say, and he was doing just fine.

One evening Larry was running a temperature and went to bed early. Kathleen and I were chatting and somehow got to kissing. But I was way too eager. I saw a look of terror on her face that stopped me in my tracks. I made coffee and we sat for a long time not saying very much.

Eventually, she broke the silence.

"Do you promise never to hurt me? Ever?"

The question hung in the air, smelling of raw meat and offal.

"Never in a million years," I replied. "It makes my blood boil to think of what he did to you."

"My brothers paid him in kind for what he did to me," she said.

She shivered, cursed and spat, in almost the same movement. Then it was gone from between us, like a burial at sea. She glanced at me and half-smiled, and the world turned blue in that back room butcher's shop, better than the Ritz.

We became friends that night. The kind that don't have to speak to be understood. When we kissed again, I could feel her body shaking. I held her long into the night, her shoulders rigid and her high back arched away from me. She never closed her eyes the whole time.

She might have scared me away in those early days, had I not been so young and inexperienced. I found myself following her movements any time she was about. I couldn't take my eyes off her, not even as she went up for communion at Sunday Mass. When she walked back along the side aisle she wore the faintest of smiles beneath the veil of hair that fell over her face.

After Mass, Father Doyle told her that he had recommended her to a tailor on Seventh Avenue in the city, who had agreed to give her a trial. Her aunt who had raised her had been a seamstress, and had trained her well in the arts of sewing, stitching, cutting and trimming. However, the 'tailor' turned out to be a factory churning out nurses' uniforms by the thousand. Most of the workers had little or no English, but they worked hard and didn't complain. They were glad to have a job.

The following Sunday, we took the afternoon bus to Coney Island and walked the boardwalk. She linked my arm the whole trip. We sat on the sand looking out to sea. She leaned her head on my shoulder. I put my arm around her and pulled her gently to me, and she didn't freeze. Instead, she laid her arm along mine, and her fingers gently moved forward and backwards on my skin. It drove me mad with desire, but I gritted my teeth and stroked her head gently.

She came to me when she was sure that Larry was asleep. It was my last night in New York. My shore leave was over. I would have to return to my ship the following morning. When I pushed her hair back off her face and caught it behind her ear, she tensed again, but only for a moment. I looked at her and she slowly raised her eyes and met mine. A red and yellow fire caught the glow from the dusty lamp. Her eyes searched my face. Then they opened a fraction, and the faintest trace of a smile crossed her lips.

CHAPTER FIVE

No one grieved at the news that Kathleen's husband was kicked to death by one of his animals. I was away at sea when the letter arrived. Larry told me that her hands shook when she read it. He said that she sat and cried tears of relief. The brute had been seen off by a raging bull.

Kathleen dusted baking flour off her hands, left a mound of dough that she had been kneading on the table and wiped away her tears. She told me later how she had grabbed her coat and cried all the way on the bus out to Coney Island. She had walked the boardwalk in the blowing rain, and tasted the salt spray that mixed with her tears. She was free. Truly free. Something stirred deep inside her.

She told me she threw her arms wide in an open gesture of embrace to the sea. A few people who walked by stared for a few seconds, and then gave her a wide berth.

Uncle Frank wanted to give Kathleen away in the Cathedral Basilica of Saint James in Brooklyn, in a ceremony conducted by Father Doyle, but she was having none of it. She and I went together to the City Clerk Marriage License Bureau and got our marriage license. I was the luckiest man alive. I knew it would kill my parents if they ever found out.

It was a simple decision to walk away from my life on the ocean and take up a job with the New York and New Jersey Port

Authority, working the cranes on the Brooklyn Piers. Uncle Frank knew a guy who knew a guy who gave me a start. I didn't need a second chance. The Da had taught me well.

We lived with Larry over the butcher's shop, saved what we could and made love late into the night. We went to Coney Island every Sunday after Mass, sat on the beach or walked on the boardwalk, until the morning sickness came and put a stop to the bus rides. After that, we sat on benches in the park or down by the East River, away from the heat of the city.

Kathleen set up a business at home. She soon grew a reputation for mending old clothes and making them look nearly new.

When the baby came early, and gave everyone a scare, yet somehow managed to survive, we christened her Grace. She had the face of an angel, one that would melt hearts. Apart from Kathleen, I had never seen anyone so beautiful. But we paid a high price.

Kathleen lost a lot of blood and had to have surgery. As a result, we were told she couldn't have any more children. She came back home after six weeks in hospital, a pale shadow of herself. I fussed over her and cared for the baby, while she turned her back on me in bed and cried herself to sleep. Things will get better, everyone said.

And they did, slowly. Grace grew into a strong child, healthy and quick. I spent more and more of my free time with her. On Sunday I would take her to the park and chase her round and round on the grass, while she tottered on her unsteady legs. I could make her squeal with a sudden movement towards her, throwing her into the air and catching her, while she laughed and gurgled with delight.

We developed a language of nods and blinks. A casual observer could be forgiven for thinking we were from an alien country. When Brooklyn Zoo opened in Prospect Park, we would spend the whole day there. Grace loved *The Jungle Book,* which I read to her every night. We would set off to see the lions, elephants and monkeys, and usually had a picnic at the seal pool, before finishing at the Bear

Pit. Grace named all the animals, and by the time she was six, could read about them on the noticeboard outside each cage.

But the only place that Kathleen would accompany us to was Coney Island. Temperatures were soaring on that Sunday in August 1936. Kathleen fussed over Grace, who didn't want to wear a sunhat, until I told her that if she didn't, we'd have to spend the day in the apartment and could only go out after the sun went down.

By the time we arrived, the main beach was full. We walked out towards Brighton Beach, before Kathleen was happy with the space to sit and gaze at the ocean. Grace ran in and out of the sea, and we built giant sandcastles with a moat, and channels for the water to flow through.

"Pops, can we buy some fankvurters fro Nahan's?"

Grace had lost her two front teeth, and the air whispered through them.

"Giant frankfurters from Nathans. World famous! Right away, my princess."

Kathleen was sitting up reading. I prepared the picnic, and then went with Grace to buy three frankfurters.

After lunch, Grace searched for buried treasure, and I worked on the moat around the castle. She filled it with water, which disappeared as soon as she had poured the seawater out of her bucket. She smiled at that and ran quicker to the water's edge. I built another castle and moat in the wet sand near the shore, and the incoming tide filled the moat and surrounded the castle. Grace sat inside the moat and watched with glee as the water flowed in and around her.

"Leh me ouh! I'm tlapped! Helf!"

It was time for ice-cream. Kathleen put a shirt and shorts on Grace, and insisted on her wearing the sunhat. Grace skipped happily beside me, and when we left the boardwalk, she held the three fingers of my left hand.

"Oh Pops, can I have a bawoon? Pease, Pops. Pease?'

I looked at her upturned face so full of light, red-blonde hair streaming strands down her back, her tiny hand holding the three red balloons that struggled to escape her squeals of laughter.

A precious moment.

CHAPTER SIX

April 1941

We sailed on the *Cumbria* out of New York harbour. I was glad to leave behind the teeming life of the skyscrapers of Manhattan and the wider sprawl of the great city. Glad to leave behind the memories of a world that was once my life. Here people lived freely every day with a vibrancy that was infectious. It was hard to believe that there was a brutal war being fought on the other side of the great ocean. We were part of an equally merciless battle being fought across the vast waters of the Atlantic which separated the two continents of America and Europe. They were worlds apart.

With the holds chock full of steel, every crew member knew that it was the very worst cargo to have on board in the event of a sinking. We'd be lucky to stay afloat long enough to launch the lifeboats. There was also a human cargo on this trip: six adults and two children. As First Officer, I had to oversee every aspect of life on board the ship. I was responsible for everything from stores to fire buckets, from lifeboats to the two-pounder gun mounted on the foredeck, and the machine guns mounted on the upper deck, either side of the radio shack. The guns were tested and the general alarm sounded when we were an hour out of port, sailing north towards the rendezvous point off Halifax.

As usual, the ship went into blackout as dusk descended in a soft light that merged the pale sky with the equally pale sea. The regular hum of the engines, and a gentle roll of the ship made for a pleasant first day and night. The sea is a peculiar kind of companion. It can lull you into a false sense of wellbeing, pretending to be your friend. It can welcome you with open arms, planting a soft kiss on both cheeks.

Mrs Ecklehurst and her two children, Jack and Jill, were to be given special treatment as she was a friend of the President, or so I was told. Her husband was a *New York Times* correspondent in London, and she was joining him there until the war was over. Mrs Ecklehurst made an impression on just about everyone. I had watched her on the quayside, her hand raised to her forehead to shade the sun, her eyes travelling the length of the ship, and then up to where I was standing at the top of the gangplank.

She wore a red blouse, buttoned low, which clung to her shapely figure in the breeze. Her long skirt swayed as she walked, revealing a slit at either side. It flowed over a pair of brown, cowboy type boots. She looked every inch a film star. She moved along the quay and up the gangplank, a woman walking in technicolour through a black-and-white movie.

Flanked by her side were two blond children. The three of them made a striking picture. As a group they reminded me of a film studio creation, designed to maximise the picture opportunities that the photographer who accompanied them snapped when the light was good.

The remaining human cargo comprised four businessmen who kept themselves to themselves. When the photographer, Jimmy Whitbread, made the mistake of photographing one of them, he very nearly lost his camera overboard, and certainly would have, had a crew member not been in the vicinity and stepped in to restore peace. The businessman growled something about national security, as a parting shot. Everyone got the message; leave these guys alone.

Billy taught the children Morse code on the gentle run up to Nova Scotia. They both took a shine to him, and he to them. Mrs Ecklehurst watched these proceedings from her deck chair, her dark sunglasses pushed high on her head. They nestled against a red and blue scarf, tied tight against the sea breeze that tried, and failed, to contain her long auburn hair.

'Dit dit dit, dah dah dah, dit dit dit.'

The two children chased each other around the upper deck, arms outstretched pretending to be planes. Billy busied himself in and out of the radio room, checking the equipment and signal lamps. Their mother had pulled her skirt sideways over her knees, as she sunbathed with her eyes closed against the bright light. The late April sun was teasing with a pleasant heat, if you could find shelter out of the breeze.

Billy found his eyes drawn to her. When he stood and stared for a moment, he was embarrassed to discover that she was watching him from under her sunglasses. Later, the wind shifted around to the north-east, and a decided chill sent everyone indoors for warmer clothing.

When Billy told me about this, it was with genuine puzzlement that he spoke about her.

"What is it, Tom? There's something about her. I can't explain but…"

"America is full of money, Billy. That's what money does. It buys you the best clothes and the best lifestyle. I hear that her family is loaded."

"And the best ships?" Billy laughed.

"No, that's what war does. Money will help you get away from war, but war is a great leveller. These fancy American women wouldn't last ten minutes in a blitz."

Billy smiled. I could see he was thinking of one particular British woman.

"And yet she's going to London, with her children."

"It's well out of London she'll be living," I assured him.

At dusk on the second day, the ship reached the assembly point off Halifax. We joined a convoy of thirty-four other ships of the usual shapes and sizes. The convoy had an escort of three Canadian corvettes, a destroyer and a converted fishing trawler – not nearly enough to give any kind of adequate protection from the menace of the U-boat wolf pack, whose numbers had grown at an alarming rate. The latest class was well capable of operating far out into the Atlantic. The U-boats lay in wait for their prey in the mid-Atlantic, then gathered into a pack and attacked in numbers from all sides, often from inside the convoy itself.

I hoped the British escort would prove to be much more substantial when the convoy rendezvoused with it at a point south-west of Iceland. In the meantime, we would have to live on our wits, and our prayers, as we chugged along at a steady ten knots into a strengthening headwind.

There was a decided chill in the wind, with more than a hint that it had passed over the ice fields of Greenland. The following day it whipped the Atlantic into a rolling sea through which the *Cumbria* ploughed and rocked and shuddered, making everyone on board who didn't possess sea-legs violently ill.

Mrs Ecklehurst and her two children, all the colour of dishwater, were confined to their bunks. The four businessmen did not stir for dinner. It started to snow. Visibility was reduced to the nearest ships in front, behind and on either side. The commodore signalled to all ships in the convoy to hold position and speed. The lookouts on the bridge were on full alert to make sure that we didn't collide with one of the other ships. It was easy to be blown out of position in the worsening conditions.

Winter had taken a bite out of spring. It poured an icy blast through the gap in the seasons to touch everything on board. It sent the ship forward, shuddering and shivering, as we ploughed through the monstrous seas. Freezing cold water swept over the bow and washed the lower deck clean. One slip and you would never be seen again.

For three long days and two longer nights, we were battered and thrown about by the storm. I brought meals to the passengers' cabins but, with the exception of Jimmy Whitbread, they remained in bed out of the cold and damp. It wasn't until the evening of the third day that the sea calmed down enough to allow them to get about without being in mortal danger of smashing open their skulls on a bulkhead. The storm had blown Arctic ice south, and we had to keep a keen lookout for that too. The commodore ordered a change of course south-east to avoid this latest half-hidden hazard. The convoy had lost two ships in the storm and one of the corvettes was sent to round them up. We were sitting ducks now if any U-boat was about.

The gods were with us this time. We reached the rendezvous point with the British escort without further incident, a day later than planned. We waved goodbye to our Canadian friends and hello to our own lads. It was special. For that moment, we were home. Billy carried the broadest grin on his face as he signalled a welcome to the corvette that bounced its way up and down off the starboard bow, protecting the southern side of the convoy. With only two corvettes and a destroyer to ward off the danger, we were very exposed to the threat of sinking from the wolf pack.

Billy was worried. He had been monitoring the radio, and although he wasn't allowed to broadcast for fear of betraying his position, he could listen in silence. The news wasn't good. U-boats were about, and there was the possibility of another storm striking in twenty-four hours. I left him to his tasks as I had a ship to see to.

The first one to go was away on the far side of the convoy. Even across the two-mile distance, we could hear the explosion followed by another bigger one, and then an enormous sheet of flame and a red angry glow against the night sky. The convoy sailed on. We lost two more ships within the hour. As dawn broke, their smoking wrecks could be discerned against the western skyline. There were no reports of any survivors, according to Billy.

Over the next twenty-four hours we lost a further six ships, in spite of the best efforts of the corvettes, who were trying to do an impossible task. The last to be hit was a huge Norwegian oil tanker, the nearest ship to us in the convoy. It was eleven o'clock in the morning. The torpedo started a fire that ran along the entire length of the ship. The crew gathered at the bridge as oil from the gaping hole in her side poured into the sea. Then she split in two, her propellers spinning madly in the air as the ship went sliding under at a frightening speed. Most of the crew jumped at that stage. They could be seen swimming slowly away from the vortex of water and oil.

The ship tilted to the almost vertical and sank in front of our eyes. Then the sea was on fire. The men in the water shouted for help, but everyone was under orders not to stop. The corvette went close, but the fire was now an inferno that engulfed even the strongest swimmers. We could hear their screams at the end. Not one made it.

I stood beside Billy and felt him shaking as we watched and listened. There was nothing to be said. Jimmy Whitbread was on deck busy with his camera. The four businessmen stood stony-faced on the upper deck. Mrs Ecklehurst and her two children stayed in their cabin, and were spared the horror. I prayed for the souls of the lost and cursed the scourge of the U-boat, wishing that the coming storm would hurry up and get here.

Blue-black clouds spread across the canvas of the western sky, obliterating the setting sun. It was a major Atlantic storm, which had tracked from the Gulf of Mexico along the Eastern American coastline. It then swung out into the Atlantic Ocean, on a path between Iceland and Scotland. The glass in the barometer dropped below twenty-eight, lower then I'd ever seen it fall. A mighty storm was coming up fast. The commodore signalled to change course to a heading south-south-east, and gave orders to maintain speed. That would be easier said than done.

By nightfall, the seas were rolling in giant waves across the bow. The skyline was lit by brilliant flashes of lightning that temporally blinded those on lookout. Then the rain and wind hit at the same time. Horizontal rain. Wind roared in from the dark and took away the breath of anyone brave enough to venture out. It howled like a madman all night long in the rigging, and in every nook and cranny of the ship.

I went to check on the passengers. They were all sea-sick and with the notable exception of Jimmy Whitbread, terrified. I tried to reassure Mrs Ecklehurst and her children that the storm would pass us by within twenty-four hours. The children were sick and scared.

It was the roughest weather any of us had ever experienced. There were many times when it was touch and go, when it seemed that the ship would be overwhelmed by the huge waves driven by hurricane force winds. In the end, the storm lasted two days. We had sailed much further south than planned in an effort to get out of its path, and now the rest of the convoy was nowhere in sight.

The chief took a reading with the sextant. The ship was two hundred miles off course. Billy listened, but there was nothing on the radio. No sight or sign of the convoy. We were alone on a treacherous ocean.

There was nothing for it but to make a run for the coast of Ireland, four hundred miles due east. Going full speed ahead, which for us was twelve knots, in a zig-zag pattern, would take the ship to Liverpool in four days. Everyone was on alert.

In the afternoon of the second day, we had a visit from an airplane. Billy was the first to hear it, a low drone that grew to a growl as the plane circled out of range of the guns. At first we thought it was one of our own, but were soon dispelled of that illusion. It was a Condor, a German four-engine long-range bomber.

The ship went to full battle stations, sounding the alarm, stripping covers off the lifeboats, arming weapons and distributing lifejackets.

Billy started to transmit an SOS Air Attack message letting others know that we were under attack from a plane. I called the passengers on deck and put life jackets on Mrs Ecklehurst and her two children. I squeezed the children in behind the bulkhead, mid-ship, with their mother standing guard over them. Jimmy Whitbread was somewhere about with his camera, while the businessmen refused to leave their cabins. As usual, they knew best.

The Condor dive-bombed in a sweep that brought it directly in front of the bow, at an altitude of three hundred feet. The ship was an easy target and our only real hope was to take it out of the sky with a lucky shot. The two-pounder and the machine guns opened up, and the plane responded with machine guns of its own. Then a bomb was released. A sickening explosion shook the ship to the core. It took out the bridge and everyone on it. The blast cut through metal and timber, sending shards of steel from the cargo, like shrapnel, in all directions.

A large part of the bridge infrastructure was blown back on to the radio shack located immediately behind it. The ship shuddered and lost all power. The bomb had dealt a fatal blow into the heart of the ship's command centre. Anyone on the bridge was now gone, blown to smithereens. I knew instantly that I was in charge of a ship sinking rapidly, well away from the regular shipping channels, a hundred miles from land.

The weather had settled down so that the sea was a steady roll. It was possible to launch the two lifeboats. What remained of the crew got to work as fast as they were able. There was a shout from the rear gunner.

"She's coming round for a second run!"

The gunner fired, and although he didn't hit the target, he managed to force the bomber to swerve at the last minute. The bomb fell short and landed in the water. The stern was lifted into the air with the force of the blast and one of the lifeboats went tumbling into the sea. The remaining passengers and crew gathered in the second lifeboat.

Mrs Ecklehurst stood shivering, an arm wrapped around each child. Her clothes had been blown off her by the force of the second blast. I put my jacket around her and left the crew to launch the lifeboat.

Billy.

I had to find Billy.

The damage to the bridge superstructure was massive. Twisted metal spars and steel plates had been ripped from their rivets on the bridge and thrown back on to the radio shack. A tangled mess sat on top of the roof and came tumbling down the front of the hut. I wriggled beneath a large section jammed against the door.

"Billy! Billy! Are you in there?"

A muffled shout was the only answer. One look at the wreckage and I knew that it was hopeless. It would need cutting equipment, and a team of men, and the one thing we didn't have – time. It would take hours to free this lot up.

Billy was ramming something against the door. After what seemed an age, the door opened a couple of inches and I could hear his voice.

"Tom, I've sent a message, and will re-send as per the protocol. You haven't much time. No chance of shifting this lot, I'm sure? You need to get everyone clear now. Tell Maggie I'm so proud of her...Tell her that I love her. And me Mam...tell her..."

I saw the lifeboat launch out of the corner of my eye. The ship was listing, and I could feel the tremble in the bowels far below deck. I squeezed myself further under the wreckage, pushed my arm in as far as the door and grabbed Billy's fingers.

"I'm here Billy. I'm not going anywhere. Do you ever pray? We could pray now if you like."

"Tom, I need you to get off this ship and safely back to Liverpool and tell me Mam and Maggie... Promise me, Tom. Look out for them for me. Now take this and get off the ship or we'll both go under. I can feel her slipping, Tom. Go, please. I'm begging you. For God and Maggie's sake, go."

He pushed a locket, like the one I had seen Mags wear around her neck, into my hand.

The ship was tipping and sinking fast. The metal above me took a jolt and shifted. We lost our grip. I knew that I had to go then or die with him.

"Maggie and your Mum are proud of you Billy," I said. "And so am I, my friend. God bless you."

There was no reply. I slithered out under the confusion of metal, and was suddenly stuck as my life jacket became snagged on a metal bar. I twisted as far as I could and wriggled back a few inches, but it was jammed. I undid the catch and freed my arm through the side of the belt. I managed to slither backwards, using my free hand to propel me, and finally my other arm came through, and I was out of the lifebelt. The ship was tilting fast. I scrambled across the sloping deck and launched myself off the side.

It was over in less than a minute. I dived off and swam as fast as I could away from the sucking vortex that was pulling the ship under. I never even felt the shock of the cold water, or heard the screams of the people in the lifeboat. They had moved away to a safe distance. I was pulled under by a current that grabbed at my arms and legs and spun me around and around until my lungs were searing with pain.

After what seemed an age, I found myself near the surface and a hand grabbed me. I was pulled on to the side of the lifeboat. Strong hands lifted me over the gunnels. The sky was bright white. I was coughing up water. By the time I was able to see again clearly, blinking against the light, the ship was gone. A jumble of wreckage and a small oil slick, rising and falling in the rolling sea, marked the spot where Billy and the *Cumbria* had vanished beneath the waves. The Condor was gone too, leaving the sky empty above the rolling waves that swept on by as if nothing momentous or unusual had occurred.

There was no time to dwell on the shock of what had happened. There was too much to be done, too many things that I was responsible for, that needed my full attention. I looked about. There were nine in the lifeboat. Mrs Ecklehurst and her two children, Jimmy Whitbread still clutching his camera, four of the crew, including two Chinese, one from the engine room, and the cook. That meant that fourteen, including Billy and the four businessmen, had gone down with her.

One of the surviving crew was an experienced sailor, a Norwegian named Rudvald whom everyone called Rudy. I put him in charge of the boat. He set a course due east for Ireland and set the sail. I stripped off my wet clothes and allowed myself the luxury of a shot of rum from the supplies on board.

Being in an open boat in a Force Three or Four south-westerly, a hundred miles from the nearest landfall, was a challenge, even for experienced sailors. The two Chinese men never stopped chatting to each other, their sing-song tone adding to the unreality of the situation. Mrs Ecklehurst was crouched shivering in the stern, her arms circling her children, who seemed to be bearing up well in the circumstances. The explosion had blown off most of her clothes. She had wrapped my jacket about her shoulders. Under that, she had nothing but a pair of torn briefs. The two children had been crouched down mid-ship behind a bulkhead when the bomb exploded and had emerged relatively unscathed. Jimmy Whitbread sat beside her at the stern, watching everything with the eye of a professional photographer.

Within an hour, my trousers and shirt had dried in the warm breeze. I insisted Mrs Ecklehurst put on the clothes, despite her protests. She had to be well enough and strong enough to take care of her children. I made do with my shorts and vest, and a blanket.

We divided the rations and ate a small meal of tinned sausages and ship biscuits. Water was restricted to a small cup each. One of the Chinese called Li had injured his arm. Rudy stitched it in the failing light with the expertise of a sail-maker. That was his father's trade back in Stavanger.

I had years of experience with big ships, but was a relative novice when it came to small boats. Rudy had sailed his whole life and was in his element. The boat responded to his expert touch. As evening fell, a shot of rum was given to all the adults. That brought the colour back to Mrs Ecklehurst's cheeks. She smiled her thanks when I checked on the two children a little later.

The watch was set and the boat settled into the rhythm of the great ocean. The sea was kind to us all night, and the next day. A cold, star-filled night was followed by a bright blue-and-white day. The wind held from the south-west and the current, the North Atlantic Drift, carried us on its journey north-east from the Gulf of Mexico towards the relative safety of Irish waters. We were afloat in a world of blue, each man, woman and child alone in their thoughts.

The children were a great distraction. Rudy showed them how to bait a hook and let out a line. The other Chinese man, Ling, was a cook. With the help of the small primus stove on board we were able to have a taste of fresh fish for lunch. The little girl, Jill, was running a high temperature so she was given a small drop of rum to help bring it down. Within minutes, she was laughing and singing *"On the good ship Lollipop."* She had to be restrained from dancing, but the song lifted all our spirits, and reminded us of happier times.

Things were going along well enough until the drone of a plane was heard in the distance. We all held our breath.

Both children grew hysterical when the plane came towards us. Their mother proved to be a lot more resilient than she had been given credit for earlier in the voyage. She wrapped one child in each arm, held them tight, and faced the threat with soothing words. Li and Ling were pointing and yelling "Plane! Plane!" as if the rest of us hadn't seen it.

The plane circled out of range of our firearms. Then it flew closer and waved its wings. It was a Sunderland Flying Boat of Coastal Command, a truly wonderful sight! The children's mood changed and they were now waving and jumping up and down. I had to grab Jack to prevent him from being lost overboard.

Four hours later, we were safely stowed on board the corvette, *Yellow Rose*, with our lifeboat in tow. It was only when I was seated in the tiny galley, with a cup of hot chocolate in one hand and a ship's biscuit in the other, watching the relieved faces around me, listening to the chatter of the children, that it really hit me for the first time. Billy was gone. I had only known him since Christmas, but he was Maggie's boyfriend, and I had grown to like him. He was a decent person, a kid at heart and a man at war, full of life and obviously in love with Maggie. Now he was at the bottom of the Atlantic.

What would I say to Maggie and Mrs Newsome? Maggie expected me to look out for Billy. She had said as much. Could I have done any more? Could I have cut through the tangle of metal to free him? But there was no time. The heavy cargo made sure of that. There was nothing I could have done. Anyone who sets foot on a ship knows the risk. Our lives are placed in trust into the hands of the gods. Everyone takes their chance.

I sat for a long time with my head in my hands. The sounds of the room and the noise of the ship bounced around me.

"Oh Pops, can I have a bawoon? Pease, Pops. Pease?"

Her upturned face so full of light, her red-blonde hair streaming strands down her back, her tiny hand holding the three red balloons that struggled to escape her squeals of laughter.

Somehow, they did escape. The spirit of air claimed them as its own. One split second they were there, the next they were gone. One split second she was holding the three fingers of my left hand, the next she had let go, so that only the impression of her hand remained. The three balloons floated off in front of the delivery truck that had skidded to a stop.

A woman screamed somewhere behind me and my princess, my precious, my treasure, my Grace, was no more. One split second she was there; the next, she was gone.

There was a red swelling at the side of her temple, otherwise not a mark. She looked like she was sleeping. The van driver collapsed at the side of the road. Then Kathleen was next to me, screaming and hitting me, while a crowd gathered round and the cops arrived. The day went dark, with just the face of Grace floating in the centre of the spinning world.

"Are you okay, Tom?"

Mrs. Ecklehurst was standing over me and put her hand on my shoulder.

"I wanted to say thanks, for what you did for me and my kids," she said. "We would never have made it without you. I'm sorry for Billy and the rest of your crew. He was just a kid himself."

I didn't look up, but she must have sensed that I was crying, because she put her arms around me, and held me like only a mother can.

Kathleen left me after the accident. She blamed me for not taking better care of our child. I would swap places in a heartbeat to have Grace live and me die. Every day afterwards was a death.

Kathleen took to the bed, refused to get up and rarely ate a thing. She couldn't look at me, didn't want to speak to me, turned away from me. The silence screamed across the bare apartment. In the end, Uncle Frank and Larry asked me to give her some space and time, maybe go back to sea for a while. That's how it panned out. I went to sea and when I returned to New York she was gone.

Frank shook his head when I told him I'd search for her. She was gone out west and didn't want to be found. She'd left no forwarding address. I blamed myself all over again for everything that happened, and for leaving her, even though it was Kathleen who left me. I heard from Larry since that she went to Milwaukee. If I survive this war, I'm going to start my search there.

"But you are still in the middle of a terrible war?"

With a heavy heart, I stood on the deck of the *Yellow Rose* as she entered Gladstone Dock. I blinked and rubbed my eyes at the sight of the city, shrouded in a thick, black pall of smoke. Fires were burning in many of the docks, and on towards the city. Pillars of choking smoke appeared to support the filthy cloud that covered most of the port, like columns in an ancient ruin. Liverpool was my city, but it was unrecognisable from the one that I knew. It was like sailing into a foreign country, a place of great catastrophe, where unimaginable terror had been visited on the population. The city was burning, abandoned by the gods.

For the record, it was Thursday 8th May 1941. My birthday. I was twenty-nine years old and lucky to be alive. I would have to make a report and see to the crew and passengers. There would be an inquiry, probably in the morning. With a bit of luck I may get up home to see the Ma and Da later today to deliver the bad news. Billy's death lay heavily on my mind. What can you say to a mother when you deliver such news? And Maggie? Poor Mags.

I opened the heart-shaped locket and stared at the two smiling faces resting in my palm.

Mags will surely be destroyed when she hears. But she must hear it from me.

Sky and Water

CHAPTER ONE

Maggie

There was a time when I believed that me and Billy would make a good life together when the war was over. It was a time that spanned the madness of war, even as my heart was blasted daily with the cold wind of death. A time when hope endured even as my soul was sucked from my body and splattered around the houses and air raid shelters of our little town.

There is no such thing as unconditional love.

There was a time when faith was blasted, splintered and scattered in the street, and the fabric of our lives flapped like faded yellow curtains, naked in the shattered remains of our bombed out homes. A time when dawn drew back the black curtain of night to reveal a city burnished in the overnight fires of hell; a city stretched to the horizon with burning, smoke-filled nostrils; sooty, black-rimmed eyes, and grimy hands battered blue and black. And teeth missing all across the face of the city.

Giant gantry cranes, their fists raised in defiance, stood along the margins of the Mersey. Rising from the fires and smoke to face a new day of toil, they reached their massive arms deep into the hearts of great ships, ripped the innards out, and scattered them to the warehouses and storage yards that crowded around the docks.

Among the sprawl of the river, the barrage balloons floated high, like alien suns watching coldly over the mayhem.

All hail the giant gods of air
Keep us safe in thy godly care
Give us this day
Give us

Love will get you eventually. It will eat at your heart, tear you apart and finally leave you broken and twisted. A heart of darkness.

And a time came when love was lost. When hope embarked with the ebb tide in the estuary and sailed, under a purple sky, out into the Irish Sea. Sailed away to oceans where dive-bombers swooped like seagulls above the decks, to where the deadly fin of the U-boat broke the surface in search of prey.

There was a time when I carried despair, hate and anger around like anchors, dragging my heart and holding it fast. I cried with silent screams to the Gods of Sky and Water.

It was a time when death walked our broken streets and poked its bony fingers into every corner of our town, stalking the smoking ruins of each morning. There men stood, exhausted from digging all night for bodies, blinking like miners in the cold morning light. They only stopped to listen when a cry was heard from somewhere below, or a limb was discovered under a pile of bricks, or to drink a cup of sweet tea.

The shadow of death went unnoticed at midday. It dodged beneath the rush of feet on the broken footpaths, as people scrambled to find food, water, shelter and clothes. The lunchtime shadow was content to snack on the scraps of random bombs, dumped by single raiders, returning from unsuccessful hunts at sea.

As the evening shadows lengthened, the spectre of death queued at the communal shelters and hung around the doors of factories and warehouses. It could be seen cowering under the arches of bridges, and huddled on the buses, trams and trains. It gathered its coat about itself on the ferries chugging on the river. The spectre sat on the Anderson Shelters in the gardens of homes in the town, and peeped in the windows of houses and tenements.

Death waited patiently in the narrow cobbled streets, in the shadow of the Overhead Railway, as it ran the length of the docks. Death lingered on the quays and harbours of the great city, heaving with toil and the sweat of trade, the smudge of oil, and the smell of life smeared with fear.

This was the time when the shadows lengthened and stretched their elongated forms away from the setting sun. The city was flooded with a terrible light under a bloody sky. If hell exists, I thought, it must surely look like this.

Then came the darkness.

And so it begins.

CHAPTER TWO

Death and destruction. Bootle, our town, is broken. Street after street, broken. Bombed-out is the wrong term. Bombed-down more like. Guernicaded, that's what. If that's not a word, it should be. Or Bootled now. A new definition: 'To be bombed from the air until there is nothing left of the civilian population and practically all buildings and homes are destroyed.'

This week alone, hundreds of people in our town have been killed and hundreds more injured. It would have been thousands if the majority of the people hadn't already moved out. What had we done to deserve this? Josie Morris and her family and now Mrs Newsome, Billy's Mum Bess, Father Breen and so many more. And that's just in our town.

I saw them all last night, all those dead neighbours and friends, marching in a line up at the factory, helping to fill the bombshells to send back to Hitler. It was a strange dream. I woke up shaking in the sticky morning air. I could hear their croaky breathing and feel their bony fingers on my arm. The mind can play funny tricks, especially with the emptiness in my chest. My hands don't seem to be part of my body at all. There's a constant battle to keep the fog that lingers around my brain from clogging up my thoughts.

The May Blitz. That's what the papers are calling it. Eight nights of continuous bombing. Eight nights of hell. Most people have moved out of town. Their homes are either destroyed or so badly damaged that major repairs are needed before they can be lived in again.

Production has dropped by forty percent at the factory this week. It's been a bad week all round. Losing the shipment for Egypt was a setback, but we have a replacement ship fully loaded and ready to sail with a convoy later today. That's kept me busy, and it's good to be busy. The trams are only running to the outskirts of the city. Cycling is dangerous in the hours of darkness, but those hours are few this May and they pass quickly.

I went round to the church this evening after work. It's been boarded up with 'No Entry' and 'Dangerous Building' signs. I slipped in the back entrance and sat on a dusty bench. The altar was intact, completely untouched. If Father Breen was right, and the bombs were Satan's work, then the devil has done a good job. He got the right people. Mrs Newsome was his enemy because she helped her neighbours, those less well-off, and those who had nowhere to live. Father Breen looked out for the welfare of the old and the young. Satan must have had it in for him in a big way. Nearly forty of them. Older men and boys on fire-watch. Women on WVS duty, hiding in a hole in the ground. But the bombs found them.

What will Billy be like when he hears the news? I have to tell him myself before he hears it from some of his neighbours. There's going to be another mass burial, bigger than Christmas. Thousands are dead across the city, and thousands more injured. Hundreds of thousands homeless and scattered. We're a lost people.

Down in the city there are soldiers on patrol, many looking scared, because there's an ugly feeling about on the streets. A lot of them are younger than Billy. Rumours abound that looters have been shot, that there were fights over food and water. Things were bad as Dad would say. Dad! Still no sign and it's been nearly a week. He must have been injured. I'm going to go around the hospitals again tomorrow.

The lists of the dead and their funeral arrangements are in the papers every day. Women and children, babies and older men not at war, and sailors home on leave. Gone. They even bombed Walton Prison. Almost twenty died inside that hellhole. Merchant sailors who missed their ship; drunk and disorderly behaviour on the streets of our city; someone taking a can of food from the docks; all locked up for the night… Then blown to kingdom come.

There was no raid last night so maybe they'll leave us alone for a while. The streets of Bootle were almost deserted this morning. It's an empty ghost of a town. Most people are now sleeping out of the city, in school halls in country towns, or in farm buildings, or under ditches. Walking, cycling or travelling by bus, they head back into the city at first light.

The whole city is coiled like a spring, wound so tight it could snap at any moment. Long lines form at the rumour of food. Ugly scenes develop if someone tries to skip the queue. These are homeless, hungry, desperate people.

I miss my home, and Dad and Mum. Tom and Billy will be back any day now. I have to hang on until they get here. *Keep calm and carry on.*

Then everything will be all right again.

CHAPTER THREE

There are moments in my life that I will never forget. Pictures become embedded in my brain, like a projected image burned on to a white screen. I saw, in the failing darkness and from halfway down the street, the outline of the familiar figure sitting on the steps of our broken home. My whole being leaped in joy. All the tension of these past weeks evaporated, like a flock of doves, suddenly released to give thanks to the heavens. Tom!

I ran as fast as the broken pavement would allow. Tom slowly stood up and I jumped into his arms.

"Oh my God, Tom…"

The words caught in my throat.

"Mary has had a baby that she called Billy, and Mum has taken them to Johnny's cousin out beyond Ormskirk, out of the way of the bombs. Dad is missing nearly a week, and we don't know if Matt and John got on their ships or not. The crypt was hit by a bomb and Mrs Newsome, Billy's Mum, and Father Breen and nearly forty others were killed. It's been a nightmare here waiting for news, Tom, and… Oh, it's so good to see you."

Tom caught my shoulders, pulled me back off him and held me tight, but at arm's length.

His eyes were those of a stranger.

"You have to be strong, Maggie. We're not going to let them break us, you hear?"

There was something in his voice that touched me, and I almost stopped breathing. He never called me Maggie unless I was in trouble.

"I did everything I could, Maggie. I stayed with him till the end. But he was trapped inside the radio shack, and the ship went down in less than a minute. There was no chance to get him out. He was as brave as a lion, and said to tell you he was so proud of you, of what you're doing. He gave me this to give to you."

Tom unfurled his fingers. The locket that I had given Billy at Christmas lay in his palm. I looked into his eyes and saw his pain. It was the worst of my fears come true. I knew then that it was real. Billy was gone. The world would never see his smile, his bright eyes and his strong body again. My love was dead. Billy was dead.

A strange noise escaped my mouth, like that of an animal mortally wounded, howling in surprise in a dark forest clearing. The pain filled my being, and my legs didn't seem to want to hold my weight. Darkness fell all around. The world was spinning. I couldn't catch my breath. My head felt dizzy, and my whole being went weak.

"Billy? Dead?"

"I'm so sorry, Mags. There was nothing anyone could do. He was so brave."

"Brave? Did you say brave? Damn him! And damn you!"

I hit out at Tom, beating him on the chest. Then I screamed. It came from somewhere deep inside, from a place I had kept locked up safe inside me, where no bomb could touch, until now. I felt myself being pulled into a black vortex at the heart of my being. It was the end.

Tom must have held me, because the next thing I knew I was through the broken house and out into the shelter. Once there, he wrapped his strong arms around me. He held me like that, long into the night.

I woke in the lamplight of the shelter out of that terrible nightmare. I'd had many nightmares before, but this one seemed so real, so frightening. Then I heard the breathing. I saw the outline of Tom sitting upright, asleep on the bench opposite my bunk. A wave of pain, fear and nausea hit me. I scrambled to the bucket at the back of the shelter and emptied the contents of my stomach into it. I was crying vomit out my mouth and my nose, until there was nothing left to come up. Still the nausea came, in violent bouts of dry-retching. Tom stood watch over me, pressing his hand into my back, holding my head, with his fingers rubbing my temple. I never wanted to open my eyes again.

Later, I lay on the bunk with the curved roof of the shelter closing over me. I was sticky with sweat, and strands of hair were stuck to my forehead. Please God, let a bomb hit me now and finish this once and for all. But there was no raid. No bombs. The door of the shelter was open. Someone was sponging my face and neck. I blinked and looked into the eyes of my mother.

"There now, Maggie love."

She leaned over me and kissed my forehead.

"Mary and Billy are doing just fine. They send their love."

"Billy?"

I cried for a long time then. The locked door of that secret place was blown wide open, and I let it go without trying to hold back. Mum held me and let the pain fill the shelter, until I was nothing more than an empty shell.

"There now, Maggie love."

CHAPTER FOUR

It was evening when Tom came out to the shelter with a piece of good news. He had organised a place for us to move to, up beyond Anfield. It was a house, which meant we could all stay together, near enough that the boys could get to the ships and I could get to the factory.

Mum never said a word about losing her home. Her mouth was set shut in a kind of friendly grimace that could turn sour with the flick of a switch at the mention of the war, or Germans, or the fact that we now had nothing. The one thing that wasn't mentioned was Dad.

I got up, collected my few belongings that were left and pushed my bicycle out the road, with a scattering of things balanced on the back. Tom had commandeered a hand truck and filled it with the remnants of our lives: photographs, pots and pans, the contents from the Anderson Shelter, and little more.

The evening was warm and a pale blue sky mocked us up the gentle rise of Breeze Hill, and on beyond Goodison to the higher ground at Anfield. From there you could see the ruins of our town. The docks on both sides of the river still smouldered in places. Across the river in Birkenhead, cranes worked in the dockyards. There was movement on the river. A convoy had arrived and was dispersing to the docks that were still open. The business of the port and the business of war went on.

I turned away. So many people had lost loved ones. There would be a mass burial again. This time it would be huge. This time.

There had been no more bombings. The city was able to breathe once more. Our town was another matter. It was destroyed, with hardly a street that hadn't been badly damaged. People returned from the country to find their homes destroyed, or their roofs gone, or their houses condemned as unfit for habitation. There was no sewerage, no gas and no water. In some parts there weren't even any roads. Almost thirty thousand people from the town were homeless. Our own home was classified as 'badly damaged but repairable.' The houses on the other side of the street were deemed 'beyond repair' and would have to be demolished.

The docks were more down than up.

I got all this from Tom, while I sat eating my breakfast in the half-light of early morning. The food tasted like cardboard. Tom had been systematically checking every hospital across the city. He heard that some injured patients had been brought to hospitals outside the city, even as far away as Warrington.

Some people were beyond words, and that was me. I kept what I had to say for work, checking orders and giving instructions, ticking boxes and seeing that the dispatch operation recovered from the setbacks of the past few weeks. I was called in to the office.

"Maggie, I'm sorry to hear about the troubles in Bootle," said my manager. "I understand that you have lost people close to you, family and friends. Please accept my condolences."

He put out his hand and I shook it. Then, with a nod of his head, he changed the subject.

"Production is down, as you would expect, but in spite of everything you have managed to keep up the schedule at your end. I just wanted to say thank you and well done. I will meet with your team this afternoon as they go off shift to let them know. You can be very proud."

I liked talking about production. It was the closest thing I got to actually firing one of these shells, or dropping one of these bombs. I loved to see the lines of shells turned into bombs, loaded on to a ship or train and sent on their way.

I loved my job.

All the bombs that had fallen on us, all that had happened to me, and to our city and our town, only served to make me love it more. It was the reason I got out of bed in the early hours of the morning and walked in the half-light to catch the Simonswood tram. It was why I worked extra shifts, when necessary, without complaint.

I didn't want to hear about Mary, and her baby who had colic, and how she was back home in her own place. I didn't want to hear when Tom confirmed that Matt and John had sailed with their ships on that dreadful morning when the *Malakand* exploded. I didn't want to know that they were as safe as you can be at sea in this mad war, when in reality you weren't really safe anywhere. That Luke and Pat were due back in port tomorrow. What did it matter?

"The Lord Derby War Hospital, north of Warrington, was used to evacuate wounded during the May Blitz."

Tom was talking to Mum, who had just made a pot of porridge and was dishing it out to us in the cool that you get in the early mornings of late May. The strangeness of our new home was softened in a yellow light that shone through the open back door. Someone else's home, with ghosts on the stairs that creaked in the night. Mum stopped her chores for a moment. She pushed back a strand of hair that had fallen across her face. I could see that her eyes were shining. Was it tears, or anger? She had never said a word about Dad, not since the ship blew his dock apart.

Everything was destroyed in the Huskisson Dock, blown apart. Docks, warehouses, ships, cranes, quays. All gone. In their place were heaps of broken metal and piles of bricks. They were twisted into gruesome shapes by the force of the blast and the ferocious fire that followed. It truly was a scene from hell.

I stood looking at the devastation all around me, and tried to take it in. My hands shook as I held on to the clipboard and waited. The soldiers gave the all-clear to a few bombs that had sunk with what was left of the ship's hull into the dock, and hadn't exploded. Like children rescued from a lifeboat, after a terrible ordeal following a great catastrophe, these bombs were hauled on to the remnants of the dock from the oil-filled water.

"Have you had any word on your father, Maggie?"

I looked at the weary face of the Chief Fire Officer. It was a face that had seen too much death and destruction.

"My brother Tom is checking the outlying hospitals in the off-chance that he was brought out to one of them," I said. "Thanks for asking, Chief."

It was the morning of the burial. Tom had taken a look in Anfield Cemetery where a trench a hundred yards long and twenty yards wide had been dug. The remains of over eight hundred men, women and children, were to be placed within that vast space. Three hundred of them had not been identified. Tom had taken a look at all of them as far as I knew. Bits of Mrs Newsome. Bits of Father Breen. All mixed up. What did it matter now anyway?

After work I cycled out to Our Shore. It was good to be alone with the high blue sky streaked with wisps of see-through clouds that veiled the heavens in places. I found a quiet spot out beyond the bunker and parked my bike. I sat on a sand dune and let the soft sand invade my toes. I could see the glint of barbed wire standing exposed by the ebb tide. The beach was reported to be mined and it was now forbidden to bathe.

I wanted to feel the wet sand under my feet. I hitched up my skirt and set off walking in long strides towards the water. There was a shout from the bunker, but I ignored it. I could see a convoy stretched across Liverpool Bay. The lead ships approached the Queen's Channel. They had made it safely home. Another shout. Someone ran down the beach behind me. I was close to the wet sand now. Shining coils of barbed wire were suspended by rusty metal and wooden supports, each one leaning like a drunk against a lamp post. Cool rivulets ran around little diamond-shaped islets of sand. I anchored my toes, like diggers, into the soft earth.

I looked at Our Shore, at the sea that ran away beyond the barbed wire, through the line of ships, and on out to the horizon.

"Billy!" I cried.

But the name did not come. It was just a sound like a ghost caught in the sea breeze, carried away to the wisps of clouds that ran out over the horizon.

"Miss, stand still. Don't move. There are mines about. Be careful where you put your foot."

He was panting. A trickle of sweat ran down his face from under his helmet. His eyes were pleading with me to take hold of his outstretched arm.

"You can't be out here, Miss. Come along with me now."

Another soldier stood behind, his gun at the ready.

I dropped the flowers into no man's land, flowers that I had gathered by the roadside at Our Shore. It was astonishing that flowers had bothered to grow in the middle of all this, but they had.

I turned my back on the cruel sea. The soldier took my arm and walked me back up the beach. The sergeant took one look at my face and softened. He offered me a cup of tea and sent the other lads off to collect my bicycle and my shoes.

No words were spoken. He put a cup of sweet tea into my hand. The warm, sugary taste filled my head with thoughts of home. But where was home? Our home was gone and our loved ones with it.

It was time to go.

I smiled my thanks through watery eyes.

With the sea breeze at my back, I cycled away from the shore.

There would be no more tears.

CHAPTER FIVE

Miracles. That's what's supposed to have happened wherever Christ went. Curing blind men and lepers. Casting out devils. Feeding the hungry with loaves and fishes. Changing water into wine. Raising dead people back to life.

I don't believe in miracles anymore. I've seen too many dead people stay dead, and hungry people stay hungry. Too many. They're just stories from a time of superstition, written down many years after the events themselves. People have a great capacity to reinvent the past to suit their own purpose.

These days Mum spends most of her time reading the bible, when she isn't out with her WVS duties. The church hall is being used again to home those who had none. It was turned into a temporary church on Sundays. A new priest, Father Hickey, took Father Breen's place. I didn't want to go up there.

Then a true miracle happened.

Tom was shipping out on Monday and had decided to use his last afternoon of leave to check out the hospital in Warrington. I'd never been to Warrington.

I knew that the glass roof at Lime Street Station had been badly damaged at the beginning of the May Blitz. I hadn't been in there since that day in March when they had marched the U-boat Captain Kretschmer and his crew from the prison. They came down through the city centre, and up to the station to catch a train to London, where the top brass were waiting to interrogate them. Billy was home on leave that week. He dragged me down to see the captain, and told me that he was a hero in Germany. He had sunk many of our ships, but had been caught napping by the destroyer *HMS Walker*, and sunk out in the Atlantic. Billy insisted that we go down early to get a good view.

It is possible to feel hate. I don't mean my own. There was hate in the air that day. Light rain fell like spittle from a grey sky. Thousands of women lined the streets, filled them with their anger and pain. Here were Germans in the heart of our city, Germans who had taken away our sons, husbands and fathers. They had destroyed our homes, schools and churches. Because of them, our children were sent away to the country. They had terrorised us from the air, and from under the water.

There was a communal shout as close to pure hate as it would be possible to feel. People had their arms outstretched, pointing an accusing finger at Captain Kretschmer. He held his head in the air like some kind of conquering hero, instead of a prisoner of war. He was young, and probably considered good-looking back in Germany. He looked like he was smiling. The sight of him drove the crowd mad. There was a push forward, and some of the children threw stones that missed. He would surely have been torn asunder, had we got our hands on him.

The police moved as quickly as they could to stop the stone-throwing, but they couldn't stop the wave of pure hate that followed the crew into the station. I remember how Billy had shouted with the rest of us, only louder. He shook his fist in the air and let out a kind of howl. After all, he had seen the U-boats in action. I howled too, as loud as I could.

On Sunday I went with Tom and stood on that station platform under the partly shattered roof. I needed to get away from our temporary house, full of old ghosts from someone else's life. Being with him brought me closer to Billy.

"Mags, the Lord Derby War Hospital was used to evacuate some of the wounded during the May Blitz. There may be a chance he's out there."

I had learned not to get my hopes up.

It was a bright, sunny day in late May. The hospital was out in the country where hedgerows were buzzing with insects. Bees and birds spent their time flitting here and there. Overhead, trees were bursting with new leaves.

The building was originally built as an asylum. It had the look of a mad house. Once they got hold of you inside those thick red-bricked walls there would be no end to your stay. The inmates had been shipped out to other "loony bins" (Mum at her best) and it was now a war hospital, nursing the wounded from the nearby army base.

I wasn't getting my hopes up. I had spent many fruitless days searching in and out of hospitals all over the city, with no luck anywhere. It was as if Dad had vanished off the face of the earth. If he had been in that dock when the ship went up...

I sat outside on the grass in the warm sunshine while Tom went in to make enquiries. I was thinking of the time before Easter when I went with Billy on a picnic into the countryside. We had parked our bikes out of sight behind some trees at the base of a steep hill. A path hidden in the undergrowth wound its way up to the crest. At the top there was a clearing with bushes and trees all around us like we were in another world.

"No one will disturb us here," he said.

Billy had brought a blanket, and I had a basket with sandwiches, a drink and some biscuits. I could feel him tense when we kissed. I laughed and lay back and opened my cardigan. Billy took it as a sign. We lay there for what seemed like hours in each other's arms, kissing and caressing each other.

"We have to wait Maggie," he said. "We'll be married as soon as this war is over."

I wished I had that afternoon to live over again.

Tom came back with a strange look in his eyes. His voice cut through my dreaming like a bomb.

"Mags, you won't believe it. I've found Dad. He's inside. A bit shook up, but not seriously injured. He's lost his memory though. Doesn't know who he is. Took a heavy blow to the head, according to the nurse in charge."

Tom looked every bit the brave officer who had been awarded a special medal by the king. The newspaper reporter had arrived up at our new home. He asked Mum what she thought of her son being awarded the George Medal, for "outstanding bravery and leadership under fire at sea." Mum didn't know anything about it. Wasn't that just typical of Tom. The report in the paper the following morning was under the banner headline: *'George Medal for Local Hero'*. The sub-heading was *'Mother knew nothing about it'*.

Typical Tom.

Dad was in a ward at the end of a long corridor. Tom had spoken to him for a few minutes. He told me that Dad had forgotten his own name and history, his family, his home place. I had heard that a blow to the head can do that to you. Without thinking, I raced across to the bed. I was about to launch myself at Dad, until I saw his bandaged forehead and the empty look in his eyes. Tom put his hand on my arm.

"Da, this is Maggie, your daughter. I'm Tom. Your name is Michael Brady. Your wife is Margaret Brady. She was Margaret Byrne before you married her. You have ten children. Me, Tom, I'm the eldest, and Maggie here is the youngest. In between you have John, Luke, and Martha who's a nun, and Liam, Matt, Pat, Peter, and Mary who's just had a new baby, Billy."

Dad looked confused. A nurse came over and said we would have to leave, as too much information all at one time wasn't helpful. Tom wanted to get Dad discharged straight away, but the nurse said to wait and see if our visit might start to bring back his memory.

"Come back in a few days, and bring some papers, or a photograph," she said.

I tried to find out what had happened to him, but no one on duty knew. He was brought in, they said, with hundreds of others on that fateful Sunday morning of May the Fourth. It was probably as a result of the explosion on the *Malakand*. He had no jacket with him, which explains how he had no papers, as he always kept them in there with his pipe.

I suppose that I was happy to see him. I just didn't *feel* happy. I didn't feel anything.

On the train journey home, Tom was silent and that suited me. We had found a shell of a man that looked like Dad, but there was nothing inside. The filling was missing. The nurse said to remain patient, that a positive result would probably come.

How could I remain positive? It was all my fault. The ship. All my fault.

I would gladly swap places. To be emptied of all memory.

I have decided to work nights from now on.

CHAPTER SIX

Summer 1941

I don't remember much about the summer of '41. The bombs stopped falling and I began to work nights and sleep during the day. Mum started calling me Mole at some stage, and the name Mo stuck with her. The boys were mostly at sea. The news was continuously bad everywhere. Dad came home after a month, and was able to remember most things "when it suited him," Mum said. He went back to work and the house settled down to a sort of rhythm.

There were times when it was filled with the voices of sailors, returned from the perils of the sea, and times when it held its breath waiting for news.

I was getting ready to go to work one evening. The boys were eating dinner. The talk was always of the war.

"Just because Hitler has invaded Russia doesn't mean he won't try to invade us here. And Liverpool will always be a target for the Luftwaffe."

Liam was home for a week having been in the Mediterranean as far as Malta. It hadn't gone well, as far as I could gather. He looked worn out, with rings under his eyes. I'd never seen him like that before.

"If Hitler was going to invade he would have done so this summer. There's no chance of that happening now. He's moved his attack force east. Even he can't attack Russia and Britain at the same time. He's pinning his hopes on starving us into submission."

"Starving!"

Tom's earnest face burst into a great smile when Mum put the dinner on the table in front of him. He jumped up and gave her a twirl about. She hit him with Sting, but you could see she was delighted to have some of her boys' home.

If it is the case that love exists separate to ourselves, a force of good in the world, then the opposite must also exist. That makes sense now. Hate and love must balance. If you can love, you can hate. They're the opposite sides of a coin. Flick it in the air and it lands on Love. Flick it again and it lands on Hate.

I had another name for it: production. We made bombs for aircraft to drop on targets, shells for artillery guns and shells for tanks. Every night I organised the next day's delivery, checked, cross-checked and packed, ready for shipment. Lines of shiny messengers that would send out our love to the enemy. *Many happy returns!*

The earth spun into autumn and on into winter. The nights grew long and cold. Jerry had only on a few occasions returned to bomb the docks, but nothing like what had happened in May. If the truth were known, the whole world was on edge. Our home was being repaired and Liam had had a good look. He declared that the Germans had done us a favour. We were getting back a much improved house.

The war in Russia was going Hitler's way and he was reported to be on the outskirts of Moscow. For once the sea had been our friend. Most of Europe and North Africa was lost. Then another miracle happened. Pearl Harbour. The United States of America declared war on Japan. Germany and Italy declared war on America. According to Tom, who has been in America lots of times, and had lived there for a good few years, this was the one thing that could save us. I had listened to endless arguments about this in the kitchen.

"Now we have a real chance, Da. Just wait and see. We can beat Hitler yet."

Dad scratched his head and the mark of the scar over his ear was angry red from the cold. My heart burned with the hunger for revenge. Maybe now it would be our turn to make them pay for what they had done to us. For Billy's sake.

After work, the next morning, I cycled out to Our Shore. It was a bitter December morning with a raw sting bringing the cut of Arctic ice on the wind. The sea and sky were joined as one in a grey-and-white moving canvas. The Americans were out there somewhere.

"The Yanks are coming."

That's what the girls in the factory were saying. They were thinking of them as men, flesh and blood. Men who could bring you on a date and give you a kiss, and more. Men who were good dancers. Men who might give you a present of stockings, or chocolate, or cigarettes.

I thought of them as killing machines. Millions of them, with the best of equipment – ships, aircraft, tanks and guns, and soldiers. This was a war machine that would be carried across the angry sea and make landfall here in this very place. The Americans would have their own bomb-making factories, but we would need to make even more now. For Billy's sake.

The soldiers watched me from their bunker, but I had no intention of stepping foot on the beach. I stood and faced the icy blast that stopped my breath and made my eyes water. I had never before noticed that the sea could look so cold. The sky was a dirty grey, but the sea was a grey-black, heaving monster which spewed the white tops of its waves on to the beach. Such a cold, watery grave.

I shivered and turned my back on the coast. The cycling was easy, with a strong wind behind me. I could feel Billy's hand on my back, pushing me home to bed.

CHAPTER SEVEN

December 1941

That Christmas fell hard on us.
Shall I compare thee to a summer's day?
I was done with Shakespeare. Nothing lasts forever. I had learned that much the hard way. Not life nor hope nor... But what about love and the memory of true love? Sometimes, in the cold light of morning on my way home from work, when I was sat on the tram with my eyes closed pretending to sleep, I couldn't see Billy's face clearly. It was fuzzy at the edges, a photograph in memory with a smudge, out of focus. Then I'd panic and grasp our lockets that I carried around my neck. I'd open his, and look at the smiling faces of the two of us that day in the city before the world went dark, and I could breathe again.

Mum was mad at me, I knew. But I couldn't make myself go to see Mary's baby and listen to her love talk to him and call his name, "Oh Billy, Billy, Billy..."

I felt like a useless sister. Mary might never forgive me and I wouldn't blame her for that.

The memory of last year's Christmas twisted in my gut like a bayonet. Not the bombs falling, or our house damaged, or my dress. What do I care for a stupid dress anyway? No, none of that. It was the sweet memory of that day in our old house that had been bombed and patched back together, like the fabric of our lives. Me and Billy going to check on his house and our few precious moments together, before we were stilled by those filthy thieves. And afterwards, Christmas dinner with Billy and his mother joining us. Everyone smiling. We were a real family in that oasis we called home.

I remembered Dad carving the turkey, with all his wits about him, not like now, as Mum would say... Billy being handed around the family with a red face. If he was nervous, he didn't show it. The sweet smell of turkey and stuffing filling the room. Talk of football and the shock of Billy even thinking of playing for Liverpool. Giving Billy his locket as a present so that we could always be together. Why did he give it back to Tom in those last moments on the ship? Was he trying to save me the pain of what was to follow?

What was he thinking in the seconds after Tom left him, the tilt of the room already a steel coffin? Sliding towards that watery grave, and the great noise of the water sucking him to his death?

What was he feeling as the slimy water filled his room until there was nothing left but sea? Then the cold terror must have hit him in those panicky moments, with no escape from the choke of water, the searing pain in his chest, and his last thoughts of me.

I love you Maggie. I will always love you.

You have one life and one love.

Tom had told me all about their days in New York, how Billy was so excited and wanted to take me there, so that he could show me the skyscrapers and visit the Statue of Liberty together; how he had taught the two children on the ship Morse code.

I often closed my eyes in bed in the mornings after work. These scenes played out in my head, in the dreamy time before sleep overtook me. Then I would jump with a fright as I'd feel a cold slap of water hit my face. There would be Billy, the last breath leaving his body, and a look of panic that said, 'This can't be happening to me.' But it was.

After that it took ages to get some sleep. I often woke up tired and agitated. Then it was time to get dressed, and off to work, to keep sending my regards to Jerry.

Luke, Pat and Peter were home this Christmas, while the rest of the boys and Mary's husband Johnny were away at sea. I had volunteered to work over Christmas. It was dinner time before I woke and came down to a noisy house. The usual food parcel had arrived a few days before Christmas from Ireland, so it was a feast similar to last year's dinner. But of course it wasn't the same.

Mary was nursing Billy in the front room, and I went in with Mum to see them.

"Well, here comes Mo, Mary!" said Mum. "Mo, this is your sister and your nephew. I don't believe you have met."

Mary looked up from her feeding time and covered her breast. Here was an amazing sight. A child with his mother's eyes, Johnny's face, her smile and a mop of curly black hair. Mary looked tired. There was a hint of tears in her eyes.

"Don't stand there gawping Mo, take your nephew and give your sister a minute to fix herself. He doesn't bite, you know. Come on, what are you waiting for?"

With that, Mum took the baby up and held him in front of me. He giggled, looked at his Gran and looked at me. Then he reached his two arms out to grab my hair and somehow, I was holding him. He was strong and almost threw himself back out of my arms so that I had to grab him again. I gasped, and he gripped a lock of my hair. Then he pulled himself close to my face and kissed me.

The room was filled with blue light. The baby laughed again, gurgled something, kicked his legs hard and his whole body jumped as he waved his arms about. The world stood still. I looked into his eyes, and I swore I could see Mary staring back at me. He giggled and wriggled and jumped again. I sat down and held him on my knee. There he was, a living, breathing, thriving person, who trusted me without question. Happy and safe.

"Happy Christmas, Mags."

Mary stood in front of me, holding a wrapped present. I held on to the baby with one hand and with the other pulled Mary's head on to my shoulder.

"I'm sorry Mary. I just couldn't..."

I gulped back tears and the baby must have sensed it because he gave a yelp of surprise, and started to whimper. Mary took him back, shushed him, and sat him on her hip. They looked like they were slotted together, as if he was growing out of her like a stubby branch that was an extension of herself.

"Even a mole has to put her head over ground some time," Mum declared. "Come on in everyone, dinner is nearly ready."

She was smiling. I hadn't seen her smile in a long while.

Luke was just back from a convoy to Murmansk in Russia, which hadn't gone well from what I could gather. I remembered the cold out at the shore, with the icy blast in the wind, and I shivered as I tried to imagine what a journey that must have been.

"If we don't stop Hitler in Russia and North Africa we're for it."

Peter had been in the Mediterranean for the past two months and that had been hell too. The whole world was on a knife edge.

Mum banished all talk of war with a flourish of the carving knife.

CHAPTER EIGHT

Summer 1942

Vera Lynn was on the radio singing *'We'll meet again.'*
"That woman hasn't been to Liverpool recently if she
thinks there's any bluebirds left, after this lot have done
with us. What is a bluebird anyway?"

Mum liked Vera Lynn singing about the Cliffs of Dover. I even
heard her hum *'Yours'* when she thought no one was listening. She
was right about the destruction of our town, and much of our city.
For me, the place of peace was out on Our Shore, where sand and
tide met. Until recently it was out of bounds. I didn't need to go to
other places to meet him. All I had to do was close my eyes and Billy
was there, smiling, handsome, waving his arms, as a ship sailed down
the Mersey and on out to sea.

"We're losing ships every day now. How long can that go on?"

That's what Tom said to Dad one evening after tea as he smoked
his pipe, sitting out on the steps of our home. We had moved back
into our house at the beginning of June. Mum said that Liam was
being optimistic when he said it had been rebuilt well. The houses
opposite had been cleared, the gap in the street a permanent
reminder of what had taken place last year. Still, it was nice to be
home.

I sat half-listening to the song on the radio, watching the pipe
smoke spiralling like signals to the god of sky. The war had moved

away, and turned into a series of exotic names in distant places. Singapore, Rangoon, Tobruk, and the Gazala Line in Egypt. It didn't take a genius to know that we were doing badly everywhere. And the Russians were holding on by going backwards.

"The Yanks will have to call a blackout, and use convoys, or we'll lose the Battle of the Atlantic."

The talk was of the new class of U-boat that could range across the whole Atlantic Ocean and stay at sea for weeks.

"They're picking off American ships against the lights of the American shore like a child knocking over a toy."

I was listening but "distracted by the radio," as Mum would say. Tomorrow was our three-year anniversary. June 24th 1939 was our date, me and Billy's. I will never forget that day over in the church hall getting ready for the Midsummer Fete, Billy with his hand outstretched to help me down off the chair, his eyes and his smile. Three years. It seemed like yesterday.

"Penny for them."

Mum had carried out cups of tea for the men. She sat beside me and put her arm around me. It was comforting to feel safe, even for a passing moment.

"You can't wait around forever," she whispered.

She spoke so softly that I barely caught what she had said. The men were busy discussing the new American airbase they were building out by Warrington, near where Dad had been in hospital. The runway and apron of the old RAF Burtonwood were being laid with concrete. The airbase was being upgraded to take the heavy bombers that had started flying in from across the pond. The base was going to be where the American Air Force would look after their planes, as far as I could gather. Tom said that when it was finished, it would be the biggest airport in Europe.

"There are a lot of Yanks in Warrington now, Mo," Mum said. "Perhaps you should go out there to the dances with some of your friends, Molly or Tess? You need to have friends, you know, especially in times like these. There's one on this Saturday afternoon."

I looked at Mum and she was being serious, telling me that I needed to get over Billy. I stood up and stubbed out my cigarette end.

"I'm off to work. See you all in the morning," I said. "Ta-ra."

After work the following morning I cycled out to Our Shore and watched the gulls circling overhead. They spun like a giant, screeching, ever-turning wheel on some secret spying mission. Billy used to say that they were Liverpool birds, and only went as far as Southport on their holidays. Watching them wing across, they were at home with the wind and sky. The sea danced in waves, backwards and forwards, trying to force the land under water.

A steady stream of ships steamed down the Queen's Channel and off to face real danger. I overheard Tom say to Dad 'Anywhere but Murmansk!' so that must have been particularly bad. The threat of invasion was more or less gone now, according to Tom, and he was usually spot on. The water looked so inviting. Part of the beach had been cleared of mines, and the barbed wire moved back to allow a space for swimming within a safe area.

The sea was cold on my feet. I shivered a little, but walked in until the end of my dress touched the water. I reached down and stretched my hands in the clear liquid and felt its exquisite coldness pour around my fingers, connecting me to Billy on this special day. Our day.

The first time I heard Vera Lynn sing that song it touched a chord. I thought that my heart was about to break. War makes you hard on the outside like a shell, with the angry stuff packed deep inside, ready to explode. I have felt like that for the last twelve months. Mum says that moving bombs out to strike at the enemy is good Christian therapy. Tom says to take it day by day. Working nights suits me. There are not many people to talk to, coming and going at dusk, or in the early morning light. I feel a sense of panic if I can't remember his face clearly.

"Time is a great healer."

Who said that? Whoever it was didn't know their arse from their elbow, as Dad would say. It is true that time puts a distance from the great sadness, but the chasm in my chest opens up every moment I think of Billy. It's like a swirling sinkhole at the centre of my being, like black water pulling me down into the abyss.

Leaving the shore behind, I cycled home and fell into a fitful sleep, filled with empty sky and cruel sea.

I was sitting on the floor in Mary's place, playing with young Billy. He looked at me with a quizzical smile that stopped my heart. He found joy and wonder in the simplest toys, like this set of wooden bricks that he was building up into an unsteady height. The lot came tumbling down, which thrilled and frightened him at the same time. He jumped, and his whole body moved as he kicked his legs. I smiled at the comical look on his face. Then he laughed and almost cried, and in that moment my spirit jumped with him. It made me laugh too, but when I went home, it made me cry dry tears to sleep.

Life is like that, really. I love to watch Mary feed him as he sits in his high chair, spoon in hand. He gets very excited as he tries to feed himself, with the food going everywhere. Mary is patient, with his goo and gaa in the room, chock full of nursery rhymes:

Half a pound of tupenny rice, half a pound of treacle,
That's the way the money goes, Pop! goes the weasel.

"A bundle of pure joy!"

That's what Mum calls him. Her face lit up when Mary brought him into the house. She whisked him into the back kitchen to mollycoddle him. I sat on the steps with Mary in the morning sunshine, having a laugh together. At times like that the world felt a little saner. I'd spent all night getting a shipment ready for Egypt, where the news was bad again, according to Dad.

Birthdays and anniversaries came and went. I had dreaded Billy's anniversary at the beginning of May. A whole year dead seemed a lifetime, and yet it was like yesterday. The fact that it was also young Billy's birthday was a distraction. Seeing the world through the eyes of a child and the wonder of a candle on a cake... seeing the bombed out city one year on... Tom was right. We will never let them beat us, but at what cost? The city was a distressing sight. Most people didn't have much more than the clothes on their back. Hundreds of families were still in requisitioned homes. Hundreds more were spread across the city or away staying with relatives. Mum spent her days chasing the rumour of food from queue to queue. She had a network of spies and a means of communication that were a mystery to me. Yet somehow, she managed to have food of some sort on the table, and a small amount of bread and butter, on account of her large family bringing in a few bob. Rationing was hard and getting worse. The shops were almost empty.

She never once mentioned Ireland.

The work of the port goes on at a great pace now that the bombing has stopped. All the action is out on the waves. I overheard Tom telling Dad about the new tracking system, which can pick up a submarine from air or sea. It was top secret, but if it does what they say it will do, it will swing the war back in our favour again.

Liam told me that the convoys to Murmansk were a nightmare. Twenty-four hours of daylight up there inside the Arctic Circle. The Luftwaffe bases in Norway went at the ships around the clock. In his last convoy, only six out of thirty-one ships got through. That figure shocked me. Twenty-five ships lost with their crews and their precious cargoes of tanks and shells and fuel. That's probably one thousand men gone to the bottom of the Arctic Ocean. If that continued we would lose the war; it didn't take a mathematical genius to work that out.

Tom said that the Luftwaffe lost nearly fifty bombers on their last raid on Liverpool, the night they destroyed our town. He believed that was why Hitler put a stop to them bombing us and decided to invade Russia instead. Liam said that he needed the Russian Steppes for food and the Caucuses for oil. I think Hitler is just mad for power, and wants to prove himself the greatest, even better than Napoleon Bonaparte. I hope that he comes to the same end. Maybe he didn't read the history books before he burnt them. Or maybe he didn't want his army to read about what happened to the last major invasion into that vast and frozen territory, before they set out on the same journey.

There was always hope, as Father Hickey would say. He was a great man for the hope of peace and love of your enemies. He had come over from Ireland after the May Blitz. I liked his smile and the way he nodded his head when he was speaking to you. He made you feel that you were the only person in the world that he was talking to.

With its doors flung open to let in the fresh July air, the Church Hall, which had been transformed into a temporary church, was nearly full for Sunday Mass. I couldn't see how God could move so easily next door from the original Church, which was still boarded up with *Keep Out* signs. Who would want to go in there anyway?

After Mass I cycled out to Our Shore. I had a sandwich and a bottle of water in my bag and that would have to make do. It was one of those midsummer days when the weather couldn't make up its mind. Grey clouds covered the sun without a hint of rain, and moved across on the sea breeze, their silver edge glinting so that I had to shade my eyes. Then the sun burst out and it was warm. I lay back on the sand and felt the heat on my skin. Then just as suddenly, the sun disappeared again and the temperature dropped. It was as if someone had switched off the light and opened a door, sending the warmth out and bringing the chill in.

I closed my eyes and tried to hold a picture of Billy in focus, but it kept flickering on and off at the back of my eyes. I sat up.

"Blast!"

I thought that the clouds had covered the sun again, but then the cloud spoke.

"Pardon me Ma'am. I didn't mean to block the sun. I was just wondering if you could tell me, is it safe to swim here?"

It was the first time I had met a Yank. I shaded my eyes against the glare. The silhouette of a young man barely older than me, with a smile that showed a mouthful of white teeth, spoke again.

"Me and my pal Harry, we were thinking of going for a swim. Is that okay?"

He gestured across to where another soldier was gazing out to sea, just as Billy had done so many times. His voice had a drawl to it that didn't seem to be in any hurry to get to the end of the sentence.

"Just stay between the flags," I said. "The rest of the beach is mined. It's still pretty cold in there."

He was gone with a 'Thank you, Ma'am' and an annoying swagger. His friend Harry waved his thanks too. I watched them as they peeled off their uniforms. They had their bathing suits on underneath. They sprinted down the beach, disappeared under the waves and swam about as if their lives depended upon it. When they were finished, they ran back across the sands. The other soldier, Harry, came across halfway to where I was sitting up, pretending to eat. He waved again. Sea water glistened on his body and he ran his hand through his short fair hair.

"It's lovely in," he said. "Thank you for letting us use your beach. Maybe you'd like to join us for our picnic."

I laughed out loud at the cheekiness of him.

"It's not my beach, as you well know, and I have a picnic of my own, thank you very much," I said.

"Yes Ma'am. We just thought we might share some of our chocolate with you."

I had heard the girls talk about the presents these Yanks carried about with them. It had annoyed me then to think that we were so easy a conquest. Not today.

"As I said, I have my own picnic, thank you," I said. "Don't you have some Germans to go and kill, or did you come over here just for a holiday?"

His face dropped a fraction and he turned and walked quickly away. He was tall. Even taller than Billy, and more muscular.

The clouds were gathering darkness into their midst. The sun disappeared and the edge of the cloud shone golden like a curved necklace. Then that too disappeared. Out on the water, a shower of rain was crossing the estuary, a slanting connection between the gods of sky and water. Then half a rainbow suddenly hung there, like a magic waterfall of light. It appeared between the clouds and ended in an arc of brightness, gliding in front of the dark stage of nature's show. It settled on an incoming ship that sailed through the pool of multi-coloured light and broke the waves in a splash of white and blue. Another American troop carrier. Excited cries were carried across the water on the strengthening breeze.

A squall was coming. I gathered my things and made a dash for the bicycle. On the way, I pulled on my jacket and hat. A smack of rain hit with the freshness that only a summer shower can get away with. The Yanks were running down off the sand in their bare feet. By now they were both naked to the waist, their shirts, jackets and boots in their hands. How they laughed! I hadn't heard such laughter in a long time. They reached their car, pulled up the hood and jumped in, just as heavy drops of rain fell about like incendiaries. But not incendiaries of course... The opposite – water bombs.

"Ma'am, come in and shelter out of the rain," Harry called. "Come on, Ma'am. You'll catch your death."

He was leaning out the window and waving his strong bare arm, calling me over. If it had been raining fire, I wouldn't have accepted the offer.

"Thanks," I called back. "I'm fine. I like the rain. It makes me feel connected."

With a wave of my hand I jumped on my bike and pushed hard to try to get ahead of the shower. When I passed the car, Harry was smiling and his eyes shone. He shouted after me.

"See you again sometime. We'll be here on Saturday morning – if we're still alive."

Well, that's what I think he shouted, but I couldn't be sure as the words were drowned in a flap of wind. The boys beeped their car horn as they passed me again, about a mile down the road. Harry was halfway out the car window, this time in full uniform.

"Come down to the dance on Saturday afternoon," he bellowed. "It's the Glen Miller Band. I'll be waiting outside at three o'clock. Please come?"

The car was driving on the wrong side of the road. I shouted a warning and waved and he waved back. Then they disappeared around the corner, still on the wrong side of the road. When I reached the bend in the road they were nowhere in sight.

We'll meet again. Some songs just stick in my head, and I can't get them out no matter what.

Now the Yanks are here, and they're going to change the war in our favour. That is, if they don't kill themselves with their dangerous driving before we even get started.

The Yanks are here.

CHAPTER NINE

Hamlet was a Danish Prince. He was a great man for ghosts, and for raising the question of whether there was life after death, and if ghosts were good or evil, or both. He even dragged along his friend Horatio to witness the ghost of his father, wandering around the castle walls, looking for his son to command him to avenge his murder.

"Mark me!"

Mary was fussing around the hem of a dress she was lending me for the dance.

"To be or not to be – straight!" she said. "Hold still."

"That, my dear sister, is the question."

"Princes can be such idiots. Come to think of it, most men can be idiots."

"From what I hear down at the factory, many of the girls are being more than idiots with these Yanks. Anyway, I'm not sure there is anything after death. When you're dead you're gone and that's that. Just another piece of dust on the wind."

"Mags, stop being so morbid. And remember, 'There are more things in heaven and earth than are dreamt of in your philosophy.'"

"Yes Hamlet would say that, but he was mad, remember."

"Only North North-West! Hold still or I'll stab you with my sword."

Mary was finished with the needle and smiled as she stood back admiring her handiwork.

"Mags, there's not a pick on you," she admonished. "Are you eating at all? This dress never looked anything as good on me though. You'll knock 'em dead."

"Alive is better, thanks," I said.

I don't often hug people, but I loved Mary more than anyone, except maybe Tom. She was my support. Not once a cross word, all those months, when I went away from the world.

"Tell me what he looks like again," she said. "Maybe I should come along, just to keep an eye on you."

"He probably flirts with every girl he meets," I replied. "Most likely, he won't be there and even if he is, he won't remember me. I'm going to the dance to make Mum smile again."

"It's good to see you smile again," said Mary. "Now off with you to meet up with Molly and Tess."

The bus was full of noise. Squeals and shouts of excited girls from the factory filled the air, as they called to each other across heads and seats. I sat quietly letting the sounds of the moment roll over me. There was a split second of guilt that I felt happy for even thinking about thinking about someone other than Billy.

I could feel the light touch of his locket wrapped around mine beneath Mary's blue dress, the one with yellow flowers that spoke of a peaceful summer long ago. Tess and Molly linked me either side as we walked from the bus in the bright afternoon light, through the crowds of young, smiling American soldiers in crisp uniforms. There was no sign of Harry or his friend. I hadn't really expected that they would be there.

A hangar had been transformed into an enormous dancehall. The band was definitely not Glenn Miller, but that wasn't a surprise either. These Yanks didn't seem to take life seriously at all. There was a holiday atmosphere that could suck you in and swirl you about. It was impossible not to be infected by the vibrant sound and the movement all around. There was a high energy in the air, like electricity.

"It was a gathering of young stallions let loose in a field of fillies."

That's what Tess said afterwards, and she should know; she came from the country and could ride a horse. I looked at the wide circle of eager eyes and knew in my heart that I had made a colossal mistake.

"I'm going outside for a smoke, girls."

Molly and Tess were being asked up for a dance. I turned before an approaching soldier could get to me. They were sucked into the mass of dancers and disappeared.

Outside, groups of soldiers gathered around jeeps parked on the green area to the side of the hangar doors. All heads turned as I walked past and somebody whistled. If he thought I'd be flattered, he was wrong. It made me angry.

Then I heard: "You can't go here, Ma'am. Sorry Ma'am.'

"No smoking in this area, Ma'am. It's forbidden."

I breathed in and counted to twenty, just as Tom had taught me to. When I turned, Harry was standing a few feet away.

"You came – I can't believe it!" he said. "I'm Harry. Remember, from the beach the other day? Come away from this section. It's a fuel depot. You can smoke over here."

There were jeers from the jeeps.

"We're not the enemy, you know," he said. "I'm just Harry."

He put out his hand. I shook it, then pulled away.

"You do have a name, I guess?" he added. "In America, we usually tell each other that much without giving away any war secrets. Unless you're a spy, then you'd probably give me a fake name, and I'd never see you again."

His smile almost took my breath away.

"It was a mistake for me to come," I said. "I should go back inside to see my friends."

"Whoah!" he said. "Whatever you think, I'm not the enemy. I came over here to help you win the war, and that's what we're gonna do. Together. Just not today. Today we can dance and enjoy ourselves."

Molly and Tess appeared out of the blue, slightly out of breath.

"Maggie!" said Tess. "We were worried. Where did you disappear to?"

Then they looked at Harry.

"Ah, Maggie. So that's the state secret!" laughed Harry.

He was smiling again. He turned to the girls, his arm outstretched.

"I'm Harry, I'm here to win the war."

He shook hands with Molly and Tess, who stood there staring.

"Don't you take anything seriously?" I asked. "You seem to think that the whole thing is a joke. You've probably never been in action, or held a dying child's hand, or..."

The girls linked me either side and spun me around. Molly winked at Harry.

"See you later inside – and bring some friends with you," she quipped.

She guided me to an area where a crowd had gathered and smoking was obviously allowed. With tremulous hands, I lit up a cigarette.

"I'll be fine now, thanks," I said. "I'm going to stay here for a while. I'll follow you in a bit. Really, go on and have fun."

The opening bars of *Chattanooga Choo Choo* caused a mini stampede into the hangar. The girls waved and promised to return.

I sat on a low wall near the line of jeeps, struggling with my thoughts and memories of Billy.

"Would you like a cup of tea? I believe that the English drink tea."

Harry stood in front of me, looking like a child who had lost his favourite toy. I gulped a long breath of air and smiled. Harry took my hand and guided me into the hangar, to an area where they were serving tea.

Molly and Tess were back, checked I was fine, and were gone again before the band started up the next swing number. The whole hangar was swinging, defying death and the shadow of death.

There is something about sweet tea that gets to the very centre of your being. It is impossible to drink it and remain angry for any length of time.

"If you'd like to walk outside, or sit and talk, or anything?" he said. "I could keep you company."

I looked at Harry. He was the perfect gentleman. The anger fell about my feet like a discarded shell case.

"I'm sure you'd prefer to dance with some of the girls," I said. "I just need some fresh air."

I walked away quickly and didn't look back. He must leave me and my heart of darkness alone. Surely he would get the message. But he didn't. His long strides brought him alongside me again. Then he skipped in front and spread his arms, pretending to be a plane that buzzed about and circled me as I walked. The silliness of it made me laugh. He stopped fooling around, and I could see that he was pleased.

"Are you a priest or something?" I asked him. "Don't you Americans take no for an answer?"

"Actually, I'm Jewish," he replied, "so technically I'd be a Rabbi, which I'm not. I'm a pilot. And you're right. I haven't seen any action yet. But that's going to change soon."

I glanced again at his smiling face. There was something in his eyes that spoke of truth and kindness. We had walked to an area where a construction compound blocked our way. The grass around was turned to mud by the heavy trucks. I wasn't watching where I was going and walked right into it. My shoe sank and was held fast by the sticky brown glue. I tried to stop and leaned backwards. Then my foot went from under me, and I lost my balance. I would have fallen on my back had Harry not grabbed my arm. His giant hand held me suspended in air. Then somehow he swept me off my feet, swirled me around, and placed me on dry land, minus my right shoe. I was rarely lost for words, but if the world had slapped my face, I wouldn't have felt so betrayed by fate. The shoe was one of Mary's best that matched the dress. My first instinct was to go in after it, but once again Harry was there, and had fished it out with a 'slugg'. I was a sorry sight. One foot covered in mud up over my ankle, the pencil seamline Mary had drawn up the back of my leg all smudges and ruined.

Harry tried not to laugh. I did see the funny side and, although I was fit to explode, it came out as a giddy laugh.

"Come on, I'll clean you up," said Harry. "But you have to tell me your full name."

Afterwards I remembered the strength of his arms, how he had lifted me like I was no more than a leaf or a feather. He carried me into a deserted medical centre, found me a chair to sit on and fetched a basin and warm water. He threw me a towel and disappeared into a side room. A few minutes later he re-emerged with Mary's shoe washed and cleaned as best it could be. It was too wet to wear. He said he would carry me back to the hangar, but I would have died first. Walking in a wet shoe isn't the worst thing, once you squeeze your foot into it and don't walk too fast. Just ignore the little squeak that it gives off, and the squelch every time you put your foot down.

"Thank you Harry, sorry what's your second name?" I said when we got there.

"Cohen."

"Well thank you, Harry Cohen. You Yanks are not all bad, it seems. And sorry you missed your dance. A bit of a disaster really."

"I'll be out at the beach on Tuesday morning," he said. "If you're there we could share a picnic between the showers. That's if I make it to Tuesday."

"What do you mean 'if you make it'?"

"We start operations tonight. Like I said, we're here to help you win the war. Now it's our war too."

Molly and Tess were back, took one look at my shoe and laughed.

"Maybe we could all meet up there?" said Harry. "I have to go now. It was lovely meeting you, Maggie Brady. And Tess and Molly."

"I'm Molly," said Molly. "She's Tess."

"Of course, sorry Ma'am."

His friend who had been with Harry at the beach was calling from a slowly creeping jeep for him to hurry.

"See you Tuesday morning, rain or shine?"

Harry Cohen jumped into the moving jeep and was gone, leaving behind a cloud of smoke that hung in the late afternoon air like a shroud.

It rained all day Tuesday. It would have been madness to cycle out to the shore and be drenched in the summer storm. I was close to going at one stage, but then the heavens opened and that decided it for me.

When I told Tom, I could see his eyes drop a fraction. It wasn't good for an English girl, who had lost her boyfriend to the sea, to date a pilot. Neither was it a good idea to become attached to someone who had a very short life expectancy. His chances of survival were even worse than those of a sailor, according to Liam, but you weren't allowed to say that. I had overheard Liam say exactly so to Mum on that Tuesday night.

Outside, thunder rolled and lightning flashed. I was getting ready to go out to work. In spite of myself, I jumped with every crack. That was followed quickly by the long rumble of thunder, like the growl of the planes overhead. I ducked when the flash came. Then I held my breath, waiting for the next crash. Even though I knew it was coming, it still made me jump. My heart was racing as I set out for work into the cosmic blitz.

Maybe the Gods were trying to tell me something.

CHAPTER TEN

Summer 1943

Four years. It's hard to believe.

The factory is busier than ever making bombs and shells by the thousands. As fast as we can make them, they're shipped out to Egypt, or brought over the channel by Bomber Command to pound the factories and industrial heartland of Germany. The news is getting better, as the boys argue endlessly about the progress of the war. We have won in North Africa. Everything is ready for the invasion of Europe. Liam says it will be through Italy, but Tom and the others say it will be Sicily first. The best news for me is that the Yanks have made a real difference, especially with their bombers.

I often think of Harry, flying missions over the Mediterranean. His last letter, two weeks ago, was from Egypt. He'd been to the pyramids. He was full of them – giant tombs of the Pharaohs and the Great Sphinx sitting guard over their graves. Mary had shown me pictures of them in the library. They looked out of this world. Over two million giant blocks to build a headstone for the great Pharaoh Khufu. Mum said he must have had a very big head. And what were they doing, only building a connection to the next world... a channel to the stars?

Mum was looking after young Billy while Johnny was out at sea, so that Mary could go back to work. Billy was tearing around the place, constantly babbling his baby talk. If he wasn't strapped into the pram he'd jump out. He took all of Mum's time and energy, but she was loving it, I could tell. Still, she was happy to let me play football with him for an hour in the morning when I came in from work. Then she was away out with him strapped in, sitting up in the pram, off to scrape together food for dinner. I dragged myself to bed, exhausted, blackout curtains pulled against the light.

Four years. Friday June 24th 1943. I had worked ten nights straight through to get the time off till Sunday night. I could feel the two lockets swinging loose under my dress as I cycled the shore road in the early morning sunshine. Yellow light shone low out of a red sky, glancing down the river, across the sand and on out to sea. I turned my back on the glare of the sun and watched the red clouds, stretched high across the sky, run out in fluffy streaks to the west. Below, the sea lay flattened like a mirrored sky.

It took only a minute to park up and carry the bicycle on to the sands, undress and run free with the cool sand damp under my feet. I had the beach to myself. Even the soldiers on lookout weren't bothering at this hour, probably asleep, or eating breakfast.

Four years. Two of them stolen from me by Hitler and his scum. I stood looking west, staring out into the deep with barely a ripple, just the slow, gentle lapping of the shore. It was hard to believe that the sea could be anything but kind.

I waded out, slowly feeling the water rise on to my knees. Then a shock of cold on my thighs forced me to stand on my toes. Fear exploded as I submerged, followed by a sense of liberation, freedom, of being in another world. Liquid was present above and below me. I was in a world without wars, bombs and death at every turn. It was a world where nothing mattered but the need to breathe. I forced myself to stay under, stayed down for as long as possible, but eventually I broke the surface and gasped air so fast it seared my lungs, my eyes popping in the watery light.

Afterwards I lay on the sand, closed my eyes and tried to capture his face. The harder I tried, the more the edges blurred. I panicked then, ran to my clothes and opened the locket. It was hard to recognise the two happy faces, now faded, from another time, another life.

CHAPTER ELEVEN

Summer 1944

The beginning of the end.

That's what Tom had said to Dad, sitting on the steps in the cool of the evening.

I'd watched them moving out over the past months. The Yanks. Thousands, from their camp at Aintree, the air buzzing with planes. This was what they had come to do. This was it.

Now they were in France and Hitler was doomed. It was only a matter of time.

The Battle of the Atlantic was won too. That didn't mean it was over, but the great danger that existed when our ships were being sunk on a daily basis was over. There was nowhere for the U-boat to hide from our radar. No more sneaking around without being found from sea and air. Between the Americans, Canadians and ourselves, the skies above the great ocean were now covered from shore to shore. No more Mid-Atlantic Gap for them to hide in. Once a ship remained in convoy, there was little chance of being sunk, unless it was unlucky and hit a mine, as one did last month a couple of miles off the mouth of the Mersey. That ship went down without a trace, not even a drop of oil washed ashore.

Now it was a matter of numbers. We had millions of shells and bombs that were shipped off to France or Italy. Someone loaded them into a tank, or a gun, or on to a bomber. They were fired or dropped and then… I often had a dream where I was one of the shells. I always got that far and then woke up with a fright. I listened to the stories being told by whichever of the boys happened to be home of an evening, and I never grew tired of them. The gliders being towed by our planes and then released somewhere over the Channel. Those gliders, filled with human beings in full battle dress, passing silently over the coast. Outside, the wind whistling, inside, eyes wide and a knot in the belly. Then crash-landing in fields behind enemy lines. How terrifying would that be, to be inside one of those? Then to re-group and attack the enemy from the rear, with the main force landing on the beaches of Normandy. Jerry on the high ground dug in with machine guns, mortars and God knows what. Shells screaming overhead from the battleships offshore. It sounded great when Pat told it. I was thinking just how bloody and messy it probably was, with Jerry having had years to prepare the ground defences. War was mad. The world was mad.

I slept most of the night in my own bed, now that I was back working days. There was no real chance of them bombing us. They were too busy trying to stop us bombing them.

It was our fifth anniversary, Saturday 24th June 1944. This was the first year I worked through the day, but I cycled out to Our Shore after work. It being Saturday evening, there were people about. By the time I arrived, the heat had gone out of the sun. Most were leaving. I sat and watched the sun go down in a warm glow that spread across the horizon. It was reflected in the landscape of fire and water. It was hard not to believe that some kind of God was in charge of the planet. It was mankind that was making such an unholy mess of it.

Out on Our Shore, the evening fell in softly. The light was fading in a bright, high sky with no moon. I stood knee-deep in the water with the tide running in around me. If I stood my ground, it would come and take me to him. Then there would be a certain kind of peace that could take the ache from within me, open me up, pour it out and make me whole again. Make me the person I used to like, the person that was me before the Blitz.

The water was in danger of touching my skirt that I had hitched up into my knickers. Ophelia sang while she was drowning. She was driven mad by the way Hamlet treated her, even though she had lied to him, and spied on him for her father Polonius and his political ambition. Polonius made the big mistake of trying to rationalise love.

It could be the nicest way to die.

"You feel no pain, only a lightness, as if you were flying towards the light."

That's what Liam said some sailor, who had nearly drowned, told him it was like. He said it didn't feel like being in water at all. Mum had put paid to the conversation, with a call for no more talk of death in the house. It being Good Friday. We were all going off to the Stations of the Cross.

I spread my fingers in the cool water and wished for an end to the pain. A rogue wave hit my thighs and woke me from my slumber.

Mum says that if Hitler doesn't kill us, the rationing will. I didn't care how little there was to eat, so long as we paid them back for what they did to Billy and his Mum Bess, Father Breen and Josie Morris and all the thousands of others. I remembered the terror of the night raids during the Blitz. Now these flying bombs are hitting London and I know they could come here, but it's not likely, Tom says.

The numbers are on our side. It will be only a matter of time before we fight our way into the heartland of Germany and kill the poison that lies at its centre.

I haven't heard from Harry in a long time. I pray every day that he's safe somewhere, which is ridiculous, as he's a pilot and therefore is hardly ever safe. Still, if he gets through this, he might come and see me, and I could go with him to visit New York. You never know what might happen, but I'm glad that we've remained just friends. I suspect that he believes me to be a bit mad, and in need of someone to look after my sadness, as he calls it – to be for him the sister he never had. It's complicated being a friend with someone who's on the edge of death on a daily basis, and being in love with a person who's been dead for three years. I feel that my head has been screwed on tight to a body filled with rancour. It's stayed that way for years now. Probably rusted, stuck, never to be removed. Mum says I have my head screwed on all right.

That's what war does to you.

CHAPTER TWELVE

Afterwards
1945-1947

So it ends. After the end, is there the hope of a new beginning? Churchill is gone, dumped by a country he saved from annihilation. So much for his 'Our greatest victory' speech. After the joy and dancing in the streets, after the street parties and speeches, there was only a short time when it felt good that we had won.

That summer of 1945 was filled with bittersweet days and nights of dark dreams. Men came home from the war to a fractured country. Damaged men, broken men. Some were shipped back out to the Far East, where the war was still going on. Women were turned out of their jobs to make way for returning servicemen. War jobs, like mine in the munitions factory, were gone. It was a time of hope and change.

My brothers had all survived the war. They argued with Dad and with each other about the New Britain and how it should be shaped. The welfare state. A fair society for all. After a while I got fed up listening. Littlewoods took us girls back and I buried myself in work, a supervisor with twenty-five girls under me. The Pools. Mum said that it was all a fix. It was easier to say nothing to that.

The boys spent hours arguing over who might score, and which team would have an away win the following Saturday. They put their money on forecasting the results of football matches the length and breadth of the country. It was supposed to be good fun. I always felt that it was driven by a desire to win. Then the winner could get the hell out of Liverpool, or wherever they happened to live. Out! Mum said that it was better during the war because we had someone else to blame for the lack of food and clothes and the high prices in near empty shops.

"Now it's just the government, God help us, that we have to worry about," she said. "They want to rule the world. I can't even manage to buy a fresh loaf of bread without having to use our ration book to buy it – and I have to queue for the privilege. And now we're feeding Germany too."

Mum was on her hobbyhorse and there was no stopping her. I quietly reminded myself that nowadays she baked her own bread, and never had to queue. In essence, she sounded what many people felt. Disappointed. Let down.

Harry never came back. His plane was shot down over Germany in February 1945. That's all I know. He might have been on the Dresden raids. They wouldn't give me any more details. He was killed bombing cities that were full of people just like us, except they were German and worked in factories just like I did. It was our turn to pay them back, to give them a taste of their own medicine.

It wasn't like when Billy was drowned. War makes you hard, and I always knew that Harry might not make it. I liked him for his innocence. I liked him when he laughed, and when he made me laugh. I liked the fact that he was a perfect gentleman. It could have been so different between us, in a different time.

I didn't cry a tear for him, not until I went out to Our Shore, the morning after I heard the news. It was early March. There was a wind chill in the air that froze my ears and made my eyes water. The sky was grey and the water almost black. There was a sting in the north wind that tasted of Arctic ice. I hadn't brought a hat. The cold made my head ache, as I watched the dirty grey clouds scud across the estuary and on towards the hills of Wales.

I remembered the sight of him the day we met. Standing there on the sand, water running down his chest, a war hero with a soft centre, like Humphrey Bogart in *Casablanca*, but without the wisecracks. He was a true gentleman, and I regretted not having told him that I liked him a lot. I never even told him that I liked him at all. Harry Cohen of New Jersey, with impeccable manners. I kept him at arm's length and he accepted that. He called me his big sis because I was two months older than him. He was a special human being. I prayed that he may have been captured somewhere in Germany, and that we'd meet up after the war is won. I looked at the cruel sea and a shiver ran the length of my body. Tears came and made my eyes sting in the biting air.

Gulls screamed and squawked and flapped around me, looking for scraps of food.

Then it started to rain.

Spring 1945 was dawning all across Europe. The world moved on, little by little, ever so slowly in the direction of peace. The 'Victory in Europe' celebrations in May were special. I saw Mum and Dad kiss. I hadn't seen that for a long time. The celebrations were hard because they stood on the graves of millions of people, including over thirty thousand lost at sea like Billy, with no grave other than the vast ocean. A great leveller.

Life returned to a new normal. It was almost worse than the war.

It was a summer of horror stories. Stories of death camps and millions of Jews dead. Stories of the suffering of prisoners of war in Burma, and their treatment at the hands of the Japanese. Stories of mass executions of prisoners as the Allies advanced on all fronts. Terror stories. Then, at the beginning of September, the atom bombs, and the end of the war in the East. I shudder to think what Hitler would have done had he developed the A-bomb in time to drop it on us. We would have been wiped from the face of the earth. Atom bombs would have been dropped on every major city in Britain. We would have been the prime target after London. I have no doubt that he would have annihilated us.

I don't want to talk about it anymore.

1946-1947

Another year. Life was supposed to get better, but there was never enough food to go round. Rebuilding had started, but it was slow. The whole world was dark and dreary. Tom went back to live in America. I heard stories that he had a family in New York, but that was beyond belief. Tom never talked about it. When the war ended, he packed his few belongings and left. He said that he'd send for me when he got himself a place of his own, but he didn't write. He was never good at keeping in touch. It broke my heart again.

By Christmas 1946, talking with Molly and Tess, we'd all had enough. We'd saved our money because there was nothing to spend it on. We planned to take a week-long holiday in Ireland in the summer of 1947.

Then the winter came. When the first snows fell in January 1947, it was something of a novelty to see the black ruin of the city covered in a cloak of white. But the novelty soon turned sour. Snowfall upon snowfall, ice and gale force winds were followed by even more snow, until we were buried under two feet of it. And still it came, on and on.

Mum blamed the Russians. Roads and railways were blocked. Stockpiles of coal froze in the mines. Everything on the docks froze. Then the ground froze, and the sea began to freeze. This freezing weather went on for months. Power stations ran out of coal. Electricity was cut off for hours every day. Radio and television stations were closed. Factories closed. Food froze in the ground.

People were freezing or starving to death. It was grim in our town, and in the city, and even worse in other parts.

And then there was the football. Liverpool doing so well, Everton only middling, and the matches frozen and flooded off. Billy would have been in his element.

It was the coldest winter since records began. When it was over, and the thaw came in April, the ground was still frozen. The snow melted and flooded half the country. If God had been trying to tell us something during the war, he was repeating the message loud and clear. Get the hell out!

That's what Molly and Tess decided to do. They were going to Australia. It sounded so far away, and I wasn't set on the idea, but they convinced me to come along with them. In the end, when I hadn't heard from Tom, I just gave in. So it was decided. We'd have a week-long holiday in Ireland in July, and take the boat to Sydney in September.

Mum wasn't impressed.

"You be your own person now, Maggie Brady," she said. "Things won't always be this bad here."

But things were bad. Everything was rationed – bread, meat, sweets, even potatoes. There was nothing in the shops to buy, so we saved all of our money.

Ireland in July. A different world. Just a boat trip across the Irish Sea to a land of plenty.

I'd warned Molly and Tess not to eat, but they didn't listen. They feasted on cakes and tea in the restaurant, while I sat up on deck, watching the familiar shoreline sink below the horizon, feeling the pitch and roll of the boat as it set a course for Dublin. By the time we arrived, the girls had been sea-sick for hours. I sat up on deck with my eyes closed, thinking of Billy, and then of Harry. No news from Tom either. I had to hug myself hard to stop myself from crying. I was done with crying.

Waking in the half-light of a strange room was a thrill that stopped my heart for a second. Then the realisation hit me that I was in a hotel in Ireland with no end of possibilities. The full week of my holidays stretched ahead, a foreign country waiting to be explored.

Our room had a small balcony overlooking the seafront. The suck and slap of the sea repeated on and on through the open French door in the still night. The rhythm called me out of sleep and drew me outside into the pre-dawn light. I hadn't watched a sunrise over the sea since the time I came to Aunty Maggie's funeral. I could see an outline of what must be the hills of Wales – tiny, backlit shapes on the eastern horizon. So different from the early mornings at home.

Then a faint glow in the sky garnered itself to orange. It spread across the curve of the horizon like the bright wings of a giant bird, glowing red against the pale blue sky. The outline of a bandstand on the esplanade stood black against the light. As I watched, the whole sky caught fire, and was reflected in the still water. The sun broke the horizon and a shaft of light hit me between the eyes, like a bullet. I had to turn away towards the mountain at the end of the promenade. A hump of black rock sat brooding over the sea, crowned with gold.

A rattle of a milk cart in the street below was the only disturbance to the cosmic event. The girls remained asleep in the stuffy room, a faint whiff of vomit in the air.

Later, I sat alone in the breakfast room listening to the chatter, surrounded by the clatter of the morning meal. Afterwards, Molly and Tess joined me. We walked the length of the promenade to clear their heads. 'Round about, families who all seemed to know each other took their morning walk. People shouted greetings; *Lovely day!' 'Yeah, going to be a scorcher.'*

Groups of parents stood talking, or sat on the pale blue seats, with children licking ice-cream cones or munching candyfloss. The bandstand was invaded by an army of musicians, setting up for a concert. Deckchairs were arranged in rows in front, inside a roped-off section on a wide expanse of grass. On the far side of the bandstand, a Punch-and-Judy show was in full swing.

A policeman was waving a truncheon about. I couldn't hear what was said, but, sitting on the grass in front of the stage, all the children laughed. Up on the promenade, a hefty man with an enormous handlebar moustache was pulling a cart filled with delicious smelling shellfish. He wore a pinstriped red-and-white apron, and a broad-rimmed, white hat. My lips watered in anticipation. I tasted some periwinkles, and the salty taste stayed in my mouth, even as we climbed the lower slopes of the Head. The girls turned back for food, not having had any breakfast. I followed the throngs of people up the path that snaked its way through the trees, on to the shoulder of the mountain, to a tearoom with magnificent views of the bay. It reminded me of a scene from a picture book of Italy that Mary had shown me once. That was when Harry had been flying missions from Sicily, during the dark time.

The view from the terrace was breathtaking. Rolling mountains, in hues of purple and green, filled the western horizon and tumbled across the landscape, ending in the sea. Islands divided the near bay from the next one, which must be Dublin, because I heard a man pointing out Howth to his children. The town was tucked into the bay below. It stretched from the promenade, which ran the length of the beach, inland for a mile, before disappearing into the countryside beyond. England and Wales lay over the eastern horizon, lost in the shimmering air, out of sight and almost out of mind.

The high blue sky was streaked with thin white clouds. They ran out to the horizon and disappeared into the mix of sky and water that ran backwards in laughing waves, back to the shore beneath the cliffs below. I sat for ages, drinking in the freedom. Bray. It was as far from Bootle as I could have imagined.

The Vikings had come here too, those warrior men driven by their Gods of the North. They came in search of treasure, hunting in the Glens of Wicklow for Christian gold. The female warriors, the Valkyrie, if they had taken the time to look around, must have felt that they had come home. This was Valhalla. It was paradise.

I was all dolled up. There was something lovely about having the girls fuss over me. The ballroom was packed. It had been a long time since we'd seen so many boys our own age. Not since those dances in the Burtonwood airbase all those years ago.

Out of nowhere, we were asked to dance by three dapper lads dressed to the nines, looking like something from the movies. My guy looked like Bing Crosby, only better looking, and he was a dab hand at this dancing lark, without a doubt. The best mover I'd ever danced with. When he took me in his arms, I was transported to a safe land, where I could leave all the troubles of the past behind.

With each beat of my heart, Australia and its shimmering red haze, began to submerge over the distant horizon. Ireland, a far more attractive place, was real and present and green. So green.

And so it begins.

A bout the author:

Keith Ryan is a retired teacher and Secondary School Principal. He was born in Bray in 1956, the fourth of seven children to his parents Vera and Ollie. Vera was born in Bootle and lived there throughout the war before meeting Ollie, while on holiday in Bray after the war.

He has also written *Blue Star Rising* (2019) available in your online bookstore, in ebook and paperback.

Thank you for supporting independent publishing. It would be greatly appreciated if you could take the time to post a review online wherever you read books.

A cknowledgements:

Thank you to my editor Celine Naughton for her wisdom and guidance. Her encouragement combined with her unerring suggestions and corrections were invaluable to me. You can catch up with Celine at www.celinenaughton.com

Thank you to Ann Glynn of *Ann Glynn Design* for her creativity and her friendly and efficient service, as she worked on the cover design of this book.

A special thank you to my children Conor, Barry and Emer and their families for their support, encouragement and love. Finally, special mention for Ava and Noah for their inspiration, and to my wife Miriam for everything.

Blue Star Rising

A novel

Keith Ryan

CAMADERRY

PRESS

Blue Star Rising, a literary novel set in the autumn of 1993, tells the story of Richard (Dickie) Boyle, a member of the Dublin Gaelic Football Team who face Kerry in the All-Ireland Final. As a child, Richard was fostered from his birth family in the inner city to a middle-class family in the suburbs.

He starts a temporary teaching job in a sheltered workshop where he meets Dee. This tale of young love is set against a background of life-threatening violence, social imbalance, and family opposition. The journey of self-discovery takes Dickie back to his birth family in Dublin's flatland, and their involvement with drugs and paramilitary violence, forcing him to confront his past - a past that threatens to destroy all that he holds dear.

Blue Star Rising is available to order from your local bookstore. It is also available on Amazon.co.uk and Amazon.com both as a paperback and as an e-book. The ebook is available to download in Kindle, Apple, and in all good online stores such as Kobo, Barnes and Noble, etc.

You can read the opening chapter

CHAPTER ONE

October 1993

I'm doing a lifestyle piece on you - you know, likes and dislikes, what you eat, where you hang out, where you buy your clothes… Will you do an interview with me sometime this week?"

Orla had been in his class in UCD.

"Look Orla, I don't want to appear rude, but I'm not interested in any of this."

"You may not be, Dickie, but our readers and your supporters are clamouring for this. It's going to be written with or without your help. I just thought you'd like to have an input, that's all. We're starting with your biological family, your life in the flats and moving on to…"

"What?"

"Dickie, my editor is very clear about what people are asking for in this article. You are an amazing person and the readers want to know what makes you tick. They want to know everything about you, including your early life in the city. I was hoping to give you some control over the direction of the story. I can meet you anytime you like. Give me a call soon."

Richard noticed his hand was shaking as he replaced the receiver. Family! What the hell did that mean? A mother who drank, smoked and gambled every penny that she could lay her hands on. Three sisters who were interested only in themselves, who despised him for leaving, resented him for having a house, money and an education, envied him for making something out of his life and tried to make him feel guilty at every turn.

Well, he had moved on from that life for good. If he gave his mother money, what would she do? Straight down to the Horse and Jockey for comfort. And his sisters wouldn't speak to him because he was sent away and they were left to try to cope with life in the flats. His eldest sister Scarlett was living with some low-life in the city centre. What chance for her three-year-old son that Richard had never even seen? Bruce, she called him. Probably after Springsteen or Bruce Lee, or a character in one of the soaps that she spent all day watching on her giant television screen. Her partner, a loudmouth covered with body tattoos and gold jewellery, had a reputation on the streets. As for the other sisters, Elizabeth and Marilyn were rough diamonds, but they must have had it tough. Family!

He'd have to call Orla. An involuntary shiver ran down his spine. Beads of perspiration trickled down his forehead and into his eyes, making him rub them awake into this living nightmare.

There was a carnival atmosphere in the flats. The blue bunting trailed from every balcony and every lamppost, onto railings and washing line poles, as Orla and her photographer got to work. They had insisted on doing the photoshoot on a Saturday as they wanted the flats full of kids. Richard liked that much of the proposal and secured their agreement that no photos would be taken inside the flat. His car was surrounded as he drove through the entrance and parked. The kids were excited to see him and delighted to be asked questions by a reporter. Richard was beginning to relax and enjoy the adulation when his mother and two of his sisters appeared.

They were dressed like they were going for a night out in the pub. Hair, nails, heels (Lizzy and Marilyn), short skirts and fishnet tights (Lizzy and Marilyn) and tight, low-cut tops (all three). Ma wore a leopard-print top, black leather mini skirt and a fur coat.

"Darlings, you look amazing!"

It was Marc Paul, the photographer, snapping away. All the neighbours were out to watch the show. Jason, one of the lads, had decided to act as spokesperson.

"It's all right living here, but we need more facilities, a proper playground, somewhere to play football, and a youth centre. That would help to prevent young people from getting involved in drugs and crime. Most of the time there's nothing to do."

Richard could see that even Orla was impressed.

"Jason, how old are you?"

"I'm twelve. Just started secondary school this year."

"Did you say there's drugs and crime here?"

Jason looked about as if they were surrounded by drugs and crime. He lowered his voice.

"It's the way we're brought up. No one has a chance. What do you expect? How could it be any different? We need help!"

Orla stood with her mouth open as Jason, who was interviewed on a regular basis for TV, radio and PhD studies on poverty, crime and drugs, reamed off his polished routine. When he finished, he smiled for the camera. Orla lapped up every word, then turned to the family.

"Can we get one family photograph with Dickie in the middle please?"

"Richard."

"Pardon?"

"You called him Dickie. His name is Richard. I named him after Richard Burton, you know. But you're too young to remember who Richard Burton is, I suppose."

"Richard?"

"Yes, that's it. He was married five times, you know. Twice to Elizabeth Taylor who I called my daughter after. I loved *Where Eagles Dare*. Have you seen it?"

"Eh, no, sorry, I haven't, but I'll look it up. That's lovely. Just look straight at the camera. Can you all smile, please? Thank you, Marc Paul. Do we need any other shots?"

Richard could feel his mother's hand shaking as she grabbed hold of his arm. He couldn't remember the last time she had touched him. She never touched him. But he could feel her shake and he felt sorry for her.

"Are you okay? Do you want to sit down?"

His whisper was brushed away by his sisters who grabbed him for a last photograph with them. Marc Paul gave the thumbs-up sign and he and Orla were done. His mother grabbed his arm and whispered in his ear.

"You have to get Bruce out of the crèche immediately. His life is in danger. Someone fired shots through the window into Scarlett's flat last night. She's gettin' ready to go to Spain later today with that Cobra one. Richard, she can't take Bruce with her. It's too dangerous. Can you go down and collect him and bring him back here now? We'll take care of him till things settle down again."

"Ma, he doesn't even know me. Can't Elizabeth or Marilyn do it?"

Her grip was surprisingly strong and she twisted his arm till he was looking right into her face.

"You have to do this. I'd never forgive myself if anything happens to him. Richard, I'm begging you! They'll be watching for the girls, but they won't stop you. Please, Richard."

He didn't have to ask who would be watching. There had been a movement of anti-drugs activists and it was rumoured that the paramilitaries were pulling the strings. A question that you don't ask. You just know.

"Okay, Ma. I'll get him. But Elizabeth will have to come to hold him in the car."

So it was that Richard found himself sitting next to Lizzy, who didn't usually talk to him at all, now shouting directions and yelling at him to hurry on through the crawl of lunchtime traffic. She rolled down the window to hurl abuse at every car, truck or bus that blocked the way. Richard's nerves were frayed when he pulled up across the road from the crèche. There didn't seem to be anybody about, but that could change at any time.

Richard insisted Lizzy come with him. The crèche staff seemed happy to give up Bruce who eyed Richard with suspicion until he saw the car.

"Beep-beep. Me-drive-me-drive."

He was bouncing in Lizzy's arms in the back seat. She had to struggle with all her puny strength to keep him from jumping into the front as they snaked their way back to the flats.

"This is your Uncle Dickhead, Bruiser. Say hi to your Uncle Dickhead."

Richard didn't think they'd been followed, and breathed a sigh of relief when they reached the flat. His mother had the door open and was outside sweeping, a thing he had never seen her do before.

"Say bye Uncle Dickhead."

"Bye-bye Dickhead. Bye-bye Dickhead."

Bruiser repeated it and seemed to like the sound of it as he shrieked with joy to see his Nana.

"Bye-bye Dickhead."

He had the face and build of a boxer and even at three years old, Richard could see that the three stripes cut into each side of his head by the barber suited him.

"You've had your fun, now piss off."

It was amazing how his sisters could turn nasty in the twinkling of an eye – and just out of earshot of the Ma who had gone inside with the precious bundle of joy.

On his way to the car, Richard passed 'Drugs Out' signs on vacant doors and windows. He had read about the candlelight marches to the homes of drug dealers and of the violent confrontations there. He lived just four miles away, amid leafy, tree-lined streets and whitewashed houses with ordered gardens and middle-class neighbours who played golf and tennis and sailed out of Dun Laoghaire on the weekend. A different world, a different universe.

Orla was waiting patiently outside his house. She greeted him with that professional smile she reserved for her special assignments.

"Hi Dickie, or should I say Richard!"

"Drop it, Orla. Sorry about the delay. I had to do something for my mother. Okay, Marc Paul. No photos outside the front of the house. Let's go inside."

Orla smiled. This was going to be a great article. She could see the headline: *'Blue Star Rising'* with great photos from the flats and then this. It was perfect. Dickie was such a gentleman. She couldn't help admiring his physique as he walked to the front door. "Drugs and crime." That's what that child Jason had said the future held. She must do a follow-up article with him on life in the flats.

"Can we talk about your foster parents?" she asked. "How old were you when you came to live here?"

Richard walked through the sitting room, opened the patio doors and stepped out into the autumn sunshine that flooded the decking and bathed the garden with its ethereal light.

Later, when the photos were done, Orla sat across the patio table and broached her final subject.

"I know you said that talk of Dee was taboo, but I have to ask you for a comment on reports that she's back in Ireland. Have you guys been in touch?"

"Taboo means taboo, Orla. I'm sorry, but that's all I have to say."

"Yes, but this is the one thing that readers are dying to know about. That and your trip to Sydney. Where to from here for Dickie Boyle?"

Richard stood up. The interview was over.

Lightning Source UK Ltd.
Milton Keynes UK
UKHW010705160221
378865UK00001B/54